I0667333

GENTLEMEN OF THE SHADE: VOLUME I

BY TOD CROUCH

ISBN-13: 978-0615621869 (Self_Untitled Publishing)
ISBN-10:0615621864

i

This book is dedicated to the gay kid in the middle of nowhere who doesn't feel like being stereotyped and wants a (hopefully) entertaining introduction to gay history. Every homosexual character in this book, save for one, existed and contributed to the progress of society in one way or another. I encourage you to research the individuals mentioned herein who strike your fancy.

VERY Special Thanks to:

Dimitri Portnoi, Ryan Doyle May, Christopher Red Martiny, Hal Lanse, Adam Baran, John Russo, Indigo, Vicki Gilpis, Dan Bach, Victor Scott, Jory Dominguez, Nathaniel James, Peter Bauman, Ted Crouch and Karen Klinzig, and all those far too familiar with what it takes to keep the wolves from my door.

I've had nights I will never forget.
I've had nights I will always regret.
But I can take it on the chin,
and say "Boys Will Be Boys"

I felt driven and I felt obliged,
I've had feelings like a thorn in my side,
I hope you never let this down now,
 "Boys Will Be Boys"

> "Boys will be Boys"
> Goldfrapp

Tod Crouch

Prologue

> *Endowed with inextinguishable life, in*
> *spite of all that has been done to suppress it, this*
> *passion survives at large in modern states and*
> *towns, penetrates society, makes itself felt in every*
> *quarter of the globe where men are brought into*
> *communion with men. Yet no one dares to speak of*
> *it; or if they do, they bate their breath, and preface*
> *their remarks with maledictions.*

"A Problem with Modern Ethics"
--John Addington Symonds

Munich, 1880. A young Doctor Magnus Hirshfeld nervously walked into the Ministry of German Jurors to give his long awaited speech concerning an undiscovered social phenomenon: Homosexuality, an obscure and elusive medical condition. Dr. Hirshfeld delighted in finally discussing the trend with reasonable and decent people of the Christian court with civility and understanding. Surely, the elected officials of the German high council would not shake the same bigoted fists which blackmailed and beat the good doctor.

Magnus entered the cavernous foyer of white marble and oak, into the crowd of black-robed bureaucrats, clouds of lice exploding from their powdered wigs. Magnus, now in his mid twenties, kept both a trim build and a full head of curly black hair, despite the stressful life he lived as a campaigner for manly man love of men. At the appointed lecture hall, His heart dropped, nearly blowing out his bowels in the process. The well-lettered placard outside read:

Decimating the Homosexual Plague:
Protecting Civilization
From Total Collapse.
A Lecture by Dr. Magnus Hirshfeld.

Before the jurists entered the empty hall, Magnus plopped into his chair and looked dumbly at his naive collection of Greek poetry. The faint echo of footsteps bounced off the high ceilings as a stout clerk greeted Ulrichs with a smile, "So good of you to come, Herr Hirshfeld."

"Thank you," Hirshfeld said through a haze, "However, I believe you are misinformed—"

"--We simply cannot wait to see how to curtail these unnatural acts. Truly deplorable, it is. I do hope you deliver a rousing speech. If I may say, I seem to have seen some of these (ahem) *homosexuals* flitting about in anticipation for your lecture. I do hope you show them the error of their ways and lead them to a cure, for the sake of all the German people. Good luck!" The coordinator said flitting off, as the color ran from Hirshfeld's face to pool in his shoes.

Doom overcame the Doctor as his life's work lay skewed by convention of a contemporary self-righteous society. It could be so simple to give them what they want, lest they twist his words to their own perceptions, with or without him. *Give them what they want, get out alive.*

Dr. Hirshfeld looked at the quickly filling room. An audience of jackals sat with jagged smiles, preparing for the circus. Old women with worried faces sat side by side with a quiet, effeminate minority. Monocled scientists frowned in skepticism. *Give them what they want, get out alive.* Fourteen righteous men, saddled with hearing the will of the people, filed in and took their seats far above the civilians. As the gavel dropped its commanding order, the fever pitch broke. Magnus stood, sucked in a deep breath, and gave them what they wanted.

Magnus cleared his throat. "Gentlemen of the jury, you have invited me here to understand what has not been discussed openly, for fear of persecution and oppression. This action has not been given a proper name or proper acknowledgement until this day. Only those who do not know of it have not experienced it, though it remained unnamed until now. I ask you to keep an open mind, for only then can we come to a civilized conclusion. I speak of an intimate love between two men, or two women."

The head councilman leaned in with a haughty, blubbering voice as his ball-sacked waddle violently swung, "You mean… girls who fornicate with boys who copulate with boys… who comingle with girls who philander with boys like they're girls, who conjugate with girls like they're boys?"

"—Always should be someone you really love, your honor." Magnus added. The crowd gasped and twittered objectionable nonsense.

"Whatever are you saying, dear boy? Are you suggesting my own boarding school antics of being hosed down with my schoolmates man seed is not shameful…but encouraged?" The head Juror said, veins knotting tightly upon his forehead. "How can you, Dr. Hirshfeld, stand up and believe in something that I can't even begin to understand?"

"Esteemed colleagues, I have here many fine examples of historical Homosexual loves from some of the greatest minds throughout history--" Dr. Hirshfeld said, quickly rifling through his history books.

The Chief Juror laughed. "I don't suppose you're going to tell me next that we all came from monkeys, or that flies don't spontaneously generate from rotting meat, or that the air is full of tiny invisible creatures! How could you be such an expert? You waste our time with this nonsense. You might as well dissect a unicorn while you're at it." The other jurors throatily mumbled in contemptuous agreement.

Dr. Hirshfeld felt the fires of defiance engulf him as he proclaimed, "Sir, I am such an expert, for I am a homosexual!" And I maintain my status as a law-abiding citizen and of a peaceful humour." A woman in the crowd shrieked at seeing such a supernatural creature and feinted fast away, still clutching her handkerchief to her forehead.

The hyenas in the peanut gallery raged.

It was useless to continue. The jurors gave in to braying chaos. A soothing calm came over Dr. Hirshfeld as he looked into the unmasked face of society. It was not so much an action against him or his kind—but the shame of confusion among lesser men. It was the society who scorned a loving God's permissiveness. Who did not bark in lunacy smiled with silent optimism.

The clerk gripped The Doctor by the arm. "Come along. I think you've done enough damage." He turned to the crowd, letting the hateful faces burn into his retinas. A few men with heads held high gave the slightest of nods, and Dr. Magnus Hirshfeld was convinced: There would be sexual equality in his lifetime.

Part I:
The Fairy Godfathers

Tod Crouch

Chapter 1:
Turn of the Trick

> *I am an orphan, an orphan boy.*
> *I've known no love, I've seen no mother's joy*
> *A dirty doorstep my cradle laid,*
> *My fortune's made: I'll shake you from your sleep To hear me weep,*
> *Your day will come indeed. For I am a poor and a wretched boy,*
> *A chimbley chimbley sweep."*

Chimbley Sweep
The Decemberists

1880, London. Edward Shelley, barely in his teens, lifted the brow of his flat cap as the morning sun hit heavy eyes. He rubbed soot from his ruddy face with blackened hands, stretching his legs out from the doorway he slept in. The rats, on occasion, passed him to see if he were yet dead yet, prompting Shelley to spasm regularly in his sleep, scaring off more timid vermin. The door opened behind him in and the well-groomed homeowner said, "Move along, you sodding wanker!" The stray hissed and ran off.

After stealing brushes from his abusive mentor, Blogwart Grimstench, Edward kept an eye behind him for that twisted monster. Grimstench fell off a roof, costing him an eye and a leg before hiring Edward as an apprentice. Tired of beatings and badgering of a bitter drunk, Shelley stole Grimstench's tools and worked the claustrophobic chutes at the old age of 14.

The only thing left in this world for him was a desperate, joyless freedom. He waited patiently for death when descending into the flue's trappings. On occasion, young married women took him in to clean and seduce him, but Shelley knew these days would not last. His rosy cheeks and white-blonde hair only appeared when the old ladies took a fancy to him and washed him. Otherwise, Edward scraped soot from his face with his jagged fingernails. The boy only saw his own true face every other month, if lucky. There must be a better way.

Hungry, Edward waited until the cramps grew intolerable enough to allow spending his money. The soggy London sun groaned up from the horizon as a few shopkeepers swept debris from sidewalks before setting out their wares, ignoring Edward as he waited for his customers to wake.

Edward spent his early morning searching for edible food, when a young chap not much older than himself stepped out from a house of prominence. Startled, a caught look flashed across the older boy's face, quickly altered by a peculiar smile of many subtleties: confident, malicious, compassionate, and intimidating. The grimy, lice-ridden sweep looked to the tall lad dressed in a beaver hat and elegant morning coat. The strange boy descended steps, tipping his hat to filthy child. Edward cautiously nodded back, sinking in damp shoes, knowing it was best to keep this chase from dragging out. Shelley pulled a brush out defensively, "Please sir, I have no money. There is no reason for fisticuffs." Edward said, knowing he could not take down such a ruffian. The stranger merely smiled.

"I mean you no harm, friend," the stranger said. "I was just looking at your eyes."

"What of them?" Edward replied.

"I think they are very pretty. Like a china doll's. Have you ever seen a china doll's eyes?" The older boy said. Edward's heart pounded in his chest. The little chimney sweep had no friends, and cried to sleep at such an unfair loss. To look into this strange boy's eyes, as if it were home, if Edward ever knew such a place. Edward was too confused to run. The stranger asked stupid questions. "Are you a sweep? Is that your brush? Do you clean chimneys this early in the morning?" He smelled clean, even from a distance. The other lad wiped a curl of black hair from his flawless cheek.

"Go away. I have work to do," Edward said, walking away.

"Nonsense!" The boy said, cheerily, "I like you, little one. My name's Henry, Henry Newlove. Surely you can go to the country with me today. What is your name?"

"I haven't the money. And I don't know you." Shelley's forehead ached from frowning. He buckled, "Edward. Edward Shelley."

Henry Newlove reached into his pocket and pulled out a fistful of shillings, a king's ransom to young Edward. "It would be my treat. Come on, then. Even a sweep deserves a holiday, Edward."

"No."

"Suit yourself," Henry said with a shrug and turned away.

"Wait!" Edward said, "Where would we go?"
Henry turned around with a smirk, "Just a few miles out. I know a great little orchard where the farmers would never even know we're there. We be back by nightfall. Do you have to be back at a certain time?" They both knew Edward didn't. "Let's go!"

Newlove even bought Shelley a change of clothes, and, springing for the bathhouse, making Edward feel quite decadent.

They boarded a train to the country, where tombstone grey buildings passed into the sharp shadows of bright country a rare warm, sunny day blessed them outside the smog and soot of the big city. Edward looked out to scrolling English hills and spotted a creek cracking the valley, where warped trees drank with twisted roots from crooked creeks. Shelley never saw such a shade of green!

The train stopped at an uninhabited station in the middle of nowhere. Newlove beamed and said, "We're here! Go on! Get a move on!"

They stepped from the station's small awning as the train screeched and chugged off. Edward looked about. "But, Henry, there's nothing here."

Henry looked off into the deep valley from under his mess of curls. "I know! Isn't it great? Race you to the bottom!" Newlove yelled, barreling past Edward.

"No fair!" Edward cried, chasing after. Edward caught up to Henry just enough to tackle him, sending both tumbling uncontrollably down the side of the emerald hill, hysterically laughing. Already, Shelley was having the greatest day of his life.

"You cheat!" Henry said, throwing the boy off, "I would have won if you hadn't cheated!"

"You should have told me like an honorable gentleman that we were going to race!" Edward replied.

"Oh yeah?"

"Yeah! Who do you think you are? You can't beat the great Edward Shelley!" Edward said, sticking out his gamey chest. Henry laughed, goring Edward's ribcage and sending his victim into giggles. Kicking and squealing, Edward retaliated, discovering Henry was equally ticklish. Locked in their deadly tickle fight, they lost ground, hurtling down the side of the steep English mound.

"Stop! Stop! We're going to..." Edward said as the world spun about them, gravity meeting them from all sides.

"Never!" Henry said, plucking his adversary's ribs like a cello.

The two wheeled off the edge of the bank into a shallow river. Henry stood up, cold nipples peaking through his white shirt. He whipped his black hair from his face, spraying a wing of water from shaggy hair. Edward floated down river, face down.

"Edward? Edward!" Henry said, "That's not funny!" Henry dove after the younger boy and pulled the corpse to a muddied shore. "Edward! Edward! Wake up!"

Edward couldn't hold it any longer and let laughter bubble from his cherry lips.

Henry, furious, grabbed Edward by the lapels and yelled, "Don't you ever do that to me! Do you hear me?" Edward stared back in confusion.

"What do you care?" Edward answered, but he already knew when he looked at Henry. Henry released Edward to the currents and waded away. Edward always hated figuring out what people said without words.

"Just forget it." Henry said, throwing shillings to the beach. "Take your money and go."

Henry wanted to cry, but he was a big boy now that his older brother left a long time ago. This was how men did it. Boys died from anything less.

"Henry, I'm sorry!" Edward said, nearly on the verge of tears himself. In the river, Edward feared watching his only friend drift away.

Henry stopped, waiting for Edward to approach. "Oh yeah? How sorry could you be? I brought you out here. I thought I found a friend. But I don't know what you are."

"I don't know, but I know you are my best friend," Edward said. Henry looked back suspiciously at Edward.

"You mean it?"

"With all my heart." Edward said. Edward wanted to hold Henry and tell him everything that he knew. As long as the two of them were friends, life could be bearable. Edward needed that as much as he rightly thought Henry did. Trust is only true in doubt.

"Come on," Henry said, "The orchard's up a little ways. We can dry our clothes and eat some apples. I come here a lot." Henry waded back to Edward, leading him by the hand, clothes heavy with water. Their nervous silence was equally heavy. "Really? With all your heart?" Henry pressed.

"You're the only person I know," Edward responded.

As Edward weighed his affections, Henry grabbed Edward by the sopping shirt and kissed him. Edward did not fight the embrace, surprising them both. As the creek water rushed around them, they pulled each other tighter and closer until there was no question to their unity. Edward started crying uncontrollably.

"What's wrong?" Henry asked.

"I...I didn't want this to happen. But now it's the only thing that makes sense." Edward said, failing to deny truth. It was too much to process with nowhere to run, but the river ran with them. Henry took the crying boy in his arms as fish swam by. Edward's tears mixed with the river, never recovered. Henry wiped Edward's cheeks and smiled. "Ready?"

"What--" Edward said as Henry dunked him. Edward resurfaced. "You sodder, I wasn't ready!" Edward said. Henry laughed and splashed. "Stop it!"

Henry waded up, "Oh, and what's a little fairy like you going to do to keep me from splashing you?"

Edward grabbed Henry by the collar and returned the kiss. Henry stopped splashing. Henry was right.

The apples tasted great.

The two rested their heads on a log as the sun dried their bodies and clothes separately. "You should really give up chimney sweeping," Henry said. "I can already hear you wheeze. I could set you up as a messenger boy, and you could make a little extra on the side doing what we just did. Who knows? You might end up with a real job. You meet lots of interesting people."

"What do you mean?" Edward said with a sick sense of betrayal. He pulled himself out of Henry's arms and stood up, "What are you saying? Did you bring me here to... recruit me?!"

"It's not like that at all. I'm trying to help you." Henry's pragmatism appeared in the harshest light. It never worked, but maybe this would be the exception. Edward Shelley would have cried if not so angry, so ashamed. Newlove felt tainted.

Edward wept uncontrollably, "How could you? I never trusted anyone! And you pull me here and take advantage of me, you pervert! And you... you're just like me, but rather than be preyed upon, you prey upon your own kind! What kind of friend is that? I really liked you."

Henry rushed in, "And I like you, too. And you can leave me if I don't live up to my promises. But this line of work requires the use of your body, no different than sweeping chimneys. I'll do anything to protect you. Sure, our bodies may be used, but never our hearts. I can say that, because I give my heart to you—to protect and look after."

"You are a liar and a pervert," Edward said, sneering.

Henry's eyes welled with tears. "Please, Edward. Don't do this. Even if I can never win you back, don't pass this up."

"Pass what up? Being a…a…" Edward sobbed in hysterics.

"Being my best friend. It's just a body, no different than using it to get stuck in smokestacks." Henry said with a sheepish shrug.

"So, what, you'll *sell* me?" Edward said, his tears subsiding.

Henry fought his own tears, taking Edward by surprise to see such a handsome spirit buckle. "Please! You're all I have in this world! I can't do all this by myself! I've tried and it just makes me dead inside! But seeing you every day would make me strong enough to do this." Newlove wiped his tears and sucked in his sorrow. "Do what you want. I won't stop you. But please, don't leave me alone."

In Newlove's face, Edward saw his own. If Edward went it alone, it was best to go it with someone like himself. And being a chimney sweep was terrible. Naked, Edward extended his hand to Henry. "All right. Let's go on."

Chapter 2:
You Don't Have To Suck It, Just Hold It In Your Mouth

> *53rd and 3rd, Standing on the street*
> *53rd and 3rd, I'm tryin to turn a trick*
> *53rd and 3rd, You're the one they never pick*
> *53rd and 3rd, Don't it make you feel sick ?*
>
> *53rd & 3rd*
> The Ramones

Henry gave Edward an address to a small office. Edward Shelley checked the Soho address as nervousness set in. Newlove once said, "Now don't worry about Adolf Brand. He's in charge of the whole operation. He's well established in Berlin and just started a branch out here in London."

The longer the hesitation, the more anxious Edward grew. The boy opened the door to an unassuming office, leaving fear for the uncertain at the door. Adolf Brand was a young, stocky man in his mid-twenties. Adolf Brand's face lacked the weathered texture of a laborer, though the faint lines of adulthood worked their fingers into the corners of his sharp eyes. Edward noticed his strong arms, his tough build and bricklike hands. Scattered on Brand's desk were several publications in German. He looked up from a pamphlet with a lengthy title. Edward recognized the number 175 on the cover. Brand set the pamphlet aside.

"Yes? What can I do for you, young man?" Brand said with a thick German accent, self-consciously stroking down the bristles of his trim moustache.

Edward took off his tattered cap, wringing it in his hands. "Henry Newlove sent me, sir. He said you might have work for me."

"Is that so?" Brand said, bemused. Pushing himself away from the desk, Brand walked over with a clinical eye and flicked Edward's ears.

"Ow! What did you did you do that for?"

"Check your tolerance or predilection for pain," Brand said, unimpressed. "Open your mouth and say 'Ah'." Edward did so and Brand threw two fingers down the back of his throat. Edward continued to say 'ah' as Brand tossed his head up and sang "mi-mi-mi-mi-miiii." Brand cleared his throat and responded, "Good. No gag reflex. Decent pitch, too. All right then. Strip."

Edward cleared his throat, "Yes, sir."

Brand walked behind Shelley, pulled the shade down and locked his door. Edward shivered. Brand pulled out a small tin. "You'll do good to invest in this stuff." He scooped out two thick fingerfuls of viscous gel.

"What is it?"

"Wasser Elaion, but you poms call it Vaseline. Don't squirm." Brand said, clapping his clean hand on Edward's shoulder. Brand wiggled his other fingers.

"Ah! It's *so* cold!" Edward said, wincing. "I hope you don't own livestock."

"Only studs," Brand said. "Well, if I had known you were coming, I would have heated it up, Princess. Stick your arm out." Brand said. Edward did so and Brand slapped his triceps, looking for flab. "Good, good." Brand pulled his fingers out and wiped his hand on Edward's back. "Well, kid, as much as those old inverts say they want a virgin, they really don't. Some

22

old MP gets a little to ecstatic and, well, nobody wants that outcome. How old are you?"

"Sixteen." Shelley said.

"Really? You shouldn't lie."

"Fourteen…"

"Practically middle aged, for the lower class." Brand manhandled Edward's vittles. "Any sores? Strange fluids? Burning sensation?"

"No."

"Good. Get dressed." Brand said. "Well, you're a little old, but better late than never, am I right?" Brand said with a chuckle. "We'll set you up over on Cleveland Street. I think that's where your boy—what was it, Newlove?—is staying. Nice place for a brothel. Have Henry show you the ropes. You pay fifty percent of your fee to the house. You got a good face and good teeth. You'll do fine. The guy who runs the Cleveland stable is a man named Hammond Rye. He's a good guy who usually takes in baby chicks, a touch soft around the edges, if you know what I mean." Edward didn't. "And just remember, anyone roughs you up, you come to me. Do you hear me? I'll kill anyone who damages my property. You don't bugger the Devil's charge. After a few weeks on Cleveland Street, we shall acquire a suitable job for you on the side as a delivery boy. Not much of a wage, but it's a good cover. You just might move up into an honest life, if you really want to. Most don't."

"Ok," Edward said. "Thank you, Mister Brand." "Please. Call me Adolf. It's a dirty business in a grim world, kid. You'll do fine. It gets easier, especially after you start pulling in around twenty shillings a day." Brand said. Edward's eyes widened. "Nice meeting you, Herr Shelley."

Edward let himself out. He felt a little better about it all, though a bit oozy in the bum. Herr Brand called him 'Mister'. Nobody ever did that before.

It took him the better part of the day to walk from Brand's office. Along the way, a new London peeled itself back. A few innocuous storefronts appeared blatantly dubious. A shabby looking bakery had no cakes in the window. The whinnying of horses were absent from a livery stable. One store had a sign merely read OFFICE. An abandoned furniture store housed only a faded fainting couch in the window--yet through the soot-fogged glass, half a dozen men milled about a fine oak table, talking. Before, he only stared at the chimneys and rooftops. Now he stared at alleys.

19 Cleveland Street in the West End of London was unimposing from the outside. A long awning stretched out from the building, reading only the word PARLOUR. Judging from the muted colors, Edward assumed it was a funeral parlor. He entered through the tall oak door, where a man with a receding hairline and a pained smile stood at a podium. Behind him: a luxurious door to the left, a paint-chipped stairwell to his right.

"Why hello, young man. Are you lost?" The host said. Edward looked down to notice his pauperly clothes.

"No," Edward said, fidgeting, "Adolf—"

The host raised his hands and closed his eyes. "Say no more. I'm Hammond Rye. I suspect you wish to see Henry, then? He speaks so highly of you." Hammond said. Hurried footsteps came from the staircase. Henry leaned over the railing, eyes wide and smile bright, "Edward! I knew it was you!"

"How did you know?" Edward said.

"Oh, we can hear everything from upstairs. Come on! I want to meet you the others!" Henry said as he swung open the fancy door, dragging Edward behind. "Nice to meet you, Mister Rye," Edward said.

"You kids have fun," Hammond replied.

Inside the showroom, Edward was surprised to see such a decadent layout. He knew little about art, but never knew it to be so lascivious. Several boys around his age stood in poses from works of art, lit with a tender play of light against their pale naked forms. Two boys froze in a wrestling move. Another hunched with a discus in hand held a perfect form until he shifted his eyes to the new arrivals. "Henry!" The discus thrower said and jumped from his pose to startle Edward. The others in the strange scene broke character and wandered forward, grabbing the nearest billowing sheet to cover their cold bodies.

"Hello all! This is Edward," Henry said, throwing a chummy arm over Edward's shoulder. Edward waved around the room, embarrassed by all the nudity.

The boy with the discus sprung to life and shook Edward's hand, "You can call me George. Pleasure to meet your acquaintance." The handshake seemed odd; George Wright fancied himself a level-headed young man of high importance in a tight temporary spot. Though odds were against him, George seemed quite intelligent for his age.

The two boys locked in a wrestling move wouldn't make eye contact. The older one, Alfie Wood, was part- time and lived with his parents. The younger one, Sidney, smiled with all the cheer in the world. Edward sensed Alfie and Sidney were more than chums as well.

The showroom door creaked open. The boys turned in a panic, afraid of being caught out of character by a client. "And who do we have here?" said a gangly man with hungry eyes and a wide, jagged smile. He wore a priest's smock and a pencil thin moustache. The boys instinctively huddled behind the eldest boy, Henry.

Henry crossed his arms defiantly. "You know the rules, Veck. No dough, no show! Get out!"

Veck laughed, "Oh, children. How precious—"

"Get out, Veck!" Henry squeaked.

Hammond entered behind Veck and said, "Edward, this is Father Veck. He just wants to see the new talent. After all, he has to know what to promote to our many customers. Your room is ready upstairs, Edward. Henry, show him about and get him cleaned up. We'll give you a few days to get nestled. Tonight, we celebrate with strong spirits and the finest foods to welcome our newest guest!" Hammond said as he mussed Shelley's hair with atta-boy acceptance.

Hammond cooked an enormous welcoming dinner in the showroom, enhanced by the extravagant Greek décor. After regaling each other with stories, song, wine, sweet cakes, and tobacco, Edward abandoned the apprehension he felt when a good situation appeared. Cozy from wine, Henry took Edward by the hand through a door in the back of the parlor, upstairs to a dimly lit hallway, where five small rooms waited.

Edward opened the door to his new home and nearly cried tears of joy at seeing what he thought he would never see again: a bed. A real bed! Edward and Henry curled up on clean sheets in the light of a guttering candle.

As sleep washed over Edward, a hand of long, slender fingers emerged from the hallway's deep shadows. Father Veck's wretched smile terrified young

Edward. The priest emerged from the hallway's darkness, his smock blending with the void. Edward buried his face in Henry's chest. Henry pulled Edward behind himself and puffed up his chest. "Sod off, Veck!" Henry screamed loud enough for anyone to hear.

"I was...just checking to see that you boys were comfortable," Veck said.

"No pay, no lay!" Henry barked. Father Veck receded like a repulsed creature of the night. Moments later, Henry and Edward heard rutting down the hall. Henry explained, "He knows a lot of people, which is why Hammond keeps him about. Sinners confess to him, and he tells them where to sin. Other than that, stay away from him. He doesn't get any freebies here, so don't let him try. Scream if you have to. He can be persistent. Too persistent. He's already on unsteady ground with Hammond, who hides him from Brand."

The next few days flew by. Edward's first client was a fat Army Colonel named Rodney Jervois, who discovered his preferences during the Anglo-Egyptian War. Shelley loved the war stories from exotic locations. The colonel was quick on the trigger, which was why he was probably still alive. The act went quickly, so Edward could hear more war stories. There wasn't any better way to spend the night without Henry. During the day, Edward stayed fit by running telegraphs between his 'odd jobs'. He made enough in his first week to afford his own velocipede, stolen a week later. He kept all his money in his over-sized shoes, so not to get it confused with the telegraph till. On legitimate runs, his footwear inspired sympathy in customers who saw a young boy in ill-fitting shoes. After packing his socks with more and more shillings, he constantly needed larger shoes, exacerbating sympathy tips.

Edward ate well, drank well, slept well, stayed busy and was quite the prize pony. It was an unexpectedly happy life.

One night while Henry was out on a job, Edward heard his door creak open. Feigning sleep, Edward blinked open an eye to see that lecherous Veck crossing his room. Soon, a weight fell down on Edward's bed. Edward flung himself into a defensive posture. "Who's there?" Edward demanded, knowing full well who it was.

"Oh, now boy, don't be frightened. It's just your old pal Father Veck. You wouldn't get upset from a visit with your old pal, would you?" Veck said.

"Get out! Now!"

"Now, now. I'm a man of the cloth. I'm sure you have some sins to confess. And you're going to have to do penance for what you've done," Veck said, his breath hot with whiskey and rotten teeth.

The child wailed, "Get out of my room right now, Veck. I'll cut you like—"

Veck snarled, "Don't take that tone with me, you little punk!" Veck grabbed the boy by his shoulders and forced him to the mattress. Burying his screams in a suffocating pillow, Veck gagged him with surgical precision. Edward didn't even have a chance and knew it. Finished, the priest replied, "Don't tell a soul or next time, I won't be so gentle. And never forget that's all you're good for." Broken, Edward conceded.

Edward laid awake, watching the night fade from dark blue to the sick yellow sunrise. Henry came home, immediately concerned. "Are you okay?"

"No." Edward replied with a face of stone.

Henry grew frantic, his hands shaking. "What happened? Who did this to you? Was it Veck?"

Edward started crying. Henry's face flushed with rage. "Don't worry. We'll take care of this. Shh...We'll take care of this..." Edward crumbled in Henry's tight arms. Though Henry pretended to be strong, this reminded him he was just a boy, unable to protect anyone from the adults who owned them all. It scared them both.

That morning in bed, Henry scribbled a note and put it in an envelope. "What are you doing?" Edward asked.

Henry gave Edward a hapenny and the letter. "Take this to the post office. Send it express. Don't wait around." Edward complied without question. The brothel was quiet for three days. Henry refused jobs to protect his lover. Hammond sensed something amiss and sent Veck to the church to find more customers and lay low.

On the third day, Edward and Henry awoke, feeling the front door slam through the building. A great bellow shook the cheap walls, "Hammond! Get your putrid, pus-swollen arse out here!" Edward never heard such volume and crept to the stairwell to see what the commotion was. In long undergarments, Hammond bolted past the two eavesdroppers and ran downstairs.

Hammond rushed past the two boys, "Go back to bed, children. I'll take care of this." Edward and Henry didn't budge. Hammond slicked his hair back and straightened his clothes, "Yes? What's wrong? Is everything on the up-and-up?"

"Don't you *dare* talk to me like that!" The man said, "This is my stable and you're just the stable hand! Do you understand me?"

"I haven't the faintest idea of what you speak of, sir." Hammond said.

"Are you paying attention to me or is this suit just floating in the goddamn air? Where's Edward Shelley?" The man said. It was Adolf Brand. Edward crept hesitantly downstairs. Brand smiled at Edward covered himself in a whorehouse sheet.

"Sorry sir, I was asleep." Edward said.

"Tie that cock up in some pants, son. We're going to church!" Brand said, stamping his cane. He turned his direction to Hammond, "You bastard! You know how I feel about third parties! If you hire these n'er-do-wells to do your job, maybe you lack the ability to perform your function. Is that what you tell me by letting that so-called priest gad about? Answer me when I'm screaming at you!"

Hammond stuttered out, "Well, I…"

"Silence!" Brand howled. Edward felt Brand's thunder through the banister. Brand stared, exasperated at Edward, "What are you doing standing around for, boy? Waiting for the lube to dry? Get that sweet arse upstairs! This is big boy talk! Chop chop!"

As Edward left, Brand released a hurricane of profanities on Hammond that could level Big Ben.

Edward dressed quickly, regretfully missing a colorful vocabulary lecture, and bounded downstairs.

Brand took a deep breath, the calm eye of a profane hurricane. Adolf checked Edward for bruises as if the boy was a prize horse. "Are you okay, son? Did that bastard Veck violate my trust?" Edward looked to Hammond, who wore guilt like a crown of thorns. Edward nodded. Brand's face reddened, "Hammond! You miserable fool! Why would you jeopardize *my* establishment? Why would you dishonor me so? If I were a less gracious man, I would castrate you for this disaster and leave you to bleed in the street, devoured by dogs! Luckily, the boys seem to like you, even if you are a pathetic rat disease unworthy of drinking bitch piss."

Hammond tried with "Well, I wouldn't say--"

"Ho…" Brand said, shaking his head, "Quite the nerve you have, telling *me* that *you* endangering *my* boys is not a disaster. Is that what you are trying to explain? Because you better pray to God that I am suffering from rage fever and hearing those words shitting out of your mouth is delirium—because I never want to hear those words come out of your mouth. Ever. Is that understood?"

"Yes. Yes, sir." Hammond said.

"Don't make me worry about you, Hammond. You're a good guy, but don't make me worry. I tend to permanently remove things which worry me." Adolf said. Shaking like a feather on the breeze, Hammond steadied himself with a hand on the host's podium. With madness in his eyes, Adolf smiled at Shelley. "Edward!" he yelled, "Let's take a walk, shall we?" As the door closed behind Brand and Edward, Hammond sobbed like a little girl.

They took a carriage to a nearby parish. Brand took a deep breath. He seemed to be readying himself by talking to Edward. "Fear not, young man, for you have done nothing wrong. No matter what you do, you are no loser scrambling along the gutters like vermin. Forget this and your life is no longer yours. Your life is not about mincing about with painted cheeks and rouged lips. Know your worth and always add interest. There's a type of happy respect in that. I suppose you could call it *gay* pride."

Adolf flipped the horseman a shilling. Upon entering the nearly empty church, Adolf walked to the pulpit. He put a finger to his lips and pulled a long blade from his cane, motioning the sparse congregation to leave. Quietly, the few members backed out. Very quietly, Brand's whisper echoed, "Lock the door, Edward." The debonair pimp approached the confessional, listening intently. When Brand confirmed Reverend George Veck waited inside for confession, Brand jabbed a candelabra into the door handle, locking the priest in.

Brand growled, "Forgive me father for the things I'm about to do." The confessional booth rattled with panicked fury. Performing his grisly magic trick, Brand jabbed his blade through the screen. A girlish shriek emanated from inside. Brand plunged the blade through again and again. Blood kissed the puncture wounds, wiping the blade clean. The back door rattled even more fiercely. Brand cut the screen out, exposing Veck's pierced figure, terrified of his imminent death among the damned. He pushed himself up into the corner, a hobbled, leaking cobweb. Their eyes locked.

Adolf snarled, "Never bugger the Devil's charge." With a surgeon's precision, Adolf plunged the point into the priest's throat. At the unholy gurgled cough, Edward unconsciously smiled. The boy watched the backside of Brand struggle against an unseen victim as an awful shrieking reverberated from the vaulted ceiling.

Brand walked out calmly, holding something in his red right hand. He dropped it on the floor and washed his hands in the baptism pool. "So the world and God shall know his crime." He sheathed his cane sword, daintily pulled out a kerchief and wiped the red from his hands and face. He removed the contents from his jacket and placed the blood-soaked wool coat on a pew.

The two walked out, Brand's arm over Edward's shoulder. "Have you ever tasted iced cream?"

"No. What's that?" Edward said.

"I think you should enjoy it," Brand said, "And I'd say you deserve an iced cream sundae."

"But Sunday isn't for another three days." Edward said.

Adolf belted out a hearty guffaw. "You're all right, kid. You're all right."

Chapter 3:
Ballad of an Aging Rentboy

Where can get my cock sucked?
Where can I get my ass fucked?
I may have no money,
But I know where to put it every time.

Cocksucker Blues
Mick Jagger

It was a beautiful day in London. Crisp air now filled Edward Shelley's lungs, now void of soot. The sun shined as if to cut shadows from buildings with a razor. A year passed since his indoctrination into the unconventional boys' club. The post office was a tolerable cover. Though his hands smelled like man parts and telegraph ink, the sixteen pounds jangling in his shoes made him happy. He turned the crooked corner to Cleveland Street, where a ruckus outside the brothel drew a small crowd.

Little Georgie Wright, the freckled boy about Edward's age, stood watch as Henry Newlove violently kicked a small boy. "You lousy snitch! You terrible snitch!" Henry yelled. It was one of the part time punks, little fifteen-year-old Tommy Winscow, getting pummeled. Little Tommy screamed for help as Henry drew long punches and bloodied the child's nose.

"Henry! Stop! What are you doing?" Edward said from across the street. Georgie, whose shoulders broadened over the past year, walked over.

"Party's over, mate." Georgie said, "He snitched us out is what. He forgot to separate his earnings from the telegraph till. Came in with three weeks' earnings. The boss asked him about it, Tommy squealed about Hammond… about this place… and us."

Edward's stomach dropped into his oversized shoes. "No! That can't be!" Edward whined. Denial was not a luxury he could afford. "What about Hammond?"

"I saw the whole thing go down at the telly office and ran to tell Henry, who told Hammond. Hammond's gone, Edward. Long gone." Georgie said with a shrug. "Probably in Spain by now." Tommy Winscow still lived with his parents and failed to understand the severity of the situation. Georgie worked the line before and would again, though he knew the imminent dangers of being an independent contractor. Several meddlers advanced to the scuffle.

Henry's rage temporarily abated, his black hair swung across his pained gaze aimed at Edward across the street. An adult swiped Henry by the scruff, pulling him off. Henry cursed himself for drawing attention so rashly in front of Shelley. Henry opened his mouth as if to say a final word and stopped short of incriminating his love, never looking back. A sudden crowd swarmed around the three teenagers; Edward Shelley stared dumbly at his entire world, gone in seconds. Seconds. Two huge hands grabbed Edward's shoulders. "Come along, son. There's nothing to see here." His heart in his throat, Edward faced the oddly familiar stranger. It was Adolf Brand again, but without his notorious moustache.

"Adolf!" Edward pleaded.

"Silence, fool! Let us cut through Tottenham before proper discourse." Adolf said, nudging the boy a few paces ahead. Edward shoved his hands in his pockets.

On Edward's right sat a park bench. Adolf coughed from behind. Edward sat. Adolf sat. The older gentleman opened up a newspaper, sitting beside the youth at a distance. "Are you all right, son?" Adolf said.

"Quite well, all things considered." Edward said, feeling conspicuous. Brand tossed him a little magazine.

"Here. Read this."

"But it's in German!"

"I'm not asking for a damnable book review," Brand barked. "Did they catch on at the post office?"

"No."

"Good. Our little community has to take a different turn. That pinchbottom Labouchere passed some anti-buggery acts here in England and the Germans pretend as if they are the ones putting the plow before the arse. A ghastly read, that Paragraph 175." Brand said.

Edward flipped through the German magazine, shocked at the illustrations of half-nude men lounging in the sun. He turned bright red in embarrassment.

Brand said, "I recommend keeping your head down at the post office and brush up on your German. When you are ready, come to Berlin, where I shall find you work. But should you move too quickly, you might attract too much attention. Though I always prefer an open life for us, you may have to remain straight-laced until you become more self-sufficient."

Without making eye contact, Edward piped up, "But... But what about Henry? What about Alfie and Georgie?"

Adolf let out a long sigh, "Sometimes the only way to stay alive is to walk away. They'll get by." With the slightest of nods, Adolf did just that, turning onto Alfred Mews, disappearing into anonymity.

Ten minutes passed since Edward's life abruptly ended. He waited for something to think. His clothes, the love letters and drawings, and that big bed he shared with Henry were gone forever. Fearing police, Edward tried to recall some of the safer rooftops he used to sleep on. A carpetbag winking in the glint of evening's gaslight where Brand sat was all that remained. Edward opened and closed it immediately, seeing valuable Daguerreotypes of naked men, dirty pamphlets—and money. At least a hundred pounds! He could live quite comfortably for quite awhile. Brand was right. He always took care of his boys.

In hindsight, Edward realized the money was to be insufficiently split among the boys. Edward would have traded it all for Henry's cocksure smirk; hear him snap his suspenders one last time—but no more. Edward checked into a flophouse, pulled the rough wool blanket over his body, placed his carpetbag under his head, and felt safe enough to cry himself to sleep.

One day at a time, weeks passed. He bought a pair of nice shoes, knowing he would spend more time on his feet than on his back. He pretended to be an adult. He made his own dinner and darned his socks. He did not trust himself to company of pubs, for fear of running into clients. But on lonely nights, he needed a glass of port to sleep. He bought the daily paper from an attractive newsie a block away from the post office. They looked to each other with desire in one eye and caution in the other. The paperboy's name was Henry, which sent a pang coursing through Edward's body.

But Paperboy Henry looked nothing like One True Love Henry. It didn't matter. Edward could barely read.

Edward knew his letters and how they were supposed to sounded togethers. He reads fairly gooder so the mails got to the right places, but is worser for writing in the good way that the orders of words was hardest--so the gossipy landlady reads him all the details of the Cleveland Street Scandal, unaware of his secret account.

Detective Inspector Frederick Abberline was on the case of *The Fall of the House of Cleveland*. Abberline asked the boys if any other teens frequented the establishment. Henry, whose name was now in the paper quite often, said no. Little Tommy Winscow buckled out of fear. Georgie Wright agreed there were no other boys involved. Edward was cleared, though a coward, hiding behind a lie. He wanted to be with Henry. After a few bleeding heart journalists admonished the abuse of child prostitutes, then frequenting them at night, several prominent names popped into place. "Fitzy" was actually Henry Fitzroy, the Earl of Euston, for one. Edward already knew Rodney Jervois, the army colonel. Hammond Rye was mentioned, but never found. Henry Labouchere used the incident to get himself re-elected to English Parliament. Edward took pride in being a pervert if Labouchere was the alternative.

Eight months passed since that day it all fell apart. During the strange year, he led the life of a lower class prisoner, existing for existence's sake without joy or sorrow, so separated from his only love. "Those fairies get what they deserve, that's what." Edward's supervisor, Alfred Dickering, said. "If I found any of those sodomites working in *my* office, I'd do quite more than terminate those poofters, soiling the very name of the Postal Services." Dickering said, snapping a pencil in two. "Those perverts are really taking over. They're worse than the Jews." Edward merely nodded, sorting the afternoon mail. "You don't seem too hot about it, Edward. Any Englishman should be outraged by what doesn't concern them." Dickering sounded jealous, being the least exciting person in England.

"You're absolutely right, Mr. Dickering." Edward said, cursing his traitorous tongue, "The mere thought of them disgusts me, so I try not to think about them." "But you should think about them, Edward! I think all of those fairies should come right out in the open! At least then, we would know their numbers and put them in camps, accordingly!" Dickering said.

Edward smiled and said, "You're absolutely right, Mister Dickering. It's bad enough that they could be living right underneath our noses."

As Edward sifted through the envelopes in the sorting room, a plain, empty envelope appeared with no return address. Edward's hand trembled, seeing his own name over a strange address. It was Henry Newlove's unmistakably terrible handwriting. Very cautiously, Edward slid the empty envelope into his pocket. Unbearable hours ticked away until his shift ended when he could examine the empty envelope.

Edward followed the address to a dilapidated flophouse. The warty hag waved a sagging arm from her greasy front desk, sending the boy upstairs out of her sight. Edward searched darkened hallways between screaming syphilitic whores and mad derelicts, until he came to the door. He knocked. As the door opened, Henry Newlove waited on the other side. His hair was too short for his weathered face and defeated eyes. Edward fell into the abandon of Henry's arms with abandon, smelling the ammonia and stale roses of his first love. With apprehension, Henry slowly placed his lanky arms around Edward. Neither had known such happiness since that tragic day.

"Henry! I've missed you so much!" Edward said, laughing through his tears. Henry pulled Edward into the room, smelling sweetly of dead rats. Edward felt as though he, too, escaped prison. They sat on the bed beside each other.

"I have some news," Henry Newlove said. The pain of Henry's absence surged up on once again.

"What troubles you? I met Adolf shortly after the incident. He said we should travel to Berlin and get better jobs. I studied German in my off time. We could leave this filthy town and start life anew! We can travel by train, like we did when we first met!"

Henry's gaunt frame transformed him into a sickly wraith. From a mouthful of sores, He said, "Have you accepted Jesus Christ as our Lord and Savior?"

"What?" Edward said.

"I've been converted from my wicked ways in jail. They brought in priests to talk to us boys. They lectured us for eight hours a day, telling us how our sinful lives would cause us nothing but ruin. I don't want your soul to be ruined, Edward, because I love you."

Did they hurt you in that way?" Edward said.

"They punished us every night. It was the only way to learn the pain of our wickedness."

"Oh, Henry, no. No. No no. No no no no no no…" Edward whined, his eyes welling up with tears,

"What did they do to you! You don't actually believe that nonsense, do you?"

"With all my heart." Henry said, "Please. Join The Church with me. I am joining the holy life."

"No! You simply mustn't!" Edward screamed, "What about us? Why would you do this to me? I love you!"

Henry's eyes were cold. "I love you, too. That is why I want to save your soul. We were exploited, Edward. Only Jesus can save us from our past."

Edward, devastated, slumped on the bed.

"But all this time..." Edward said, "You were the only thing keeping me alive."

"Come to the rectory with me tomorrow. It's not too late to save your soul."

"My soul is just fine!" Edward cried, "And so is yours! How could you let anyone tell you what's best for you, when you alone know what's best?"

"If you don't want to join me in the church, you should leave. Jesus never associates with sinners. Neither will I."

"What are you talking about? Jesus loved a whore!" Edward said, "This can't be happening!"

Henry said in a detached monotone, "It was hard for me. But now, I understand. I wish I could show you the error of your ways."

"But you know those priests will bugger you and you won't even get paid!" Edward screamed.

Henry said, "Will you keep your voice down?" Edward paced the tiny room, trying to find an exit that was not the front door.

"God would never want you to break my heart like this." Edward said.

Henry said, "You don't know the Bible the way I do. You're just a dumb whore like I used to be. I want to help you. I'm sorry I ever introduced you to that lifestyle."

Edward wiped rivers of rage from his eyes. "I'm not a dumb whore! I was smart enough to not get caught!" he sniffled. Finding no other exit, he walked to the front door.

"Wait!" Henry Newlove said, taking Edward's arm. In a final act of desperation, Edward attacked Henry with a final kiss. Henry's lumpy lips stayed cold as he shoved Edward away. Only a sliver of who Henry used to be glinted in his eyes. "I can still save you," Henry begged weakly.

"You can't save with one hand and condemn with the other," Edward said, grabbing his coat and walking out. Edward watched the legs of his body stumble down the stairs. Edward heard his body's ears hear Henry call to him. His hands shoved the door open. He felt his breath sharpen to the cool twilight air. Outside, Edward wiped his cheeks—how dare he shed tears! He calmed down by the time he reached his flat.

That night, Edward Shelley packed a bag and left for Berlin.

One of the pamphlets in Brand's bag gave a street address in Berlin. The trip was longer than expected. His travels to the countryside with Henry seemed so long ago. Edward stared out the window, spoke to no one, barely slept or ate. The happy tourists attempted to chat him up, but Edward could only respond with the chilly silence of a refugee.

In Berlin, Adolf Brand sat behind a desk piled high with submissions to his publication, *Der Eigene*. All the money he collected as a pimp went into this financially disastrous venture. With the crackdowns on brothels, Brand spent all his earnings on publishing something he believed in. *Der Eigen* needed everyone. Everyone needed *Der Eigen*.

Brand's office door opened. A young man held an old familiar suitcase in his hand and pathetic expression on his face. The suitcase fell from the traveler's hand, and composure fell from his face. "Herr Brand?" Edward's bottom lip quivered.

Adolf recognized him immediately. "Why, little Eddie Shelley! How are you doing?" Brand greeted the young man. Edward rushed to Brand, sobbing. It broke the hardened pimp's heart.

"Henry's gone to the monastery," Shelley choked out. The body in Brand's arms was as fragile as crushed tissue. "Why? Why would he do that to me? Please Mister Brand! I... just... don't know... I don't know what to do..."

Brand held him close and patted his blonde, dirty curly head. Poor kid braved isolation long enough. Brand sighed and said, "You have to walk away sometimes."

"But it's so hard!" Edward cried, becoming even more wretched.

"I know, son. However, we must move forward. We make our own choices as others do. We can't take those who don't want to go with us." Brand said, gently patting child's back, "We chose this destiny because it was who we are, not because it was easy. Shh, now..."
When Edward's tears subsided, Brand offered him scotch, which Edward slammed quickly. "I don't even know what I'm doing here," Edward confessed, "I just had to get out of London. I failed to give notice to my boss."

"Don't trouble yourself with that, now." Brand said, "We take care of our own because everyone else wants us dead. The options are wide open for you here."

43

Edward sniffled. Brand gave him a handkerchief. Compassionate as Brand was, he silently hoped this reunion would quickly conclude. A 'sexologist', Dr. Magnus Hirshfeld, sent word of his arrival in Berlin to carry a discourse on the plight of the sexually inverted. The good doctor was late. Brand continued, "I have yet to complete some articles for my magazine. Rest up on the couch for now, as I am sure you are knackered from your long trip. I know you've had a long day." Adolf said. Edward's eyelids dipped in agreement.

Edward's eyes barely closed when a heavy fellow entered with an even bigger moustache than Brand's. Small spectacles rested on his large nose. In one hand, he carried a thick folio.

"Dr. Magnus Hirshfeld, I presume?" Adolf Brand said with a smile, "I am quite pleased to finally meet such an esteemed sexologist."

The doctor said with heavy breath, "Terribly sorry I'm late. I just received a telegram from Hanover—and they require our assistance concerning—a murder!"

Chapter 4:
The Werewolf of Hanover!

Hanover, 1890. Fritz Haarmann was a gentle soul to look at. His baby face held a constant expression of a kicked puppy as he fidgeted with the Deutschmarks in his pocket. Nervous and excited, he cruised the Hanover train station, where all the line boys gathered.

He felt like a faceless tourist. He nearly chickened out at the last minute again. In the constant battle of shame and lust, lust wins the battle and shame wins the war.

The lineboys struck careful poses. Fritz never liked the girly ones. The young ones who feigned innocence thrilled him. They had lithe bodies still growing into masculine features. Looking down the line sullenly, Haarmann's gaze landed on *that* one: the boy in an undershirt and short pants, showing a sliver of leg above the high sock. Blonde haircut with rusty shears, the boy seemed more bored than aroused. Feeling someone's eyes on him, the boy fixed on Fritz.

Haarmann stopped as the crowd's currents eddied around him, claustrophobically. The timid, fat man drowned in the shallow of his breath. The streetlamps flickered with bitter wind. Trains wailed an endless banshee shriek. Haarmann's heart pounded in his ears. He looked away. He looked back. The boy smiled. Fritz looked around. Everyone silently scolded him, seeming to point and laugh at him. The boy, too, started laughing. Cops wouldn't arrest him. He was too pathetic. Fritz wanted to cry. They were right. He was pathetic. And desperate. Everyone thought so.

Even pigeons mocked him.

"Hey mister," the boy said, now standing before Fritz, "do you have a cigarette?"

Fritz took a shallow, nervous breath. "Yes, young lad. I do believe I have one around here." The boy smiled like a wolf. This john was going to be an easy roll.

As was the signal, Fritz took two cigarettes in his mouth and lit them, passing one to the young man. The boy took a drag and spat out the pubic tobacco shavings. The boy sized up the feeble man, saying, "What's your name?"

"Fritz," Fritz said, unaware of his own intense frown.

Flinching a suggestive eyebrow, the boy cocked his head back, "You're going to miss your train, Fritz. The name's Ernst. But you can call me Ernie." Ernie said. Fritz swallowed hard. "And how old are you, young man?"

"Sixteen," Ernie said with a smile. At thirteen, he wasn't fooling anyone.

Fritz said, "Awfully young to be out here by yourself at night, don't you think?"

Ernie took Fritz's hand and said, "I'm working on fixing that."

Fritz smiled. The boy smiled. The two walked among the crowd. They passed a policeman, who saw them as nothing more than traveling relatives. They smirked at the foolish officer.

The crowds stopped and clapped. The lights grew brighter and brighter until there was not a shadow at the train station. The boy loved him. Everyone loved him. Even Fritz loved himself. The boy squeezed Fritz's hand. Fritz squeezed back. It was going to be ok. He could live with himself. The boy gave life purpose. It was all Fritz could ever want--a pleasant young man, who didn't find Fritz ugly. Or fat. Or old.

They could do the thing and cuddle all night.

"You know it's going to be 20 marks up front, right?" Ernie said.

"Anything. Anything for you, my sweet little Ernie." Fritz said, beaming. A boy this beautiful changed everything. Maybe Fritz was a winner, after all.

At the little apartment door, Fritz fished out his keys to the little apartment. "Sorry. They always seem to get stuck in my pocket."

"I wonder why." Ernie said. Fritz felt his heat swell. The key bucked the lock loose. The older man smiled sheepishly and entered, letting the boy follow.

Haarmann never paid for sex, but always bribed loneliness.

"You'll have to excuse the mess. I rarely have company," Fritz said, hanging up his shabby coat. Ernie already looked for escape routes to crawl out of in the middle of the night with everything he could carry. The tiny room had one window. Climbing out a second or third story window was easy at his size. A little tin toy train fresh from the train station gift shop sat on the nightstand. Ernie rolled it gently across the nightstand.

Fritz Haarmann trembled as the boy stripped. Embarrassed by the size of his belly, Fritz extinguished the lantern before wrapping around Ernie. Ernie struggled against Fritz's roughness, before frustration overtook the large man. In the darkness, Fritz bit into the boy's throat and ripped away the flesh. The child squealed as red spattered Haarmann's face. Haarmann swallowed the flesh, eyes wide and wild. Ernie scrambled helplessly.

Haarmann mewled, "You'll tell! You'll tell them I was a bad man! You'll tell everyone! You'll never tell! You can't tell! You think I'm weak! But I'll show you! You're just like the others!" Haarmann tore at the child's neck again. As Ernie's struggles and screams turned to twitches and wimpers, Haarmann climaxed. He leaned back in near exhaustion, holding the nearly dead boy in his hands. Ernie now seemed as gentle and soft as a rabbit Haarmann crushed as a child. The rag doll body landed on the floor with a hollow, soulless thud.

Haarmann relit the lantern. The walls, ceiling, and floor glistened with blood. His eyes burned white-hot from behind a glistening, red mask. Calmly, Haarmann smoothed his hair of the excess fluid, warm as his own fever. Ernie's trapped eyes still moved. Sickened by their judgment, Haarmann plunged the toy train in each soft socket. Dragging the limp body by the ankle to the kitchen, Fritz Haarmann got out the tools.

***

Adolf Brand, Dr. Hirshfeld, and Edward Shelley arrived in Hanover the following day, where Inspektor Kurt Hagen greeted them. Hagen was in his late 40s. Interrupted by an eye patch, a bright pink scar ran down the left side of Hagen's face. He sneered at the world through his disfigurement. Young Dr. Hirshfeld walked up and extended his hand to Hagen at the rail station. "Inspektor, It is a sincere pleasure to meet you. These are my associates, Adolf Brand and Edward Shelley. They have done extensive field work concerning the matter at hand."

Hagen stuck a cigarette in the twisted end of his mouth. "No need to mince words, Doctor. I know of Brand and I assume this is one of his rent boys. From that Cleveland Street debacle, I'm guessing?" Hagen said. Shelley looked about nervously. "It makes no difference to me. As for you, Herr Brand, I have no concern for your activities. Your actions are far outside my jurisdiction. You should feel lucky that other officers do not have such a vulture's eye as mine or they would swoop down on you like the carrion you are." Inspektor Hagen said, staring though Brand. Brand stared back, his moustache covering his snarl.

"Gentlemen!" Hirshfeld said, "We have a crime to solve."

They walked a few paces through the Hanover Station Promenade, where a few line boys already waited. Inspektor Hagen paid them no mind. Shelley sized them up as competition, finding most quite handsome. They reminded him of Henry's sharp eyes and black hair. A few returned a wink and a pucker.

Adolf Brand nudged Shelley disapprovingly and whispered, "We are in the company of the law. Refrain yourself!" Shamed, Shelley hung his head and stared at his shoes.

Brand looked to the same lineboys and sized them up for his stable. Most of them looked underfed and bony, but their creamy skin and pouty lips sent his imagination racing. Dr. Hirshfeld nudged Adolf Brand and whispered, "We are in the company of the law. Refrain yourself!" Brand hung his head and stared at his shoes.

Dr. Hirshfeld looked to the same lineboys and saw herpetic pustules along their lips, syphilitic discharges crusting in the crotches of unwashed pants, the yellow eyes of hepatic livers. He shuddered.

At the police station, the four entered a small room with a large, empty evidence table. Hagen pulled a rucksack and emptied the contents onto a dirty table. An enormous pile of corpse remnants clattered onto the slab, releasing an unbearable stench. Hagen passed around a tincture of camphor. Brand swabbed his moustache with the balm, cutting the acrid odor. Hirshfeld picked up a leg and examined the joints. Shelley counted the skulls. Hagen said, "These were found in a dumpster only a few blocks away from the train station."

"My word, these are the bones of teenage boys!" Hirshfeld said. "Much of the meat has been cut from the bone with some sort of serrated knife, but this is too sloppy for a butcher's work. Not only that, but he failed to saw down the femurs. Many of these *lustmord* types are much more meticulous with their handiwork. I'm guessing disposal was an afterthought, leaving the primary objective to be sexual in nature."

Inspektor Hagen said, "Boys have been disappearing from the Hanover railway station. Fairies or not, these are sons of mothers. Murder is murder and I will not stand for it."

"How honorable of you," Brand said.

"I'll have you know, Herr Brand, I'm the only one working this case. Do you know what the other members of the force say when I show up with a bag full of dead line boy bones? 'Good riddance'." Inspektor Hagen said.

Dr. Hirshfeld interjected, "Herr Brand meant no offense, Inspektor."

"I should hope not," Hagen replied.

"How do you know these are, uh, line boys?" Edward said, shyly concerned with his own wellbeing.

Hagen smiled, "That's a good question, young man. We have ten missing persons reported over the past two weeks—Nearly one boy a day. Friedel Rothe, 17. Fritz Franke, 16. Wilhelm Shulze, 17. Roland Huch, 15. Hans Sonnennfeld, 18. Heinrich Strauss, 18. Fritz Wittig, 17. Heinrich Koch, 16. Heinz Martin, 14. And Friederich Abeling, 11. All these boys disappeared going through Hanover Station, but they are too young to travel alone. I know what occurs in the shadows of that station. Naturally, the boys who work the line have no strong trust for the police."

Shelley looked at the contents on the steel table, noticing a much smaller skull, brown hair clinging from a shoddy scalping job. Hirshfeld examined where a few vertebrae still affixed to the skull. The Doctor squinted through his tiny glasses and reported, "There are human teeth marks on the back of this skull."

Hagen cleared his throat. "Unfortunately, this is potentially less than half of them. I've got fourteen other missing person reports, all last seen at the Hanover Railway station."

Edward Shelley took a seat, his arms turned limp as he said, "Why would someone do this? Why aren't there police officers there? Why isn't anyone telling them to be careful?" Shelley blinked and two tears raced down the sides of his cheeks. Dr. Hirshfeld put his hand on Edward's shoulder, but the doctor's bedside manner failed. Magnus' other hand held a greasy tibia.

Adolf said with cold sobriety, "Because they want us dead, Edward."

"But why? It's not right! It's not fair! It doesn't make sense! We didn't do anything to them!" Edward cried. Magnus nodded to Adolf.

Brand sighed, "Come on, son. Allow me to indulge you to a nice meal and a pint."

"How could you even say that?" Edward squealed,

"Someone's killing us and no one cares…and you have want to have *dinner*? You're as bad as the rest of them!" Edward stormed out, slamming the door behind. The Inspektor, the pimp, and the doctor all looked at one another.

Dr. Hirshfeld asked, "Do we go after him?"

"Not yet," Brand said. "It was foolish to include him. After all, these could have been his bones."

"He won't go far," The Inspektor said, "not with the Werewolf of Hanover loose. He'll be back, dead or alive."

Brand charged Hagen. "Listen, you son of a--"

"This is no way to act!" Hirshfeld bellowed, "I begin to think the young lad is more mature than both of you! If you refuse to be civilized, at least be professional."

The door opened quietly and a newly collected Edward entered. The adults looked to the floor, guilty of their outbreak. "Well?" Edward demanded, "What are you going to do about this?"

Hagen answered, "Son, we're still figuring that out."

"You're going to need a lure, right? And the local boys would never cooperate with police. So allow me to put my services to legal use as jail bait."

Brand said, "Absolutely not! You are not going to endanger yourself, not after what you already endured."

Edward looked to the grownups and said, "This is more my battle than yours. I shall be the lure and you shall be the reel."

Brand cried, "This is madness!"

"Madness begets madness." Dr. Hirshfeld added, "Have you a better idea?"

Hagen hesitantly agreed. He said, "Allow me to contact my informant. He's a bit slow in the head, but he knows the underworld of Hanover quite intimately." At the informant's house, Inspektor Hagan knocked on the upstairs apartment door. A portly man with hard blue eyes answered, drying his hands with a red towel. The man smiled kindly, "Why Inspektor Hagan! It's so good to see you again."

"Gentleman, this man has provided us with some of the greatest underground intelligence in all of Hanover. I introduce you to Fritz Haarmann."

The informant looked to Edward Shelley and said with a toothy smile, "So nice to meet you all."

Chapter 5:
When the Hunter Gets Captured by the Game

> In *little children's heavy heads*
> *My dreams erupt while in my bed*
> *Innocence is dripping red*
> *In dreams I walk with you*
> *In dreams I talk with you*
> *In dreams*
> *You're mine*
> *All of the time*
>
> Love's Secret Domain
> Coil

"Please, have a seat," Haarmann said. Magnus Hirshfeld, Adolf Brand, Edward Shelley and Inspektor Hagen searched for seating in the tiny apartment as Haarmann closed the kitchen door. To his guests, he seemed to be a polite simpleton ambling around with a sad look in his eyes. "Hello Mister Hagen. How are you today? I'm glad you came to visit me." Haarmann said. "I've made some meat pies if you are feeling a bit puckish."

No thank you, Herr Haarmann. We won't be staying long. We're investigating a series of murders," Hagen said. Previously, Fritz nosed out three bank robbers, a forger, and two murderers in the Hanover area. "Line boys at the Hanover Station have been getting picked off. We wondered if you heard anything."

Shelley noticed on the nightstand a little tin toy train, flecked with brownish-red rust. Edward gave it a push. The wheels failed to roll.

"You can have it, if you want it," Haarmann said to Edward. "It was mine when I was last... visited by youth."

"Thank you, sir," Edward said, tinkering with it to get the wheels moving.

"How are you going to catch this fellow?" Haarmann asked with a worried expression.

"Edward here is going to act as bait. But we have few solid leads. Have you heard of anything new? Any new gangs crop up with distaste for the rent boys?"
"No, no..." Haarmann said, "I haven't heard anyone making sport of it."

Magnus scanned the room. Not a hair was out of place. It smelled powerfully of bleach and lye. The mattress was recently reupholstered, and the floor shined with a vibrant luster. Hospitals were not this spotless. Inspektor Hagen stood from the chair and said, "Well, thank you for your time, Fritz. We don't want to trouble you."

Edward led the way out, feeling uncomfortable around *real* criminals, even if only reformed petty thieves. Brand pocketed the toy train Edward forgot. Dr. Hirshfeld noticed a brown water stain next to the bed, confused as to why the stain came from the center of the wall and not the ceiling. Haarmann appeared next to a startled Hirshfeld, "Is everything all right?"

"No, no. I was just on my way. It was a pleasure to meet you." Magnus said, feeling embarrassed for letting his intellectual judgments of a lower class thief leak through. Outside the apartment, Hagen laid out the details. "Brand? Hirshfeld? Attend to the evidence room to discern if those bones tell you anything new. Edward and I will head to the Hanover Station to start the bust."

"Why the hell should I go back with Maggie?" Brand said.

"There's enough pimps on the street." Hagen said coldly. Brand didn't argue.

From his apartment window, Fritz Haarmann watched the team divide. From the bedside table, he pulled out a piece of piano wire.

***

It started to rain. Hard. Within a few minutes, Edward Shelley was soaked to the bone and freezing at the Hanover Station. The rain drove the prettier ones away, thinning the competition. It was no different from the years wedged in a London chimney or delivering letters from the post office in the freezing rain. Still, it was hellish to be so cold. Hagen stood in a crumbling alley, watching Edward from a moderate distance.

At the police station, Magnus stood over several femurs, picking out pairs like mismatched socks. Bored, Brand watched the doctor attempt to solve an impossible riddle. It embarrassed Magnus to be inept at the crude forensic sciences. Something poked Brand in his pocket, where he retrieved a small tin toy train. He set it on the evidence table.

"What do you have there?" Magnus asked.

"A toy Haarmann gave to Edward, but Edward forgot to bring it with him." Brand said. Magnus accidentally bumped the wobbly table, sending the train over the side. Brand huffed and picked up the train. "Honestly, do I have to pick up *all* your toys?" Rust chipped off the train, revealing a bright paint job underneath. A sharp pang of dread weighed in both bellies. Magnus and Brand exchanged the same horrified expression.

Magnus ran his fingernail over the toy. "This isn't rust! It's blood! Grab your coat, Adolf," Hirshfeld said, "I know who the Werewolf of Hanover is!"

At the train station, Inspektor Hagen watched a train push through howling rain. He checked his pocket watch. A footstep scraped cobblestone behind him, but it was too late. Two gloved hands holding piano wire came down fast over the Inspektor. Hagen threw his elbows back hard, only to hit something dense as a tree trunk. Hagen struggled for breath as his vision faded when, with a quick slice, the wire opened his throat. The train whistle wailed.

Moments later, Edward saw a familiar face in the crowd. "Hello, Mister Haarmann," Edward Shelley said, trying not to shiver.

"Hello, little Edward," Fritz Haarmann said with a vacant stare and a slight smile. "I spoke with the Inspektor and he told me to escort you back to my place, as I have found a lead. It is not safe for you out here. The doctor, the inspektor and your friend are all waiting at my flat. They sent me to come and pick you up."

"That is wonderful news!" Edward said, "I'm freezing out here." He wrung the rain from his soaked shirt.

Fritz said slowly, "I think I might have some clothes that would fit you perfectly."

***

Brand and Hirshfeld exploded out of the examination room. Brand yelled, "We need an officer's assistance!" The police dismissed them.

Magnus grabbed Brand's arm, "We don't have time for this. They won't help our kind." They hurried to the livery stable. "Get me your two fastest horses, now!"

The stable boy looked at the two men and exclaimed, "But sir! It'll take a few minutes for me to strap up the horses!"

Brand waved his cane menacingly at the stable hand, "Make it quick boy! I never ride bareback!" The stable boy's hands worked fast. After servicing so many police officers, it was like tying a shoe.

"What is the meaning of all this?" the Komissioner bellowed, storming in with lackeys tight in tow.

"Civilians stealing state horses is a federal offense!"

"There's no time!" Brand said, mounting his horse, "Lives are on the line! Get to the Hanover Railway as soon as you can!" Brand's horse reared up and let out a heroic whinny as the two men jumped the stable doors. Bewildered officers looked to the cold, birdlike visage of the Komissioner.

The Kommissioner watched two men charge headlong into danger, he nodded and said, "Do it."

Magnus' dumpy body barely stayed in the saddle, though Brand held the reins like a master equestrian. Magnus yelled, "I'll hit Haarmann's place. You hit the rail station!"

"Hell no, Maggie!" Brand said, "That bastard is mine! No one buggers the devil's charge!" Their eyes locked. Magnus nodded. With a rap on the hindquarters of his great galloping beast, Adolf Brand swooped down a side street with an Eagle's grace.

At the rail station, Magnus brought the horse to a trot, hoping the trains wouldn't spook such a marvelous animal. Dr. Hirshfeld's breath froze in the air. He passed the wall void of line boys. A crowd gathered at the far end of the promenade. He knew why.

Magnus rode through the parting crowd. Blood diluted in the wet pavement, raked into the gutter's grating. Rail workers gathered around the nearly decapitated body of Inspektor Hagen. Two police officers were surprised to see Magnus arrive on a stolen police horse. Before they could object, Magnus commanded, "Get to 18 Liebenstrasse! The Werewolf of Hanover lives!" He turned away from the crowd and felt a rising terror. Edward Shelley was nowhere to be seen.

***

The carriage dropped Fritz and Edward off at the small apartment in driving rain of twilight. Haarmann seemed distant and bashful, assumedly his disposition around rent boys. Many treated escorts with curious suspicion and Edward was familiar with such awkwardness. Fritz said, "Hagen and your friends are waiting inside."

The boy walked into the small apartment and heard the door close behind him. His instincts screamed in the empty room. Edward saw through Haarmann, whose stupid smile now turned demonic.

Haarmann's heavy arm knocked Shelley across the room, through the kitchen door. Edward looked up in horror as dismembered children's legs dangled from hooks. Knives lined the walls. Arms reached out from bloody buckets. Haarmann chuckled, grabbed the boy's ankle and drew him close with a spider's malice.

Outside Fritz's apartment, Brand hopped off the horse and ran up the stairs. He took a deep breath, drew his cane sword and shattered the flimsy door with a kick. Inside, Haarmann was predisposed, reaching up his fireplace. The Beast turned with a bloodied eye socket, growling at the new intruder. Brand drew his cane sword, blade bobbing in Brand's terrified hand.

Adolf swung his blade at Harmann, who blocked it with a splintered plank from the front door. Haarmann threw the plank aside, along with Brand's wedged blade. The beast lunged, tossing Adolf through a stained, flimsy wall.

Adolf landed in an elderly couple's living room, where the old woman continued knitting and her husband read the paper. Brand jumped to his feet with a table leg in hand and swung it at Haarmann. The cheap wood shattered into sawdust against the The Beast, who licked his bloody lips and shoved Brand through a French door into a small kitchen. The pimp picked glass out of his face as the behemoth advanced. Brand reached into a drawer, looking for a knife. Haarmann slammed the drawer shut. Brand felt something snap. Haarmann kicked the trapped Brand before hurling him through the neighbor's front door and into the hallway.

The elderly woman continued knitting among the ruins of her quaint abode, "See? I told you we lived next to a murderer. But no, you wouldn't listen." The old man grumbled, rattling her away with his newspaper.

Brand, delirious in pain, rose from his wretched state in the hallway. A flash of lightening at the top of the stairs illuminated the path to the rooftop. Light-headed, he ran up the stairs while his busted wrist grinded bone fragments. Collapsing on the tarpaper and gasping for breath, he heard the thunderous hooves of The Beast advancing. Cold, hard rain gave him focus. He struck a boxer's stance. Haarmann stepped from the red light of the stairwell like a demon from hell. Blood traced Haarmann's footsteps on the rooftop. Lightning flashed, further distorting a wicked face. Brand stood his ground in futility.

"Come on, then!" Brand yelled above the rain's applause. "Everyone knows it's you! You can't win!" Haarmann smiled with red teeth and chuckled. Adolf threw his mightiest punch into a granite hide. Haarmann countered, sending Brand flying through sparks of pain.

"Is that all you've got?" Brand yelled, getting up to throw another sad punch. Haarmann landed a direct hit to Brand's face. The pimp spun back like a rag doll. His nose broken, his eyes began swelling shut. Still, Brand pulled himself up, wavering. Another blow sent Brand skimming across the rooftop puddles like a stone. Brand lifted himself up, delirious, when a blackened shadow struck The Beast.

Downstairs, Edward Shelley climbed down from his hiding place in the chimney into the destroyed room. For all Haarmann's girth, he failed to pin down the wiggling little Shelley, who bought some time by planting a wooden splinter squarely in Haarman's eye. He scampered up the brick chimney, but could only hold his position for so long. As the thuds from the small room moved to the rooftop, Shelley searched the debris to find both cane sword and scabbard. Running through the broken glass and splintered wood, the youth bounded to the roof, where Haarmann stood over Brand. Shelley tossed Brand the blade before shattering the scabbard over the aggressor's head. Unfazed, The Beast turned to the defenseless child.

Adolf spun up and sliced Haarmann's left thigh. Haarmann roared and lurched back.

"Get out of here, Eddie!" Brand said.

Blind with rage, Brand took a fencer's position as his peripheral vision began to fade. Limp wrist behind his back, Brand repeatedly jabbed Haarmann into a corner of the roof. The wounded creature howled at the multiple punctures coming too fast for retaliation. The pimp drove the blade through to the hilt and growled, "Never bugger the Devil's charge."

Haarmann stepped back, off the ledge to death. The last howl of the Werewolf abruptly ended on the cobblestones below. Brand slumped, exhausted and shaking on the roof. He tried to see through the agony, but the colors of pain shined too bright.

"Stay with me, Mister Brand. Help is on the way." Edward said, swabbing Brand's various wounds.

Glass flecked Brand's face. His mouth was a bloody hole and his eyes swelled shut. "I'm all right! I can't see. Is it over?"

Before Edward answered, a squad of police officers stormed the rooftop.

"Dr. Hirshfeld!" Shelley cried, hugging the large man.

"Dear boy, are you all right?" Dr. Hirshfeld said.

"I'm fine, but Mister Brand is deeply wounded." Shelley said.

"Dear sir, you look positively wretched." Magnus said to Brand. "But fret not. Everything shall be well taken care of."

"Please be advised of improving your bedside manner, Maggie." Brand said, feeling the loose teeth in his mouth, "This night is far from 'well taken care of'."

Brand heard half a dozen officers on the roof with dogs. The dogs confused him.

Magnus said, "Let's get you back to Berlin."

"I agree." Brand said, "*Hanover ist Sheizen*."

***

Adolf Brand, bruised and battered, took on Edward Shelley as an assistant, and Shelley took him on as a mentor. They never returned to London.

Dr. Hirshfeld, never far away, visited the *Der Eigne* office, avoiding the police and detractors staking out his medical practice. Arm still in a sling, Adolf Brand examined submissions to his magazine, while Shelley studied his German. "How goes the magazine, Herr Shelley?" Dr. Hirshfeld asked.

With a pile of papers in each hand, Brand said, "We have a few subscribers here and there. Contributors are usually anonymous. Quite a lot to process. How goes your attempts at creating at Scientific Humanitarian Committee to openly address the problems of sexuality?"

Dr. Hirshfeld sighed, "Hrm, slow coming. There is no shortage of people requesting aid, but I have only so much aid to give."

With Magnus holding his medical files and Brand cradling the month's new submissions, the idea came to them simultaneously. Dr. Hirshfeld said, "Do you find it plausible to combine our efforts? Surely, these documents reveal that there are more of us out there, and to combine our strengths could only come to benefit us all."

"I'll begin compiling a list immediately." Brand said.

"We must, however, advance with great trepidation. Such a dossier would be far too dangerous to be available to the general public. We must proceed with incredible caution. My participation would endanger the Scientific Humanitarian Committee, as well as all those involved."

"How else could you continue... if without subterfuge?" Brand said with a wry smile.

"Perhaps an unadvertised social club?" Dr. Hirshfeld said. "My research shows that in Italy during the Renaissance, inverted sexual acts were so prominent, a separate police force was created to keep the buggering limited in the streets. The police were called Officers of the Night, who rounded up so-called Gentlemen of the Shade."

"What a marvelous title," Brand said, putting the two piles together.

Dr. Hirshfeld said, "If we are to carry through this, we must begin a letter writing campaign immediately."

PART II:
Oscar and the Wilde Boys

Tod Crouch

Chapter 6:
The Importance of Being Urnist

Always do what you are afraid to do.
--Ralph Waldo Emerson

The SS Arizona celebrated the New Year of 1882 with a day left at sea before docking at Ellis Island. The sharp wind sliced unhindered through the huddled masses on deck, where Oscar's bright purple suit glared out from the earth tones of peasants. He heard the French were building a massive statue for the small island off the coast of North America, but between the Americans and the French, Oscar wondered if they would ever get the damned thing built.

He found a deckhand and asked how long it would be until docking.

"Oh, it's a pleasure to meet you, sir," the shivering sailor said, "We dock in about five hours." Oscar's famous one-liner fell absent, disappointing the sailor. Truth be told, the poet felt out of sorts from his element. The sea was merely a backdrop to his choppy suspicions. A little parlor trick such as himself was on his way to New York city; His head swam with delusions of grandeur, calcifying with each refuted doubt. As his ship came in, Oscar Wilde never anticipated it to be so massive.

He returned to his suffocating quarters and pulled out his trusty recipe box of index cards. The poet studied his famous quips and anecdotes for scant minutes before falling fast asleep. A deafening horn rattled him from slumber. Charging through the iron belly of the ocean liner, he pushed his way up to the crowded deck. Manhattan in the distance seemed smaller in person. As they approached Ellis Island, the ship passed the construction of The Statue of Liberty-- only a pair of naked legs stood proud and meaty, as the dress had yet to be constructed. Oscar smiled, hoping they would stop construction completely at the thigh.

A small collection of boats cluttered the Ellis Island docks. Oscar asked a deckhand, "What are those boats doing out there?"

The annoyed sailor replied, "They are newspaper reporters, sir."

"What would newspaper reporters be doing in the harbor?"

"They're here to witness your arrival, sir," the sailor said.

"Why on Earth would they want to witness my arrival?"

"I don't *know*, sir. Perhaps you can ask them. We'll be docking momentarily." The sailor said.

"Don't New Yorkers have anything better to do than hound celebrities?"

"Apparently *not*, sir." The chafed deckhand answered.

Tugboats guided the small floating city of a ship into the harbor. The Arizona's deck erupted into a cacophony of unintelligible commands, screeching metal, and engine protocols. As Oscar descended the gangplank, a throng of small rowboats rocked in the rippling swell. The ravenous reporters howled, fighting broken waves among a few capsized boats. One screamed, "Oscar Wilde has arrived! Oscar Wilde has arrived!" Sketch artists scribbled the dapper Irishman's queer detail who indulged them slowly. The screams and splashes of journalists transformed them into wildebeests dying in the maws of submerged crocodiles.

Oscar pushed his way through his fear of Americans. *Surely, they cannot all be such men into beasts*, Wilde thought to himself.

One reporter shrieked, "What do you think of America?"

"I'm not even off the boat yet, and already I have admirers." Oscar replied. Their shouts drowned each other out as customs agents herded immigrants into lines.

At Ellis Island, Wilde stood barefoot on cold tile in line for the medical examination, shoes in hand. Officials stripped him in a freezing room, searching for lesions. They scraped samples of fluid from underneath his eyelids, combed his hair for lice (finding a few acquired on the boat), punctured him with needles and packed him into a room of Europeans muttering terrified languages. Oscar brushed it off, as he did for the usual inconveniences of an itinerant lifestyle.

No one warned Oscar about spending his first night on Ellis Island, a setback he almost accepted. The following day, Oscar felt wretched. His long hair lacked product, giving him a distastefully grimy presence. He passed the second day of medical pokes and prods before collecting his belongings. The last customs agent--obviously an incompetent--asked, "Do you have anything to claim?"

Oscar snarled, "Genius. Now give me my sodding luggage." It was not going to be a good day. The customs agent stamped several papers Oscar would surely lose. The Irishman in New York shivered on the tiny boat back to South Street Seaport. As it docked, Oscar thought to himself, *Welcome to New York City.*

He looked upon stocky, ramshackle townhouses

buried in dismal clouds reeking of bad fish, unwashed masses and feces. Shocked, Oscar realized the city was built of pure filth. Winter sea winds shoved with the same cruelty of the uncivilized masses.

Twenty paces in, the crowd closed in, yelling unintelligibly. It was the reporters again, but now without the protection of the gangplank. At his height, he looked over the crowd, noticing the crowd centered on *him*. Endless chatter deafened the poet, each mouth hungry for answers. At the far end of the wooden promenade, a stout man with an enormous handlebar moustache held up a small sign reading "Wilde".

Oscar's heart leapt as he swam against the crowd's current. The poet flapped a limp wave at the nodding producer. Few poets deserved such an entrance. It was downright embarrassing.

"Mister Wilde, it is with deep honor that I welcome you to America." Richard D'Oyly Carte said, removing his stovepipe hat. The carriage driver threw Oscar's luggage atop the coach as the lanky Irishman stuffed himself into the tiny carriage. "What the bloody hell is all this?" Oscar said.

"Why, you are a celebrity in America."

"Is that all America is good for?"

"Mostly," Richard said, "Fame is a chief industry."

"Then I doubly thank you for my importation," Oscar replied, nervously accepting his newfound fate. Mr. Carte, Producer of Gilbert and Sullivan's *Patience*, also doubled as Wilde's stateside handler. Professor Browning thrilled Oscar with this extravagant trip, mostly to get rid of the young poet. Since Browning's connection with the Cleveland Street Scandal, Professor Browning grew much more selective with his 'protégés'.

"How was your skim across the pond?" Mr. Carte said.

The large bags under Oscar's eyes and crooked posture of sleeping in a shoebox betrayed Oscar's eagerness as he said cheerily, "Oh, I quite enjoyed it, sir."

"Please, call me Richard," Mr. Carte said. "Fear not, Mister Wilde. We've got your room ready at the Hotel Brunswick. You must be exhausted."

"Please, call me Oscar," Oscar said, "I am rather peckish."

Mr. Carte pulled out a flask, "Here. This should warm you up a bit. Surely, it is not as good as Irish whiskey, but it's still better than Canadian." Oscar's eyes lit up.

"Oh thank you. I traded nearly all my peacock feathers for a bottle of port on the boat. I've never been good at moderation." Oscar said, taking a long belt from the silver flask. He immediately relaxed. "So, what exactly am I doing here?"

Mr. Carte threw his head back and laughed. It was refreshing to Mr. Carte to meet someone yet to 'Go Cosmopolitan'. Oscar looked around sheepishly; he was too tired, boat-lagged, and overwhelmed to be at the top of his game. Mr. Carte continued, "Don't worry, Oscar. I'm a producer. You don't have to be 'on' with me. We're all friends here. We'll spend a few days getting you situated before heading up to Camden."

"Camden? What's in Camden? Or more importantly, where is it?"

"It's in New Jersey," Mr. Carte said, "It's where Mr. Whitman lives."

"Oh." Oscar said, "As in...Walt Whitman?"

Mr. Carte looked puzzled, "Of course. Didn't they tell you that he wanted to meet with you? We can cancel, if you prefer."

"Are you kidding ?" Oscar yelled, before regaining composure. "I'm sorry. I suppose that minute detail was lost in the itinerary. I can hardly wait to meet him."

Slipping back into his role of Wilde's handler, Mr. Carte continued. "*Patience* plays tomorrow, but you'll have plenty of time to see the sites before leaving," Mr. Carte said, "As a rule of thumb, I would not recommend leaving your neighborhood, as most of New York is reserved for gentlemen of a, ah, lower class."

Mr. Carte checked Oscar into the uptown hotel. It seemed a world away from the dump of the South Street Seaport or Greenwich. Though Oscar understood the theory of decadence, he rarely practiced it with someone else's money. The hotel lobby floored him: the Trompe L'Oeil ceiling pretended to be a beautiful sky, filled with fat pink cherubs soaring over gold-leafed molding and an atmosphere of tobacco smoke. Oscar's room was no less lavish, complete with a fireplace, hot water, and a wet bar. Over large windows hung thick draperies, when separated exposed a beautiful view of Madison Square Park blanketed in snow. After wedging his way into so many cramped salons, Oscar accepted the destiny of his decadent taste.

That night, Oscar soaked in a large claw-foot bathtub with the water nearly scalding his pale flesh. The hotel supplied sea salts, rose water, candles, and a wicker basket filled with exotic lotions. As he climbed into his tailored eveningwear, he felt a touch criminal.

Mr. Carte graciously provided $4,000 *just to show up.*

It played on Oscar's conscience, slightly. As he perfected his lengthy brown hair, he stared into the mirror. He never found himself attractive, though elegance made up for it, finally. He took a generous gulp of bourbon and felt the confidence ease into his muscles. In the opulent setting, Oscar felt natural behind his game face.

The poet had yet to lock his room behind him when guests noticed him in the yellow light of the hallway. "Why, if it isn't Oscar Wilde! How are you, sir?" The stranger said, with two attractive women on each arm. The stranger had a close-cropped haircut, powerfully broad shoulders. The guest extended a rough, calloused hand. "Allow me to introduce myself. I am John Jacob Astorhouse. This is my wife Elizabeth and my sister, Eloise." Oscar smiled at the finely dressed trio, unsure of who was the sister was and who was the wife.

"Oh Oscar, we just bought another hotel and would love to have your opinion on the interior!" The blonde-haired woman said with a thick Long Island accent, "Let's grab a quick drink in the lobby. My treat."

"Of course," Oscar said. The three trailed him into the dining hall. Before Oscar could count his money, he had too much to drink.

A pounding on the door woke Oscar, face down on the Turkish rug in his room. Groggily, he crawled to the door, where Mr. Carte was on the other side. "You're quite early, Richard." Oscar growled with one eye closed.

"Balderdash! The bellhop has been banging on your door for two hours. I feared the worst." Richard said with polite ire. "Tell me, who was that man you entertained last night?" Mr. Carte said, "I came into check on you and found you blotto in the hotel bar surrounded by an incredibly large crowd."

"Did they love me?" Oscar asked, "I can't for some reason recall."

"I did not want to spoil the festivities, but I recall a man at your side with two women." Mr. Carte said.

"Who do you mean? Mr. Astorhouse?" Oscar said, squinting.

"Oh, Oscar. Oscar, Oscar, Oscar. You must be more careful. " Mr. Carte said.

"I don't understand."

Mr. Carte pinched the bridge of his nose. "There is no John Jacob Astorhouse. My friend at the precinct said Hungry Joe might seek you out."

"Who?" Oscar said.

"Hungry Joe Lewis. He's a con artist." Mr. Carte sighed, "How much money do you have?" In a state of panic, Oscar ran to his little safe. His stomach dropped as he felt the emptied box. Back through his memory, he recalled that the sister or wife suddenly went missing for a long stretch of time.

"No! Damn! Damn! Damn!" Oscar bellowed, hoping his money was somehow adhered to the sides of the safe.

"Come on. Let it not worry you. Prepare for today and leave the mistakes of yesterday behind you." Mr. Carte said. "We will travel to Camden tomorrow, but as for this evening, allow me to introduce you to the audience of our highly successful musical, due in no small part to your fanciful character. That should take your mind off this... unfortunate incident."

Staring at the contents of the empty metal box, Oscar chuckled, understanding his artistic philosophy biting him in the ass: Live by the con, die by the con.

"Very well, Richard. Your view of the situation is quite astute. I shall busy myself immediately on preparing a speech for this evening's festivities."

Richard smiled, "Very well, then Mister Wilde. I shall leave you to crafting your witticisms."

"Thank you ever so much for your tireless assistance. I suspect to see you for a pre-theater dinner?" Wilde said, feeling his toxic blood groan.

"Most definitely, Mister Wilde." Richard said with a tip of his tophat. Oscar closed the door, closed the drapes, slid into the blackness of slumber.

It was a nice theater where *Patience* played. The seats were just as cramped as they were in England. Oscar liked seeing a version of himself, though hardly flattering. He sat in the second row with a green carnation in his lapel. At the end of the performance, the director invited Oscar to the stage to a roar of applause, which felt like a birthright. Oscar knew immediately: he must write plays. With each step, the applause strengthened Wilde's convictions until he reached the stage in a state of concrete glory. Oscar thumbed the unnatural Green Carnation at his lapel. "I would like to take this time to point out my green carnation…" Oscar announced.

"What does it mean?" a heckler added.

"It means nothing, except for those to whom it means anything." Oscar replied to thunderous laughter. On that stage, Oscar knew he was riding high on an ineffable wave yet to form. The Irishman nestled into the comforting bosom of Celebrity. Even in his last days, he would never forget that accepting roar in Chickaree Hall. When water ran, he heard that moment's applause.

Oscar awoke again, unsure of how he came to bed. He hoped it had not cost him the admirers he charmed during the after party. But today was almost a holiday: He was going to visit the old grey poet, Walt Whitman.

Pulling up to the two-story house on Mickle Boulevard, Oscar's heart raced. He stepped up to the door, where after a brief pause, the doorknob turned. Wilde held his breath tight as a bushy-bearded man opened it, just like a regular person.

"Oscar Wilde, I presume?" The old man said with a bright glint in his eye. Oscar stood stone-still and starstruck. "Are you all right, my boy?"

Oscar screamed like a little girl, fanning himself with both hands. "Oh my God! It's really you! I mean, I thought it might be you or you would have a servant answer the door but it's really you! Wow! This is such an honor! I am your biggest fan, Mister Whitman! At Oxford, I was never without my copy of Leaves of Grass! Oh my God! Oh my God! Oh, look at me, I'm so embarrassed! I don't even know what to say! Would you sign my copy?"

Whitman gave a polite chuckle at the flustered youth. "Certainly, young man. Well, don't just stand there staring. Come inside from this dreadful weather." Walt said, opening the door wide. Oscar let out a high-pitched squeal only heard by dogs. Oscar barely noticed Walt taking the book from the sweaty palm. Walt dipped his quill and scribbled a signature, leaving it open on the end table to dry.

The cozy and humble main room consisted of insulating bookshelves and a roaring fireplace. The two windows facing the street let in crisp, winter light with a whiteness matching Whitman's flowing beard. Oscar followed Walt's movements in a daze. Oscar sat on a drab, comfortable couch and stared at Walt Whitman pace the room. Walt smiled with two jars in hand. "I know I may have a reputation as a teetotaler, but in my old age I have found pleasure in local wines. Would you care to have a merlot with me?" Oscar could only register his own amazement that Walt Whitman himself was offering a glass of wine. "Mister Wilde?"

Oscar snapped out of his daze. "Of course! I'm terribly sorry. This is just happening all so fast. Two weeks ago, I was poking fun of headmasters--now I'm staying at a decadent hotel—and having wine with Walt Whitman!"

"No matter how badly you expect it, it takes you off guard." Whitman said, pouring wine into two mason jars. "You should have seen Henry. He wrote me and said, 'Wally, I leave the woods for a few months and all I want to do is go back."

"Henry?"

"Thoreau." Whitman said, indulging the boy's starstruck state. Oscar gasped. Walt smiled and handed Oscar the jar. "Take a sip, young man. It lets the blood breathe more easily."

In his trance, Oscar raised the jar to his lips and took a deep pull, where the wine eased him into the present. "That is quite good... Walt."

"It's a bit dry for my tastes, but I can't stand hard liquor. Brutish, it turns men into beasts. Wine, I find, brings out the gentleman." Walt took a sip, bruising his beard. It was a humbling image to Oscar to see Walt with wine-stained beard. The old grey poet was a baffling contradiction--both mysterious and personable. "So they tell me that you are quite the character. And poet. What is that movement you are with--the Decadent Movement?"

"Why yes, of course! We refine our words as we do our lives, seeking pleasure, beauty, and love wherever we find it!" Oscar said. Walt smiled, seeing how such a young man could be so charming.

Whitman asked, "Why do you define yourself through the movements of others?"

"I don't understand," Oscar said.

"I've loved so many people, Oscar," Walt said with a twinge of remorse, "I was... naive... in a time without defining an understood mutual compassion. It just was. The celebration of adhesion with other men never came into question. Now, detractors criticize my fondness of brethren. I live in a strange future, no longer mine. It still belongs to you. Your dalliances with members of the same sex are not unheard of to me, or anyone else in our (ahem) linked rings, for that matter." Walt refilled Oscar's jar. "You're going to have to search within yourself, if you are going to become the writer you clearly are."

"You think I have what it takes?" Oscar said.

"Only question doubt. You still have to discover a lot about yourself. You don't want to do all this work, attract attention and then have nothing to say," Walt said. "I never thought of my work as what they're calling, ahem, 'homosexually erotic'. Yet, words I wrote twenty years ago stare back at me, clear as day." Walt said. "It's a tad embarrassing, I have to admit. What seemed secretive aged into glaring overstatement. I thought my greatest work would be liberating myself. I didn't expect it to liberate such a fuss."

Walt threw another log in to the fireplace. He stood for a moment, warming his hands. "I know that you have conflict about these matters. You make light of shallow passions, only exposing depth. Are you prepared to explore such a depth, the depth of every man? Many will attack you for what you retrieve from your own abyss." Walt took his seat, hands on knees. Oscar finished his second glass, mulling both spirits and spirit. He felt the indignity of a lecture, but could not find the words to rebuke his idol. This was not the time or the place for Oscar's carefully studied one-liners.

"Come now, Walt. You of all people know the ways of men. Young love among men is mere folly. Surely I will marry and settle, leaving my adolescent tastes behind with so many other vices of youth."

Walt yelled out, "Mrs. Whitman! Come meet the famous Oscar Wilde!" The house responded with silence. "Youth is an unappeasable vice."

"There's something I've been meaning to ask," Oscar said, "Why am I really here?" Walt shifted in his seat. Oscar continued, "I must confess, this entire trip has been quite queer. I am barely a poet, yet the greatest living wordsmith offers me wine. Surely, the peculiarity does not escape you."

Walt smiled. "Like all men in their twilight years, I keep many correspondences. Several of your English and German friends have brought you to my attention."

"German friends? I have quite few notable German friends." Oscar said.

"You do... speak German, do you not?" Walt said. Though Americans never use this phrase, Oscar knew this proposition code.

Oscar's eyes grew wide. "How do you know such a phrase?"

Walt smiled and said, "I have a lot of German friends. I really did not expect to be part of this war, but a war has arrived. Judging from what your friend George has told me, both England and Germany have started up quite the cause against so precious a love." Walt said.

"I don't know a George." Oscar said.

"It doesn't particularly matter." Walt said, "That box over there. Take it."

Oscar looked over to a small oak box sitting on the mantle. Oscar pulled out a beautiful pistol. The mother of pearl handle glistened in perfect harmony with the silver barrel. "Why, it's beautiful."

"It was given to me by an old friend, Peter Doyle," Walt said, "I want you to have it. It may come in handy. What shall you name her?"

Oscar thought of an Irish Fairy tale name, one of queer Irish wit. 'Saucy inverted leprechaun' didn't have a sense of sex appeal or force to it. "I believe I will call her Fey. Fey Dun-away."

Walt said, "There will come a day when your people will call upon you to stand up for them. If you decide to stand, be sure you know who is standing in your light." Walt said.

Oscar laughed, "Oh Walt. I'm a poet, not a hero or a criminal."

Walt chortled. "Then you aren't much of a poet."

Chapter 7:
A Mild-Mannered Army

> *Standing in the line we're aberrations*
> *Defects in a defect's mirror*
> *And we've been here all the time*
> *real fixations*
> *Hidden deep in the furor-*
> *What we do is secret--secret!*

> *What we do is secret*
> The Germs

(Translated from French)

1883

M. Brand—

Stop writing me, asking me to join some feckless cause I have no wish to embolden or even acknowledge. The only reason I write you now is on the insistence of my sister, who is annoyed at the sheer volume of your one-sided correspondences. I know not what you expect of me, and I swell with offense at the slightest insinuation to exploit my friendship with Sultan Makonnen for questionable dealings with your cadre of pansy hack poets. Under no circumstance will I venture into that country of European wretches so long as that miserable beast Verlaine breathes, for surely you have drawn water from that well of despair for your insidious machinations. If I could send the scars from where I have been shot by your kind, I gladly would as a testament to my contempt.

I have my own shipping company now and live peacefully in Abyssinia with no need for writing on behalf of perverts and degenerates you misconstrue as heroes.

Why must you persist when I demand to be left alone? It saddens me that old men such as yourself insist on futile attempts to inspire me to continue a life of degradation and pitiable decadence. What I have done in my past, I have atoned for. There is no requirement for me to entertain fools who persist in fighting for some imaginary cause, created in the minds of lunatic drunkards who plague schoolyards for impressionable boys. Whatever constraint you have duly ignored in your wretched life, I implore you to search deep within yourself to reconsider this undertaking of another pitiful attempt at recruiting me for this cause you have imagined to benefit humanity.

Do not write again.

--A. Rimbaud

1883

Herr Brand—

I am surprised and flattered to find a letter from such a commanding presence such as yourself. Your proposition to organize a private collective intrigues me, though I find letter writing to be excessively cumbersome; yet, even more cumbersome rests the frivolity of contemporary salon culture. If I wanted to listen to the chattering of a hen house, I would merely step into my back yard!

My sympathies are with you concerning the erroneous legislation leading to the passing of Paragraph 175. England is becoming equally oppressive, leading me to venture into the lush backdrop of nature. I find it far gentler on my humours, but I digress. You make a valid point that the time for Uranians and other sexual inverts to begin organizing the recommended invisible infrastructure. I have recently been studying Oriental philosophies, which are surprisingly accepting of Uranians, and I intend to travel to India later this year. I may be out of touch for a considerable period, but that does not remove me from your cause.

I recently joined the Social Democratic Federation, where I have met many influential contacts through the party, though I highly doubt that they are of your specific taste. I will search out further members through my connections with the Humanitarian League. Dr. Hirshfeld may have already suggested the sexologist Havelock Ellis join our cause, but I would not recommend it. Havelock is a darling without argument, but I do not think an impotent sexologist would benefit our cause!

I'll also put in a good word with Sidney and Beatrice Webb over at the Fabian Society. They are more concerned with the progressive change of factories and economics, but surely they would employ support to an endeavor such as yours. Your desire for justice is theirs as well.

Please enjoy the sandals I have included with this package. A friend from India introduced these odd shoes to me, and I find them quite comfortable. I have made these on my own accord, for the construction is marvelously simple. I will be in touch soon.

--Edward Carpenter

1885
Dear Dr. Hirshfeld:

I know we have never met, but I found a most unusual periodical with your name in it. Most of it was in German, and your name was all I deciphered. I would have asked mummy or poppy to translate, but there were many images of a shameful nature. It was hard to find your address while going through the academy in London, but I was able to find your address through the publisher, a fellow named Adolf Brand. I have been aware that I am different from the others for many years, but it was not until I entered academy when I began having feelings for a friend of mine of the same sex. I did not know whom to turn to with this profound understanding of a truth about myself. I am barely 17, afraid of myself for what I am. As philosophers regard the truth of man's character, one truth becomes unbearably clear: I am attracted to men.

The rest of my life changes forever, and my desire obscures destiny. I do not know what will become of me as this new aberration of nature. I have tried to suppress this hunger, but it merely fans the flames desire, locking me in a cycle of self-hatred, shame, and compulsion. I am of high social standing and highly educated, and I still cannot find a cure for this malady.

Have you found an appropriate treatment to balance my nature accordingly? I know not how long I can maintain sanity, holding desire, bit and bridle, in checked demand. My family will misunderstand, and I have few who find my affectation understandable.

Please, Dr. Hirshfeld, desperate trust in strangers is the final hand played. Writing this jeopardizes my secrecy. I have none to turn to. I can't live this sickness through. Please help me.

Sincerely,
George Cecil Ives

1886
My dear boy,

I apologize for my tardiness in replying to your letter. It takes quite the time to receive mail in my current residence. I am delighted to hear from you, and sympathize with the feelings you have. Each and every one of us with these preferences is gifted, knowing something about ourselves with steely resolve.

Whereas our heterosexual peers clumsily walk through life without knowing themselves, we know an irrefutable truth. It is a hard-digested truth, but in time, we grow comfortable with desire. It is a truth of being capable of judging all other personal truths by. For being of high class and good stock, our desire for the same sex affects every stratum of class and eugenic background.

We are everywhere and retain silence, for now. I received a clipping from your home country, where the Criminal Law Amendment Act passed last year recriminalized our particular style of intimacy. At least it is no longer punishable by death. Our time is quickly arriving where we must stand up for what we believe in and risk visibility. Take heart my young friend, for you are not alone. You are not sick. Never let anyone impose their shame on you. You are good in spirit, strong. Don't let anyone tell you different. By all means, continue to write those whom you discover.

Reach out to whoever possible, just as you did to me. We are here for you.

Be vigilant. It gets better.

Dr. Magnus Hirshfeld

1892

My darling Bobby,

I do wish you would return to the House Beautiful. Constance Wilde misses you terribly as well, though my heart aches with such a new tenderness only comparable to the softness of your lips. It is too quiet here, and I resort to beastly conversations with street toughs, who threaten to rob, expose, or blackmail me. I miss the stability you provide! It has only been a year since you returned to your family, but I am still in awe that your innocence so deeply corrupted me! To give my conflicted heart's desire a name, your name, sends me aflutter like the leaves in a full summer's breeze.

How I miss your devices, your big tool! When will you return? The House Beautiful is a temple missing its altar of love, which I would lay myself upon in sacrifice.

George Cecil Ives, keeps writing to me about "big things happening." It is most peculiar, as Mister Ives shares the responsibility with Oscar Browning for my trip to the United States. I honestly have no idea what he speaks of. He is a queer one, is he not? Has he been sending you these little booklets with the addresses of strangers in them? Constance flips through them and I do not know their purpose. Do you? Alas, I have been working on quite a spectacle of theater, which I must return to. I just cannot bear to continue without writing such a lovely creature, letting him know he was on my mind. Please hurry back.

--Oscar

(Translated from German)
1893
Herr Brand,

I am surprised to hear from you, as I am halfway across the globe on a small island in the Pacific called Kilauea, studying volcanic activity. I tell you, this venture has resembled something out of a Robert Lewis Stevenson novel. A dreadful political upheaval here between missionaries and the indigenous people has threatened my research. Within three days of my arrival, I was nearly thrown into the volcano as an offering! It appears that their volcano goddess, Pele, prefers the meat of white men in her furnace. My manservant and pupil, Chauncy Litwack, tells me that the only way I could get closer to the lip of the volcano would be to throw myself in! I confess, the natives complimented my effulgent behavior. The air and temperature here is perfect for the flavor of virile adventure and companionship I so crave.

It is truly a magnificent volcano, and the native people are beautiful. We so rarely see such exotic beauty in Europe's men. We even found a gold idol in a cave at the foot of the volcano, but if I find one more idol that unleashes unholy evil, I swear I will give up this anthropological racket and go into mathematics.

What on Earth is going on over there? You mention something about an order of Greek soldiers who had their arses handed to them at Chaeronea.

Sounds dubious, Adolf. I suppose I don't really understand what manner of society this consists of. I know Hirshfeld has this notion that homosexuals are 'born this way', but it is such Darwinist flapdoodle to assume homosexuality is a disease, rather than the right of virile men. I imagined Magnus more worldly than that. I fail to see why this manly-man love has to garner attention. Is it not only difficulty for those without good legal council, social standing, or impoverished glamour? Surely, it is not a plight with to concern ourselves. The idea of combining our strengths for political power sounds like a magnificent business venture. However, secrecy and subterfuge, for which we are so inclined, has kept us from the noose's dance. Keep me updated on the details. I do see great potential in such an endeavor. This rich young man Ives you mention and his little secret society idea sound equally adorable, Adolf. Please continue to indulge me in your folly.

Bennedict Friedlander

1893

Dear Mister Wilde,

I'm sorry to be out of touch lately. I have been thinking about what you have said about John Addington Symonds' *The Problem With Modern Ethics* and reached out (and around) boys of my age. A boy I have taken a liking to, Lionel Johnston, introduced me to my new best friend, a boy named Lord Alfred Douglas. Fauntleroy could learn much about the art of precociousness from our new friend. He is a bit demanding, but his demands lead to adventure and always a spectacular scene! We've even taken to calling him "bossy" behind his back. When he discovered this, he merely sneered and said, "So? Fetch me my tea." Such a bitch! He is quite forward, and coming from me that is quite a testament. His father is the Marquess of Queensberry, so he is always buying up boys for us to share! It's quite exciting. Surely you of all my friends would love to sit down with him one fine day and enjoy his company. Not only does he have an angelic appearance, but his mind is sharp as a shard and his wit carries the sting of a scorpion. I am arranging for us to visit you at Tite Street soon. Though all these lovely boys newly surround me, I am confounded by the frustration that the young cannot be as mature as adults, though adults can be as immature as the young. I hope isolation bears the fruit of labor. I read the Dorian Gray manuscript; quite racy in parts, though certain places try too hard. Johnny Gray is tickled you used his last name. He brags constantly! . I cannot wait to see you again. Please, give my love to Constance. Her Sheppard's pie rests on my palette like the oils of a Pre-Raphaelite portrait, thick with oil. I miss you terribly.

--Bobbie Ross

1893
Bosie Douglas—

When are you coming back? I have finally finished writing *Lady Windermere's Fan*, and I find it to be a pleasant enough play for the average theatergoer. I have revised the "Portrait" again and again. I think it will be a smash success and a testament to my genius, if anyone actually publishes it. But it feels such a shame to spend all this time so lonely. Sure, Constance is a marvelous friend, though our romance has cooled, if there ever was one. You have redefined any previous understanding of love, and I find this revelation to be something to share with the world, for they should know this all-encompassing entity. It is what life is lived for. Surely, I have felt this joy for a single day with nothing to hitch my heart to, but how it gallops with you, my rambunctious filly! The ache of your absence is a reminder of my fulfillment. Please return soon. I can't stand the waning hours without you.

--Oscar

1893

Dear Mister Ives—

It was so good to have finally met you at the Author's Club social. I do hope you have taken to shaving off that dreadful moustache. A man of such boyish good looks should not waste precious years looking older than necessary! God willing, you'll have plenty of time for that.

I do see the necessity for this little group such as yours. I have taken in a marvelous young lad, the son of a Marquess. His cousin, a boy named Lionel Johnson, had some issue with a blackmailer, whom I paid off. I agree with you wholeheartedly that men of our status should step forward and protect the lower classes, regardless of the opinions of Germans. Surely, it matters not whether one is born of an 'Earnest' nature or raised into it (as if exclusivity would tidy up the intricacies of nuance) when defamation and peril meet our brothers at every turn.

Have you spoken with John Gray of late? I noticed he was spending such a time with that Raffalovich boy, whom I must say does not seem quite right in the head. He no longer indulges in the pleasures of any flesh, save for the body of Christ.

What a dreadful conclusion that Gray boy has

made, and an even more dreadful one made by his closest friend!

Please give Herr Brand my gratitude, as I have contributed to many of his young business associates. I hope to be seeing more of that fellow Edward Shelley. He has a tragic beauty to him. Bosie enjoys his company as well. I have spoken to Andre Gide, though he lacks interest in collaborating. A moody one he is, taking "inversion" to a new level entirely. Terribly sorry I have been so long in contacting you. With the newfound celebrity I have enjoyed, it has been most dreadful to maintain my correspondences. I do hope we can meet when I am back in London.

--Oscar

1893

Dear H_____,

I wish I had better news. It seems most of our lot are too afraid to come forward to aid a cause they support. The Gentlemen are comfortable supporting from the shade, expecting to reap the rewards of full participation. Reginald Turner, one from the Wilde clique, tells me Wilde's been unabashedly courting this Lord Douglas, much to the consternation of the Marquess. I, too, am at conflict for opinionated action.

If we were all to live so brazenly, we would suffer equally. It's hard to stand beside the precarious. I cannot know what Whitman suggested to Wilde, but the courage he shares embarrasses my excess of cowardice. A man who embodies spectacle cannot but turn his great passions into spectacle as well. Denying his ridiculous stance turns me to cowardice by the minute, yet supporting it turns me into a heretic by the second. Standing still sets me two steps back.

I fear for Oscar and worry for myself. After Oscar fell so far in love, there can be only another, more abysmal, fall for him. Oscar has the courage of a doomed man, and reckoning draws close.

Good Doctor, I trust your Scientific Humanitarian Committee has flourished with the influx of funding from outside sources. I have taken it upon myself to organize an English community of our kind, though our approach is less overt. I have named it after a great Greek battle of homosexual, and each of them are Gentlemen of our kind. Under the Order of Chaeronea, I do hope to combine our efforts soon.

--George Cecil Ives

Chapter 8:
Down and Out of Redding Jail

It's a possibility to live without lips
Kleenex love to fill right up with all the broken kids
I swore I drank your piss that night to see if I could live
But my wrists couldn't stand the light that we missed
And I'm still your fag

I'm Still Your Fag
Broken Social Scene

On May 19, 1897 at 6:15 in the morning, Oscar Wilde stepped out of prison. His hair turned to straw, his doughy body reduced to a pale skeleton. As the indifferent gates grinded open, Oscar ambled out. Unsurprisingly, only two reporters awaited Oscar's return to society.

"Sir?" One reporter said, shocked at the transformation, "Are you feeling well?"

"I demand neither notoriety nor oblivion," Oscar said without a passing glance. Days of morbid suffering steeped his soul in bitter stoicism. The dawn chill hit his legs like a cold, wide ocean. With sunken eyes, he searched the vestibule for throngs of lovers and friends awaiting him, but only John Gray, with his fair hair and gentle smile waited. Gray's hands were smooth, lacking labor's calluses and his face showed slight lines of his early thirties.

John said calmly, "Hello, Oscar. It's time to come home." Oscar knew this fevered dream all too well. Oscar took it in stride, ready to wake to another day of walking shackled in a penitent circle.

John hugged Oscar through the prisoner's overpowering stench. "Marc-Andre has a carriage waiting."

Wilde held himself up in somber relief. "Thank you for seeing me at such a beastly hour. Just take me home, John, wherever that is." Oscar draped his arm over his prior lover's shoulder as the two walked to a carriage. Marc-Andre Raffalovich stood by the carriage door, forcing a smile at the shambling grey-garbed mound of a man.

In his early thirties, Raffalovich's still had a boyish look to him, though his mouth still held the sarcastic smirk of angst honed by pedigree and youthful arrogance. With his fine black hair and sharp gaze, his tweed suit fit his tall, slender frame like a hooligan's disguise. Marc-Andre was once an easily corrupted innocent who thusly turned religious—the perfect Catholic boy fantasy incarnate. Oscar rolled his shoulder to the young man, "My, how you've grown, Marc-Andre. And how I have not."

"Come on, Oscar. Let's get you back to the hotel," Marc-Andre said, taking the bony rag of Oscar's hand.

John's attempt at conversation failed to hide the painfully quiet ride. John reserved rooms at Hotel Sandwich, to which Oscar replied, "Well, you little scamps certainly don't waste any time, do you?" Oscar's gaze drifted out to the cluttered city, both familiar and foreign. John told Oscar some carriages lacked horses. Oscar chuckled, "Heh, the things you miss in prison, eh?" The wind felt too fresh on Oscar's skin, like a fingernail cut to the quick.

"So what have you two been busying yourselves with?" Oscar asked.

Raffalovich replied, "I finished my manuscript of '*Urnings and Unisexuality: Study on Different Manifestations of the Sexual Instinct*'."

"Still calling it unisexuality?" Oscar said smirking, "You never cease to seem precocious."

"Well, you must understand, Oscar, that sexuality is not something a virile super-macho soldier spends idle time with, or manifests as disease much like Kraft-Ebbing would have it. I think some are born and some choose. But those chosen must overcome their desires with artistic and spiritual pursuits. I started on his *Annales de l'unisexualité*, a catalogue of everything published on unisexuality."

"What a studious little Dominican monk you've become! But you know what they say about Dominicans. They are excessively... unabridged." Oscar smirked. "And what about you, Mister Gray?"

Gray said offhandedly, "My lover converted me I bought him a church." Marc-Andre smirked and nudged John Gray with his foot.

"How darling!" Oscar said. "I simply must visit. It has been awhile since I confessed. Or even went down on my knees." Gray and Raffalovich smiled uncomfortably.

Oscar broke the awkward silence. "Am I correct in believing many of my friends won't be, ah, in attendance?"

John looked to Marc, and replied softly, "Well, ah, it's not the best season, to, ah... travel."

"It is of little concern," Oscar said morosely, "Whoever stayed steadfast to my side, deserves total admiration. I'm thankful for you both for being here. My prayers are answered by even the slightest loyalty. Both are worthy of canonizing."

"We'll get you to the hotel where we can get you acclimated. We have a boat leaving tomorrow night for

Dieppe, where Bobbie will meet us on the other side in France." John said.

Oscar scowled unintentionally as he said, "Will *Bosie* be there?"

"No. Bobbie's been keeping him at bay until you are ready. It's the same mess with him as always. One letter begs to see you. The next lashes out at your absence." John said.

Oscar covered his eyes. "And what of Constance and the boys?"

John took a deep breath, "The boys are... well. Bobbie has made sure they are taken care of."

Oscar exploded, "But Constance? Constance... I cannot regret enough of what..." Oscar covered his moist eyes. "I'm sorry, John. I indulged in being overemotional in solitude for far too long. Weeping is prison's only hobby."

Marc-Andre blurted out, "She remarried. And she's not entirely well."

Oscar's face twisted into a forgotten hideousness, "What do you mean, 'not entirely well'?"

John refrained from backhanding his clumsy lover's beautiful mouth, knowing Oscar would eventually draw out the information as if with an awl. "She's paralyzed from the waist down, in a lot of pain."

"Where is she?" Oscar raged, tears lining his face.

"It devastates me as it does you to say this, Oscar... But she does not want to see you." John said, heart breaking.

To John's surprise, Oscar sighed quickly, saying, "I should expect as much. I caused so much pain, such disgrace. I must accept this, in this new phase. Mother's gone as well." Oscar lost himself in the opiate of memory. "Let's be done with this dreadful conversation, shall we?"

John, Marc-Andre, and Oscar dined out. Nobody recognized the new Oscar, who felt the uncomfortable haze of being in public without *his* public. That night, took separate rooms and beds, much to the ex-convict's disappointment. However, Oscar's own large bed was a new form of decadence though he couldn't trust sleep for fearing to arise imprisoned.

The following day, Robbie Ross paced about his lavish French apartment. In his late twenties he secretly worried about his receding hairline. He flitted about, perfecting the sitting room for Wilde's arrival, and, on occasion, felt the pang of knowing it would never be lavish enough for his guest. Being nearly half Wilde's age also lent him another form of worry, especially since joining George Cecil Ives's curious wealthy gentlemen's club, The Order of Chaeronea.

Friends and family suggested Ross staying out of England until the Wilde situation blew over. During the interim, Ross found advantage residing in Dieppe, as many a great artist seeking representation came to him through that strange little lavender address book. As emissary to this new Art gallery, Ross spent his time seeking out new talent. In the process, he met a young Dutch painter named Hans Van Meeregen, who had an eye for emulating the painting styles of Albrecht Dürer. Yet Ross lacked concentration for tutoring Van Meeregen; Oscar Wilde was coming home.

The previous night, Ross couldn't sleep, nor expected to, plagued with unanswerable questions. What would he look like? How would he act? Should he be treated differently? How does prison change a man?

"Hello?" Oscar said, letting himself into Ross's home. Oscar placed his top-hat on the coat rack, as though merely returning from the market. Ross bounded down the steps like a child on Christmas Day, excited to unwrap his six-foot-four present. Ross bolted into Oscar's thin arms and felt the sickly ribs of his long-lost lover. Oscar smiled softly, looking down on the young man whose loyalty held the ex-convicts' sanity together. For all their waiting, such cohesion never dissolves.

Marc-Andre and John Gray followed in, smiles all around for the little reunion! "Come! Let us sit and feast the return of The Great Oscar Wilde!" Ross said, leading his guests to the dining room, where they ate roasted pheasant and drank bottle after bottle of mulled wine, regaling the sensational new undertakings and recent fashions. Oscar lacked his usual candor on topical conversation, but listened intensely. Ross carried the conversational weight with ease as he always did, and Oscar cherished Ross even more.

Robbie Ross haunted himself with what the prison governor once told him, "He looks well. But like all men unused to manual labor who receives a sentence of this kind, he will be dead within two years." Oscar sensed his own demise after other inmates beat him in the prison chapel for his immoral past.

"I have a present for you," Robbie said, pulling out a battered cigar box.

"Oh Bobbie, I don't think I cold stomach a cigar right now."

"I think you could stomach this one," Robbie said, handing the box over.

Oscar opened it. His eyes lit up. "Fey Dunaway!" Oscar shrieked at seeing his old firearm, given to him by Whitman. "Oh Bobbie, thank you. I thought they confiscated her with everything else."

"Your butler and myself, ah, rescued important documents from your study," Robbie said with a smirk.

"I wouldn't have it any other way," Oscar replied, raising a glass to his best friend.

Robbie shifted uncomfortably in his chair. "There are some pressing matters which arrived in your absence."

"Of course," Oscar said, cracking the caramelized shell of his crème bruleé, "but I'd like to work on my tan before we get to them." All laughed at the idea of a tan Irishman. Oscar holstered Fey immediately, and Robbie felt relief. Everything moved according to plan.

After dinner, Robbie set down his silverware. "Oscar, I think you should take a walk around the neighborhood. It has been awhile since you have had a night to yourself in the city."

Oscar chuckled, "Oh Bobbie, I don't think tonight is the safest of nights for me. Queensberry's thugs are probably still trailing me."

Robbie looked to John Gray and Marc-Andre for support. John piped up, "Oh come now, Oscar. You deserve a walk in the shade. You know. Collect your thoughts."

"Well, if you ladies prefer to gossip while you do the dishes, I will not stand in your way," Oscar said with wounded dignity. He stole Robbie Ross' coat and top hat and walked out the door, a parody of contempt. Robbie looked to John Gray after Wilde's loud steps faded from the front door. "John, how much time should we give him for a head start?"

John responded, "Not long. Since Queensberry's ex-boxer detectives are trailing him, we can't afford the slightest diversion. By the time we get into costume, Oscar will be far enough ahead not to arouse suspicion."

"There is always an air of risk with initiations," John Gray responded, putting his riding breeches on.

***

Oscar stepped into the fair spring night from the ground floor of Ross's townhouse. It felt good to stretch his legs adorned in real clothes. He took a deep breath of coastal air, feeling the pistol's weight comfort him. He walked down Rue Desceliers, feeling as empty as the closed shop windows.

He considered visiting the docks, but decided against it as it seemed too early in his freedom to flirt with risky trade. The familiar street of his past seemed unusually vacant for this time of night. As Oscar approached Rue Ango, he looked back instinctively to see three men following him. He was not so much terrified as annoyed. He picked up his pace and turned left onto Ango, frustrated by the lack of crowds or open shops. Hearing the quickening speed of the footsteps drawing closer, Oscar turned down a side alley--pinned in.

"Damn," Oscar growled under his breath. The footsteps stopped at the alley's lip. Oscar noticed the three men grew to six. As Oscar visually scoured the narrow alley for weapons, windows, or escape routes, he felt the frustration of injustice boil over.

The leader of the group smiled wide, his jagged teeth grisly against his blackface and foxhunter's garb. "Well, well, well. What do we have here?" The cockney sneered. "It looks like a fairy lost his way from his last shit-stinking poofter party. We don't prefer your exclusive company, nor the sexual preferences you condone."

"I do not prefer your company, either," Oscar said. "Covering your entire face is no way to apply eyeliner. However, I am flattered that you should come all this way to become the first victims of my presence." His adversaries did not know how prison sharpened senses of a newly released inmate.

"We know about you," the Foxmaster said, "We know you corrupt our children, soil your bed sheets of lust with feces, and mock our women with your cleft asshole. You're going to die, right here." They pulled out metal pipes.

"Queensberry set you up to this, didn't he?" Oscar said.

"Oh, there was no set up needed. We's independent contractors, we are." The Foxmaster said. They moved in as one entity.

"You dare pick a fight with an Irishman?" Oscar said, his eyes flaring with madness. Oscar swept a long leg under three pairs of feet, toppling half the mob. His coat tails spun behind with equal grace, as Wilde stood over the other three. He loved a good fight long overdue.

Oscar swung a brick into number four's face with the other. Number four bellowed a long stream of obscenities in German, holding his bloodied nose.

"Ah, just like my Oxford days, isn't it?" Oscar said with a smile, jabbing a bony palm into number two's face.

Wilde reared up like a great bear, lording over his attackers. Survival's focus shaved his skills down to blind, raw movements. The Foxmaster's pipe came down into Oscar's clutch, snapping the Irishman's little finger. Not the firing hand, versed with the hilt of Fey Dunaway. Oscar pointed to the assailant's face. A devilish smirk marred Oscar's gaunt expression as the trigger compressed. The blast sank the head Foxmaster. Oscar huffed, "My tolerance for pain is just as high as my threshold for pleasure." Oscar gasped to the last man standing.

The Foxmaster rose from the dirty alley, laughing loud. "Oscar, put your firearm away. It is of no use." The Foxmaster dropped his metal pipe, clattering to the ground. The other jockeys picked themselves up, laughing, save for the German holding his bleeding nose who launched into a stream of foreign profanity.

"Lower Fey, Herr Wilde," a portly Jockey said, putting on his spectacles.

Oscar squinted at the man's oily face, "Doctor Hirshfeld?"

The jockeys roared with laughter. "We pulled quite a boner on you, Osky!" Robbie Ross said, taking his helmet off.

Adolf Brand nasalled, "That cockslint broke my nose!"

"Oh pish-posh, Herr Brand," Magnus said, "Allow me to examine it."

"To hell with you, Maggie. Let me crack you in the face with a brick and see how fast you whine like a buggered milk maid."

"Well, at least with you, it's an aesthetic improvement." Dr. Hirshfeld said, "It's not broken, you big baby."

"This has been a… practical joke?" Oscar said as they all pointed and laughed at him. John Gray slapped Oscar on the back, laughing. Oscar clapped a steady beat. "All this? For me? And not even a stage! Well done! I would have preferred a comedy. Who's idea was this?"

"It was mine, Mister Wilde," George Cecil Ives said, clearing the make up from his face and returning the monocle to his eye. "You see, this was an initiation, to see if you could stand and fight for what you believe in. Oscar, I think it time we talked about your place in the Order. Have you ever heard of the Battle of Chaeronea?"

Marc-Andre winced, attempting to wipe off his grease paint and said, "Before we do anything, help me get this wretched face paint off. I can feel my pores clog as we speak. Simply detestable! Johnny, did you bring the cold cream?"

"Of course my love," John Gray said. The queer sextet cleaned each others' faces with all the exuberance of a teenage girl's slumber party. As Ross and Ives wiped each other's faces, Ives said, "Have you heard of the Sacred Band of Thebes or the Battle of Chaeronea?"

"Hold still!" Ross said to Ives.

"My Greek is unfortunately sequestered to theater, not war," Oscar said.

Ives continued while swabbing Ross' face, "In ancient Greece, Pelopidas and Epaminondas set up an elite team of lovers like us—a *crack* team if you prefer. They were the Band of Thebes, paired lovers who fought gallantly so not to die and leave their lovers alone, nor shamed by defeat in the face of their lovers. They were capable of taking down armies three times their size. Each pair comprised of the charioteer, called a Heniochi, and a younger companion, the Paraibatai. For forty years, they were the highest ranking Greek soldiers."

"Quite fierce soldiers," Marc-Andre said.

"The fiercest!" John Gray added.

Robbie Ross slapped Ives' cheeks clean in completion and said, "All done!"

Ives still daubed at Ross's face, "Unfortunately, the Band of Thebes met their end at the Battle of Chaeronea. All three hundred soldiers fell under Alexander the Great. Alexander himself honored them by proclaiming them the most formidable opponents ever encountered. He even commissioned a statue commemorating them. We draw our name from that battle, rising where they fell. Welcome to the Order of Chaeronea." Ives presented a small ring box.

"Why, sir, you flatter me. I am, however, accounted for--scandalously so, even." Oscar said. Ives opened up the box, exposing a signet ring with a simple 'c' within a circle. Oscar slid the ring on his unbroken little finger. "Doctor, would you... I think it's broken."

"Sorry about that," Ives said, "We didn't mean to actually hurt you." Hirshfeld went about splinting Oscar's other swollen member.

"You know everyone here, but our organization has spread quite wide in your absence. After an exhaustive letter campaign Hirshfeld, Brand, and myself started more than a decade ago." Ives continued, "Our collective fortunes carve out a new beginning for homosexuals everywhere. Let's walk to the docks, where we can change in private."

"I feel so underdressed," Oscar said, walking among the men in jockey uniforms.

The seven stepped onto the gas-lit boardwalk, where and men in formal eveningwear escorted women in frilly dresses. The few upper class couples avoided crossing paths with uniformed men resembling eccentric thugs. Oscar's sense of spectacle, weakened by prison life, sprung to life among his ruffians. After the pretense of salon life, the hardship of incarceration, and now his new chapter of exile, he smiled as a walking oddity among men demanding the folly of respect. The shame of freakishness gave way to the relief of confident visibility.

From the corner of his eye, dock toughs gathered, staring with cruel eyes. "Gentlemen, I do believe we have a bad review for this performance," Oscar said. Usually, sailors happily entertained the fairest sex if the fairer sex were unavailable.

"Oh, we shan't be bothered by them." Ives said.

"Are they with you?" Oscar asked.

"Oh, quite the opposite. They are quite intent on doing us bodily harm. Or at least try." Ives said with a trademark chilly smile.

"Shall we depart? They number twenty and growing," Oscar said. "I am unsure of another fight within me. Please, let us return to Ross's abode."

"Come now, Oscar. We have an appointment to keep," Robbie Ross said wryly.

"They advance, Bobbie! Do something!" Oscar said. The glaring mob picked a quick pace, turning to the boardwalk stairs. "Bobbie! Get behind me!" Oscar said. Robbie laughed and pulled a little wide-barreled gun to the air and fired. A brilliant red bouquet crackled safely down from above. "This is no time for fireworks!" Oscar yelled.

Adolf Brand muttered, "You fluttering little pansies. Must I always show you how it's done?" He fired his flare into the mob. Pyrotechnics bounced from one scorched, shrieking sailor to another. With their front lines blinded and burned, the oncoming assailants tripped over one another, scintillating fireworks shuddering shadows on sand.

"Was that really necessary?" Magnus replied as the fire above dimmed.

"Mess with a faggot and get the flame!" Ives bellowed.

"Ives, you are least attractive with an open mouth," Brand said.

The boardwalk rumbled. Oscar held fast to the handrail as terror gripped him. At the end of the boardwalk, a battalion of bejeweled men thundered towards them.

"Run!" Oscar yelled.

Robbie Ross kept Oscar from bolting and bellowed, "They're with us, Oscar! They're with us!"

"What?" Oscar said.

Oscar focused his eyes on the oncoming crowd. It was true. A skinny little queen threw a brick like a girl and sassed, "Take that, bitch!" Men with sweeping handlebar moustaches parried their swords with the limp wrists. Others threw up their hands, gingerly stepping out of the way of a drunken sailor's lunge.

Within moments, the vastly outnumbered ruffians dispersed as the battalion of beefy mangirlboys chased after. "You *better* run!" One of the sassy sailors said, catwalking back into the fold. Oscar looked to the crowd of spangled men in skimpy cut-offs nearly spilling out gravity-defying man parts.

Oscar was dumbfounded. "What manner of men are these?"

"They're *my* men," An older gentleman said, stepping through the crowd. A spectacle unto himself, the Captain wore red velvet uniform with huge dangling earrings and a peacock feather in his wide-brimmed, purple suede hat. Soft eyes added a kindness to his sun-gristled skin, while his robust white goatee separated to a smile glistening with gold. Oscar noticed his peg leg carved into a ridiculously large penis. "Permit me to introduche myshelf. I am Captain Shilvermane of the Mary Rodger, at your shervish." Captain Silvermane said, removing his wide-brimmed hat and bowing deeply. "I have heard much about your travelsh, young Oschar. Under my watsh, you shall come to no harm. Come! Let ush take shelter on my ship."

Oscar cocked his eyebrow and whispered to Ives, "You're placing faith in effeminate Scottish seaman?"

George Ives smirked, "He's not Scottish."

"I can tell. It's a horrible impression," Oscar said, "Then who is he? He looks vaguely familiar."

Ives merely smiled and said, "A man like him? There can only be one."

George Cecil Ives greeted the Captain as they walked to the triple-masts of a Corvette warship. Shocked gawkers on the boardwalk stared at the garishly dressed men prancing merrily down the boardwalk, singing cabaret chestnuts and waving to the prim society out on a terrified nightly stroll.

"Oh Bobbie! This... This is amazing! It's the future that I always hoped for!" Oscar grew teary-eyed. "Did they overturn Paragraph 175? And the CLA of '85? It's about time! Finally, it's not illegal to love you!" Oscar pulled Robbie close, planting a large kiss on him.

Robbie pulled away, "It's not like that at all, Oscar. Since your imprisonment, it has grown worse. Much worse. We have even less political power than ever. Blackmail is at an all time high. Queensbury is the least of our problems. We're all criminals now. You're the only one who got caught. Look around you, Oscar. Does this look like the grand acceptance we fought so hard for?"

"Almost, Bobbie. Almost." Oscar said. In the surrounding throng, two pirates walked arm in arm, with a hand in each other's back pockets. As the queen mob approached the wooden whale, deckhands shot off more pyrotechnics. "So, now we're cavorting with pirates? Bobbie, if I didn't know better, I would say our little group of friends has started flirting with a criminal element."

"It gets stranger every day," Robbie said. Oscar waited for a punch line.

Oscar continued, "Are you… Are you serious?"

"Oh sure," Robbie said. "I've worked my way into several galleries. I swipe out the originals to a forger named Van Meegeren, who duplicates them. I keep the originals and sell the fakes. Then I sell the originals through a third party in the black market. My biggest buyer is this nutter in Italy, Jacques D'Adelswärd Fersen. He got exiled from France for performing a Black Mass man-orgy with his fellow Parisian schoolmates. It seems like art is not so useless after all, eh Oscar?"

"Bobbie! I'm shocked that you would do such a thing!"

Robbie Ross smiled in a way that deeply disturbed Oscar, "Oscar, we're all criminals. They can take us anytime they want to, as they did with you. How many more will die victims of hatred, their bodies forgotten long before their so-called perversity? If considered criminals, let our lawlessness be our advantage to benefit our brethren. This effect has given rise to 'The

Cause'. Silence the love that dare not speak its' name and it shall have no recourse but to grow even louder." Oscar fell silent. "But let's not dwell on such topics," Robbie said, "Your welcoming party is just up the gangplank."

Oscar looked up at the massive ship of the Mary Roger, noting an elaborate masthead of a well built man with a wide grin on his face, sporting a ridiculously enormous penis. "He certainly is merry, isn't he? I mean, who wouldn't be?" Oscar said.

"Haaay sailor!" A deckhand announced, "Osky-wosky is here!" The crowd of pirates cheered in response. Oscar was overwhelmed with the rapaciousness of the lively crew. After they drew up the gangplank, they drank themselves into a stupor, venturing below deck for a true Bacchanalia. Oscar swam through a sea of sweaty manflesh to where Robbie sat, sipping a port wine on the sidelines.

"What's the matter, Bobbie? Why are you not partaking?"

Ross swirled his wine in a silver goblet, feet propped up, enjoying the view. He yawned, "Oh, once you've attended one pirate orgy, you've pretty much been to them all."

Chapter 9:
The Many Deaths of Oscar Wilde

If you had the luck of the Irish,
You'd be sorry and wish you were dead
If you had the luck of the Irish,
You would wish you was English instead.

-*Luck of the Irish*
John Lennon

Outside an alehouse in Berlin in 1899, Robbie Ross waited, heavy with dread. His umbrella shuddered with each wet shiver under a bitter drizzle. From what Robbie gathered, this was not going to be a pleasant experience concerning Oscar's conduct.

"Herr Ross?" the plump doctor said. It was Magnus Hirshfeld, carrying his doctor's bag in one hand a soaked umbrella in the other.

"An umbrella? I perish the thought of a German using an umbrella. It doesn't suit your heartiness," Ross said with a smirk, "I thought the rain improved your German stoicism."

"I shan't disturb my coiffure," Dr. Hirshfeld said, coyly fluffing his heavily oiled hair. "I trust you arrived without complication?"

"It's good to see you again, Dr. Hirshfeld." Ross said. "Though I rarely adapt my mannerisms to hide my inverted nature, a few tight spots required a certain subterfuge."

"Hrmm, I see." Magnus wiped rain from his lenses. "Is Oscar in your company?"

"No," Ross said, "Should he be?"

Magnus polished his lenses nervously, "No. I, ah, hrm, thought he might be tagging along as he is wont to do. Have you discussed this meeting with our notorious convict scribe?"

"The last information on him I have knowledge of, Oscar was in Paris..." Ross said, omitting Oscar's travelling companion, Lord Alfred Douglas, again.

The good doctor cleared his throat. The weather was not conducive to his lungs. Dr. Hirshfeld asked, "Have Oscar's earaches--Hroom!--subsided? I recall at the last meeting, they were quite bothersome."

"I'm afraid they have not subsided. He explained his plans on seeing a specialist for ear surgery."

"Ah," Magnus said, "Well, if he thinks he can endure surgery as easily as he endured prison, I wish him the best of fortune."

"Do you know who else is coming?" Ross asked.

"Hroom!—Let us get out of this drizzle," Magnus said, shaking out his umbrella.

"I never understand why Mr. Ives picks tawdry places such as these. They seem so... exposed."

"Come now, Bobbie. Shadows are darkest in the brightest day. And for your information, the shopkeeper adorns the clothing of women." Dr. Hirshfeld said with a wink.

"Dr. Hirshfeld!" Ross said, eyes darting about, "You shouldn't say such things out loud!"

Magnus shrugged, "Why should you be embarrassed? Are you wearing ladies' undergarments? Honestly, I expected more of you, Bobby. It's just a penis."

"Magnus!" Ross said, blushing.

Magnus laughed to himself, "It appears you prove my research correct that blushing in men is prevalent to homosexuals. Come along then. Allow me to purchase you an ale. None of that English swill, either."

Magnus and Robbie waited until George Ives walked in. Ives entered with his characteristic vacuous smile, spiting both the Devil and God. Ross once described Ives as a social paranoid and a romantic whore. "Good afternoon, Gentlemen," Ives said, shaking out his umbrella, monocle flecked with rain. "I trust your travel has not been impeded. Marvelously good to see you. Now all we need is for Herr Brand to arrive, and--"

Brand swerved his chair around, scotch in hand, to his late arrivals. "I wondered when you butt-holes would show," Adolf said from an otherwise empty table. A trinity of empty pint glasses and two empty snifters littered his wobbly table. "So, what's this all about?" Brand's eyelids drooped in drunkenness.

Ives signaled to the owner. The owner nodded and spoke quietly to the only other patron. The patron departed without a word. It made Robbie nervous when the barkeep said with a grotesquely thick German accent, "Help yourself to the bar." The owner flipped a closed sign in the window and retreated to the back.

The silence of the bar sank in. Ives lit a cigarette. Brand swirled his Scotch. Magnus took his only sip of beer and waited for the meeting to begin.

"Is Oscar coming?" Robbie said, feeling like he was in trouble with very bad people. Magnus and Brand shifted uncomfortably.

"Bobbie, that's why I've called this meeting," Ives said. "We have a bit of a problem, and we cannot arrive at a resolution, which is where your insight would benefit us greatly. The problem is... Oscar."

Ross sighed, "I know." He felt guilty without discernible reason.

"He's a sodding mess," Brand said, throwing up a little in his mouth and forcing the bile back down.

Ives ignored Brand, "We touched upon a snag. Nearing a new century, opportunities are opening up for us. Brand is doing a whizbang job reopening brothels and recruiting more high-ranking artists, businessmen, and politicians to The Cause. Magnus expands our base of operations with private consultations while accruing donors for The Cause. As for myself, I have reached out in America to expand opportunities for revenue. I understand you have a nice little art forgery racket going... But Oscar..."

"He's a fat, alcoholic mooch," Brand said, sloshing his scotch, "He gives Gentlemen a bad name, Bobbie."

Robbie replied, "I could talk some sense--"

Brand barked, "We're past that now! Gide's been tailing him all through Europe and the Mediterranean. You know he's buggering that Douglas boy again? You know—the one who threw Oscar in the clink to begin with?"

Ives squeaked, "Adolf--"

Brand unleashed. "To hell with you, Ives. I am quite tired of this prancy English waltz with responsibility. It's horse shit. He was supposed to be our hero, George! He was supposed to open the gates! He went to hell and back for us! And we repaid him with all of Europe. We repaid him with boys from my stables! We repaid him with a stipend! We repaid him with Swedish saunas! We repaid him with as much whiskey an Irishman can drink! We've been exhausting all our resources on him! And what does he do? What does he do? He shits on his dinner plate. Has he written anything? No! Has he stayed away from that Douglas boy? No! Has he attempted to further The

Cause? No! He just turns his back on The Cause with a childish bitterness until the money runs out and then he asks for more! We attempted to keep him from jail, and he put the crown of thorns on all by himself, without so much as a round of fisticuffs. He is a walking disaster, Bobbie. He isolated everyone with his damnable martyr complex. I tire of it to no end!"

Brand gulped down the remains in his snifter before storming off to the bar for the bottle. "He brings us all down. We suffer with him, and my boys tell me he is not hung like Christ." Brand slammed the bottle on the table before sloppily pouring another for Robbie. Ross belted down his harsh liquor. Brand continued, "I love you, Bobbie. You're a good lad and the best thing to come out of this whole Oscar Wilde rat's nest."

Ives cleared his throat. Brand sat down quietly at the hint. Robbie Ross felt like a scolded child. "So what do you ask of me?" Dr. Hirshfeld gave Mr. Ives the slightest of nods.

Dr. Hirshfeld took a deep breath, "Son, I have some unfortunate news."

Robbie panicked. "What is it? You're not going to kill him, are you?"

Adolf and Ives laughed, "Not at all, Bobbie. We do not comfort with one hand and betray with another. That would be ungentlemanly. Adolf? George? Would you allow us the room?" Magnus asked. The wooden chairs creaked and scuttled across the floor as George and Adolf stepped outside.

"Magnus, what... what is this?" Robbie said.

Magnus said, "Bobbie, I have no easy way to explain. Oscar Wilde is going to die. Gide reports--"

"You're going to kill him! Is that what this is?" Robbie said, instantly on the verge of tears.

"It would never come to that. I give you my word. Now I must ask you with the same severity, do you trust such a word?" Magnus said. Hirshfeld's eyes were kind, hopeful, serious, trusting, and vulnerable.

"Yes." Robbie said.

"You may not be aware of this, but The Order of Chaeronea is a front for a deeper secret."

"What?"

"The order is for dilettantes, for peasants. Do you know who runs the Order?"

"No, who?"

"The Order doesn't condone any activities any more illegal than buggery, but the Gentlemen of the Shade—well, that is a bit... darker. Brand's pimping is more or less an open secret. Practically every one of us is his customer. I hoped when Oscar left prison that he would take a nobler stance his current position. A Gentleman has a successor, and Oscar named you as his. Oscar and I were to balance out Brand and Ives' shadowy transgressions and promote something positive. Bobbie, a curator such as yourself, is a prime candidate for Oscar's seat when the time comes."

"Now here's the cold, hard fact," Magnus said. "Oscar is very sick. I diagnosed him at our last meeting. When they beat him in the prison chapel, his inner ear was damaged and is healing poorly, growing back wrong and putting pressure on his brain. You may have noticed changes in his behavior from this injury." It all clicked into place. "I found an excellent surgeon for him, but surgery is surgery--You know as well as I do, surgery is a dangerous last resort. In this case, the prognosis is not good."

Robbie threw his hands up to cover the tears on his face. "I know," he sniffled, "I've known for awhile now."

"I'm terribly sorry, Bobbie," Magnus said, tearing up in sympathy.

"I appreciate your understanding," Robbie said from behind his wall of fingers.

Magnus hated himself for what he was about to say. "To hell with Ives and Brand. They're both assholes of their own right," Magnus said. His candor caught Robbie off guard. "Bobbie, the Gentlemen need you, now more than ever in Oscar's absence. Each of us take great pains to ensure lines of succession stay intact. Since we have no children of our own to call family, we name our own lance-bearers. And Oscar named you."

"Me?" Robbie laughed. "Me? What about Lord Douglas? Was not he whom Oscar loved more than life itself?"

"No, Bobbie," Magnus said, "it was you. Oscar explained if any man was worthy of being a Gentleman of the Shade, it was you that should take his place. You already have power of attorney over the Wilde estate. You managed to eliminate his bankruptcy, care for his wife and children, rescue his private letters, and--above all--remain unconditionally loyal. No matter how horribly he slighted you, you still stand at his side unconditionally. Oscar has not been so far gone as to overlook your loyalty. Neither have we. Please. Robert Ross, will you join me in the Shade?"

The weight of the empty alehouse compressed.

Apprehensively, Robert Ross took Dr. Hirshfeld's hand and said, "If that is what Oscar requires of me."

Magnus gave Robbie a hearty hug, exhaling a sigh of relief.

"Thank you for joining me in The Shade." Dr. Hirshfeld said.

***

Four months passed since Oscar's surgery. He wore bandages like a Van Gogh self-portrait while the infection set in. All the top Gentlemen attended the final hours. Robbie wept while Oscar raved and bit his own bloodied tongue, the abscess pressing further into his brain.

Magnus warned, "Don't go in there, son," but Ross blew past.

Oscar let out a gurgled moan and thrashed, possessed with death throes. Robbie shrieked Oscar's name while Wilde foamed and gibbered between thrashes, pissing the bed somewhere between life and death. Silence came suddenly after a seizure of clicks before the body went limp and the pus buildup ruptured from every orifice. The priest gave last rights. The nurses pulled over the shroud. George Ives wiped a tear from each eye. Brand, Ives, and Captain Silvermane stepped from the room, leaving Dr. Hirshfeld and Robbie Ross. The stillness cut time sharply to a standstill. The wind refused to breathe.

Dr. Hirshfeld stood by the door, watching Ross process the white sheet soaking up the fluids burst from Oscar's head. Between the dust and sunlight, Ross's breath held. Robbie spun around, sitting beside the corpse, looking to his own empty shaking hands. Dr. Hirshfeld took a seat beside Ross, anticipating.

"This is all wrong," Robbie said. "This isn't how it's supposed to end." Ross was unaware of his own spilled tears.

"It never is," Magnus replied. "Tell me... how is it supposed to end?"

Robbie's body shook, exhausted from the day's stress. Robbie looked to the corners of the room as he wept, looking for an answer. Robbie sucked in his sniffles. "Knowing Oscar, he would have said, 'this wallpaper and I are in a duel to the death, and surely one of us must go!'" Ross said. Dr. Hirshfeld chuckled.

Magnus patted Ross on the knee and said, "For the sake of posterity, I thought I heard Oscar say that."

"Thank you, Magnus," Robbie said, "You've been a good friend to me."

Magnus replied, "You're a Gentleman. I'd die for you, just as Oscar did. I only hope you would die for me." It seemed too soon. "Maybe Adolf is right," Dr. Hirshfeld said, "My bedside manner could probably use some work." The two walked from Oscar's deathbed.

Robbie responded, "I think your bedside manner is just fine, Dr. Hirshfeld. It's just fine."

PART III:
The Southern Gentleman

Tod Crouch

Chapter 11:
The Strangest Trick I Ever Turned
(Overheard in a Greenwich Cafeteria in 1926)

> *I must have died alone, A long long time ago.*
> *Who knows, not me,*
> *I never lost control,*
> *You're face, to face, With the man who sold the world.*

> *The man who sold the World*
> --David Bowie

Really? Why would you want to know about that from a burned out Model-T car crash like me? Well, all right. I don't got a lot of friends, and I'm sure you'll run to the hills after I tell you a little about me, but that's a risk I'll take for a pretty little thing like you. Now mind you, this was awhile back. I'm reformed, mind you. Not that guy anymore. You sure you want to know about all that? Well, okay, if you need to know...

I was a bastard and my mamma died in childbirth. I was sent to onna them English orphanages where they shove gruel and Jesus down your throat with the same spoon and I din't have a taste for neither, so I left with the laundry one day. Bein' a scrappy pickpocket, it din't take long for the underbelly of society to come rubbin' up against me. I was a sweep for awhile, but that was worse than the orphanage. I found my way into a boy brothel. If you never had three hots and a cot, having your arse ripped open at 14 isn't so bad.

The days after the Cleveland Street bust were hazy. George Wright, Henry Newlove and a few others got pulled in, but I got a nose, see? I smell calm. If it's too calm, get out. Trust bad feelings, those sour instincts.

121

It's the only difference between being caught in a bad situation and making a bad decision.

I'm none too good with those years after Cleveland Street. Those kids didn't like me. Scared, jealous, it don't matter anymore. But they picked and they picked and they picked. Between customers and so-called friends, I set myself against the world. When they all went south, I set about my business, drifting through London, doing whatever to live. Mr. Brand always told me the most reluctant leader is most apt, and I can't disagree. I think I was about fourteen when I started helping out the little kids. I mean *little*. Five and six.

When Cleveland Street closed down, the pimps and stable hands cut their street kids loose. I couldn't let them go through what I went through. So I taught them.

In those days, everyone thought adults exploited us, but quite the opposite—we just tried to survive. If some old codger wanted to squeeze us off for a quid, it was killing two birds with one stone. I started my own little gang called the Wandering Birds. We worked a lot to stay alive. We would pickpocket during the days and seek out perverts in shadows at night. If they never saw the light of day, well, hey...

At the time, I hated Mr. Brand for leaving. I never saw the other boys from Cleveland Street. Me and the Birds never left our territory, avoiding trouble and preferred running to fighting. I'm not gonna go into that.

It was about '92 or '93 that I got back in touch with Adolf. I guess if you run in one circle, there are seven more you don't know you're in. I still hated him, but he was setting up high-end clients like Oscar Browning back in England. Brand had this little magazine for the sexual inverts, but it eventually dried up and I went back to the old trade in England, as a high-pricer for the wealthy who could afford to turn more than a few blind eyes to their indiscretions.

Soon, I was laying the upper class, mostly those in the Oscar Wilde clique. Oscar wasn't famous yet. I bounced from him to Lord Douglas to Robbie Ross to his friends at any given time. I abandoned my Wandering Birds. I was becoming a made man.

About seventeen or eighteen, the Wilde trial happened. Oscar had a crooked penis and was not hygienic. Terrible breath. They ignored my statements because they thought I was crazy as a loon. Sometimes I get confused, but not about what matters. All of a sudden, the telegrams stopped coming, and with it my income.

I picked up strangers--always a dice toss and roll--same gesture, you understand. Johns think they can do anything, so you learn boundaries fast and gouge an eye or two. It was about the sixth or seventh time I was inside, I ran into an old coworker in jail from a vagrancy charge. It took us a moment or two to recognize each other. Bodies change with the season. You can depend on that.

It was Alfie Wood. His hair grew dark. He tried to grow facial hair, but it came in a soft shadow above his lip. His back had bright red tiger stripes from growing nearly a foot in two years. Unfortunately, for me, I lacked the height for my muscular build, but I was sure it would come in soon.

"What are you in for?" I asked him. He laughed. "Actually, I'm a witness for this Oscar Wilde Trial," Alfie said.

"Oh *really?* Me too!" I responded, "How did you get subpoenaed and I didn't?"

"You know Douglas's father, the Marquess of Queensbury? He paid me a handsomely to put the innocent youth corrupted by sodomites on trial. I even stole some naughty letters to seal Oscar's fate."

"Didn't Oscar pay off one of your blackmailers?" Alfie laughed and threw up two offending fingers,

"There was no blackmailer. Burn that faggot. I have big plans, Edward. *Big* plans. I only have to do a few more high priced gigs and I'm gone."

"Why didn't the Marquess approach me?" I asked.

"Oh, Eddie. You really are quite the dolt. You are one of the most mentally imbalanced people I ever met. Don't you know everyone humored you and your simpleton ways?" Alfie said. Same old Alfie.

"Well," I said, "If you hear of any of these high pricers, let me know. I always look for work, almost a job in itself."

Alfie scoffed and replied, "Whatever, honey. I'll put in a word."

Well, as the story goes, Oscar went to jail. We all packed up and headed to France or Germany. Paragraph 175 in Germany got you six months, while the Criminal Law Amendment in England got you two years, and England came down hard. France hated the trade but wouldn't imprison you. I contacted Herr Brand to see how he could get me out of wretched London. He sent me to a wealthy fellow named George Ives. Bit of an odd duck, if I must say.

I think I scared him. But Ives arranged some forged documents to visit my "Uncle Brand" in Germany. There, I looked up Adolf Brand, who found me a few steady, reliable clients through this secret society thing. I didn't really understand what it was all about, but I was given a little velvet lavender address book of prominent Germans who would gladly pay for my services.

I was about 21 and still had most of my looks when Herr Brand sent me back to London for an errand with Mister Ives. This was a little bit after Oscar Wilde left prison. Ives threw a giant party for him and wanted me on staff for the event. I complied.

I received directions and followed them to the letter, even though my reading's not so good. Weaving through narrow London streets, I eventually came to a reeking alley, where upon closer examination rested a large metal door painted black, blending with soot. I pounded on the metal door. A small slot opened up. Two beady eyes stared from the slit.

"Password."

"If you done it, it ain't bragging," I said, quoting some guy named Whitman.

The metal slit slammed and the door creaked open with an ancient whine. *What am I getting myself into?* I thought, staring at the doorman missing an eye and several teeth.

The catering captain said, "Down the stairs and to the right. That's where your kind get ready. Look for the man in the green mask. You'll want this." the doorman said, handing me a plain little black domino mask. Mattachine, he called it.

I walked down the steep endless steps lit by a cascade of wall-mounted candles. By the time I reached the bottom of the steps, I accepted the situation I put myself in.

It was a beautiful space for a renovated catacomb: the vaulted ceiling canopied party planners flitting about, lighting gothic candelabras and the enormous chandelier. Draperies of the finest silks rippled from hidden drafts. Along the sides of the Grand Hall, where Crusaders once called their final resting place, were fluffy cots and intimate settings I knew to familiarize myself with. Clouds of incense blanketed the sweet rot baking into the walls over centuries. At the far end of the Grand Hall, a podium and row of seats looked strangely religious, presumably for a lecture.

A blindfolded band tuned up near the stone-lined staircase. I went to my appointed station, where dozens upon dozens of line boys stripped, prelubing their anuses in the nipple-sharpened chill. One old queen, pulled from the catacombs, barked orders as we prepared.

"Okay people, listen up!" The fat queen bee shrieked, "We're expecting five hundred tonight so remember—Smiles smiles smiles! This is a huge client. There will probably be a few celebrities here, but this is not a networking party. You are to be passed like hors d'oerves. That's what they pay for. If you recognize someone behind their mask, *do not* call them by their name. There are about a hundred of you, so no one should feel overwhelmed by the clientele. If you need time to go in the back and recharge, find me and let me know. If you spend too much time back there or fraternize with yourselves at the expense of the client, I will beat you. Expect to work the full fourteen-hour shift until the last person leaves. No eating, no drinking, and if you need the restroom, you must find me before I can relieve you..."

Alfie Wood approached me. The queen bee berated the underlings who unflinchingly accepted abuse without wincing.

Alfie said under the torrent of our queen bee's foul language concerning civility. "I'm surprised to see you here, after the damage you created at the trial a few months ago. Never sell out a client." I replied.

"What can I say? The price is right." Alfie said. His chin grew flab. "After this gig, I'll have enough to start over. I can't wait for this night to be over so I can begin *anew*."

The queen bee clapped his hands together like a walrus as we scattered to position. Shivering naked against the drafts, we greeted the arriving guests. Several new boys walked about with heavy iron plates of food or lead goblets of wine, scrawny arms shuddering under the weight. Guests arrived in long colorful robes and ornate masks. A parade of horrible demon faces, elongated noses, surprised eyes, and twisted mouths filtered in. No matter the effort, nothing hid the damned visages of personality or the scent of unwashed obesity. Familiar bald spots, hunchbacks and protruding bellies exposed all previous johns I knew.

The guests stood about, chatting indifferently while drinking and fisting food into their gaping maws until a masked George Cecil Ives and his closest friends took to the podium. The blindfolded band stopped. They chanted hymns of an unknown religion before George Ives spoke, "Thank you all for coming to this critical meeting of the Order of Chaeronea. It is a pleasure to see us bonded together. Of course, many of us could not be in attendance. For those of us who are not here, I hope to provide the best of indulgences for those who are, to compensate our losses. And now, allow me to introduce a man who needs no introduction, our newest and most esteemed member."

Even when being anonymous, Oscar Wilde let everyone know who was behind his peacock-feathered mask rimmed with green carnations. His deep, effete chuckle cascaded through the catacombs. "Good evening, brethren. We gather for the same reason: emancipation. Many of our countries consider our act criminal, where the only victim is law itself. It is our job to break through the back door of the common man, to spread our seed into the underbelly of society! From any position, we must be prepared to pull in and pull out from any situation. Be mindful of pinching off anyone going too deep, for the overzealous can cause us permanent damage, leaving our arses to hang in the breeze! We must speak, even when gagged! Let our reverberations of passion resonate through the tender pipe organ, so the pipes squeal with ecstasy! If we are to hide in the shadows, we must own the shadows. Our laws are our own. If they are to treat us as criminals, then criminals we shall be, until we have stolen respect itself! Do not concern yourself with violence, for power is in culture and money. I do not speak of culture in terms of poetry and art, but of community. Our very culture is our greatest asset, and we must use this to recognize that everyone here is not alone or without aid, privileged with aiding another."

It was not the carefree Oscar Wilde I remembered. As they ended the meeting, my work began. I tell you, they launched on us like starving cannibals. I usually refuse group sessions because before you know it, one is boned up like a hog on a spit. The fellow fellated before you attacks your sinuses while the brother behind knocks the wind from you. But you subdue yourself and carry on. Go somewhere else, leave your body. Shut down. For the most part, they are greedy old men—two pump chumps eager for the nightcap. Don't get me wrong, most of the guys were previous engagements--cock is unique as a fingerprint. Newer boys left soon as possible, but I stayed on. Though I was just the help, I carried conversations, doing the genital jiggle giggle all the way to the finish line.

I knew enough German to hear Mr. Brand recommend me to George, but I feigned ignorance. The crowd trickled out early in the morning and I finally took my leave, heavy envelope in hand. Ives stayed on, thanked me for participating, and handed me a plain white envelope. Inside were a few thousand and a note telling me to take a few months off. When I returned from Tangiers, Ives promoted me to full time bodyguard. I never tricked again. I didn't see Alfie Wood around after he made his big score, for awhile.

So now that I answered your question, you are obliged to answer mine: Do you, uh, live around here? I know a place.

Chapter 11:
Oscar Wilde is Alive and Well and Living in New Orleans

> *Mississauga goddam*
> *Bears the drudgery of my old man*
> *I'll be wearing my disguise*
> *Until I lead my life from Mississauga Goddam*

> *Mississauga Goddam*
> --Hidden Cameras

1905.   Alfie Wood rode the late train into NewOrleans.   Looking out the window, the country landscapes haunted him with passing visions of terror. Bioluminescent swamps painted swaying white fingers of Spanish moss, beckoning him with a mute siren's song.   Mere feet from the train tracks, a sea of burning crosses lit a ghastly tableau of pointy-headed ghosts gathered around strange fruit dangling from branches. Beady, reptilian eyes shone back from the blackest marshes, where trees passed with spectral elegance.

The train crossed a trestle spanning the Mississippi, full of gas-lit steamboats flickering on dark water.   The blue spark of the rail flashed against above ground mausoleums.   Alfie Wood wondered if he took the doomed train to a necropolis for assuming the identity of the dead man, Oscar Wilde.

The stuffy train grumbled to a stop.   The humid air hit him like a wall.   He stepped through the crowd, clothes sweat-drenched.   At the suggestion of a ticket taker, Alfie walked to the corner of St. Ann Street and Bourbon.

"What *is* this?" Alfie said to himself as he looked down Bourbon Street, where topless women jiggled in shop windows.   Down the adjacent street, men dressed in brown suede shoes and red ties flirted with rough looking men in petticoats. Café tables overcrowded the sidewalks; pedestrians overcrowded the streets. Sketch artists stood across from each other on second story galleries, drawing each other drawing. Everyone was drunk. Through the clotted streets, Alfie Wood noticed a vacancy sign in a boarding house called La Rue De La Splendour. Alfie smiled, thinking of Wilde's House Beautiful on Tite Street and found this to be the perfect substitute.

Suitcase in hand, Alfie approached the front desk and chimed the bell. A little black boy around twelve years old came out, his cap roguishly tilted. "Miss Dewey! You have a guest!" The child said. "How do you do, sir? Miss Dewey will be right with you."

Out stepped a black woman with the body of a linebacker, "Well mercy me! How do you do, sir?" Miss Dewey fanned herself, hiding rough stubble.

"Welcome to La Rue de la Splendour. I am the proprietor of this little establishment and you can call me Miss Ann Dewey." She smiled a goalie's smile of broken teeth. "How long will you be staying with us?"

"No less than a month," Alfie said.

"Ohh! What do we have here? Are you European?"

The bellhop snickered, "You're a-peein'."

"Mind your manners, L'il Orville! We got company! I will smack the black off you and beat you blue with it!"

Embarrassed, Alfie continued, "I'm originally from Ireland, but I spent much of my time in England before moving on to France."

"Ohh! You from Jolly ol' England?" Miss Dewey said, throwing a huge hand to her stuffed brassiere. "Well, it's two dollars a week and you pay upfront."

"It's really not that jolly." Alfie said, digging out eight dollars.

"Hm! Quite a high roller we got here!" Miss Dewey said with a wink. "And who do we have the pleasure of pleasuring in our esteemed house of ill repute?"

The panic of setting the ball rolling punched him in the gut. "Well, can you keep a secret?"

Miss Dewey leaned in, eyes sparkling. "Of course, Sugah."

"Don't tell anyone, but I'm Oscar Wilde." Alfie said. "You see, my plight grew quite heated, so I faked my death and relocated. I'm working on a new play and--"

Miss Dewey threw her head back, releasing a baritone cackle. "Lordy, child, you are too much!" She flipped open the registry to a random page and stabbed a long fingernail into the paper. Eight Oscar Wildes already checked in. Miss Dewey continued, "Well Sugah, you just go on and write them plays here if you want, Mistah Wilde. Your secret's safe with me." Miss Dewey slid the key over. "Orville! Take his bags up to his room! Well, Mister Wilde, welcome to New Orleans. I'd suggest you goin' over to the Old Absinthe House for a nightcap, as it's a cool night out."

Beads of sweat ran down Alfie's face. "You certainly know how to charm a lad, Miss Dewey."

"I know how to do a lot of things." She sassed, "Don't worry, child. I won't wait up."

Alfie Wood cut through the heavy crowd to the little corner bar, the Old Absinthe House. Alfie's foppish English attire exposed him as a tourist. Jostling his way through the crowd, he noticed a stairwell leading upwards to a sign reading "VIP ONLY".

Walking upstairs, a handful of women in layered petticoats fanned themselves beside dignified white-suited men, each touched with an air of condescension. They stared at Alfie with polite intrigue.

"Hello, esteemed sir, what may I assist you with? A cordial?" The bartender said with a nearly unintelligible bayou accent. Alfie cased the small room where two couples stared at the newcomer. One of the men eyed the stranger suspiciously, leaning back ever so carefully to show the butt of his revolver. The blond woman sitting next to him touched him on the arm.

"Why just admire our esteemed guest." She said loudly, crossing the bar. Strains of the brass band downstairs leaked up the stairwell. The lady with the tight blonde curls approached Alfie. "Judging from your marvelous taste in attire, you aren't from these parts. Am I mistaken?"

Alfie smiled, letting his charm ooze all over her. "Why no madam, you are not mistaken. I seek solace in such a fine city as New Orleans."

Her fan flitted faster, "My word! A gentleman from distant lands! We so rarely get to experience a truly unique flavor as yours. What may I ask is the name belonging to such a wayward traveler?" The two men at the table looked at the interaction from afar with great interest. The blond woman fanned a hand at the barkeep. "Bartender? Please, entertain this kind sir with whatever he prefers." The bartender nodded.

Alfie responded, "Something local, if I may?"

"How goes down an absinthe, sir? It don't get no more local than that."

"Much obliged," Alfie said to the southern belle. "My dear madam, I cannot permit myself to falsify my presence to a lady of such generosity. I only hope a woman of your standing can contain such a secret as I am to divulge."

Her eyes flared with intrigue to Alfie's delight. "Oh, mysterious stranger, if ever there were a trustworthy soul, there are fewer people in this fine city who hold more dangerous secrets than myself, you understand. Tell me anything, anything at all, for I am Angelique LaFitte, proprietress of this fine establishment with my husband, Mister Julien LaFitte."

She pointed to her husband at the large polished oak table on the far side of the room. He buttoned his outside coat with a nod, hiding his pistol. Another fellow, sitting next to Julien, stared incriminatingly at Alfie's prominent groin.

"I do so apologize!" Angelique exasperated. "This here is my brother-in-law and one of my closest friends, Rene LaFitte."

Alfie extended his rough hand to the queer gentleman's smooth palm. "It is... my ultimate pleasure to meet your acquaintance, Mister Rene." Alfie watched the basket grow supple and felt his own blossom.

Rene's limp handshake said everything. "I duly declare, you are quite the English gentleman!" Embarrassed by such forwardness, Alfie Wood redirected to Angelique, "It is of the utmost importance that this secret does not become common knowledge, for I am dead, and grave consequences befall me should this understanding find wrongful hands. My undoing would surely be forthcoming. Were it so, I wish to be indebted to you with the promise of your protection."

Angelique LaFitte's eyes glittered like fireworks. Alfie watched the hook puncture her cheek as she said, "Why, kind stranger, a gentleman never asks and a lady never tells. Please, explain to me the nature of your business in my fair city."

"I am quite famous in Europe for a few racy plays I wrote. But after my imprisonment, life proved too difficult. Hence, I prepared a false death, to begin life anew elsewhere." Alfie said, "You may call me Alfie. That is my new name for this new life. A woman of your intellect should know I am, ahem, earnest in my desire to not be discovered and please understand the *importance* of my *earnesty*."

Angelique's eyes grew to the size of saucers. "Permit me to indulge my suspicions. How could I possibly judge the importance of being earnest?" Angelique winked.

Alfie winked back, "Quite, quite." Angelique grabbed him by the arm and led him over to the table, barely holding her excitement in.

"Julien! You simply must meet my new friend, Osc—I mean, Alfie. He was quite an earnest playwright in London." Angelique said. "...If you know what I mean?"

As Alfie took a seat, unimpressed Julien LaFitte indulged his beautiful wife's pet project. Julien dressed in a white suit, which picked up the slightest dinge of the day, armpits already stained yellow. As Alfie Wood's research later proved, Julien LaFitte was the grandson of a famous pirate, as his wife was the granddaughter of a famous landowner and governor. Alfie Wood deduced her high-class innocence complimented his murderous thirst for power.

"How do you do, sir?" Alfie said. "Please, call me Alfie Wood."

"Much obliged, Mister Alfie," Julien said with cold indifference. "Perhaps you have more in common with my, erm, brother, Rene."

Rene smiled with more than his mouth. "I am quite a fan of your plays."

"Well, that was quite a different time," Alfie said. "I have been working on a new play. It's called 'The Fortunate Accordionist'. It involves a man with a squeezebox who invites many through the back door, pinching off those who wander brazenly without concern for the place in which they enter."

"I like the sound of it already," Rene said.

Angelique twittered out a laugh. "Oh, stop! You boys are too much!" Angelique squealed as a glass of strange green liquid landed in front of Alfie. "Surely, you recall such a beverage when you were living in France."

Alfie had no idea what she referred to, "Oh yes. This... beverage. I am unaware of the customs stateside. How do I go about drinking it here?"

Rene smiled, "Allow me to show you. Pour the water over the cube, then drink it."

"Oh yes, that is how it's done in Paris," Alfie said, conceding. "I never want to appear a tourist, even in exile."

The other woman sitting at the LaFitte wore pants. She fisted her beer mug down with the subtlety of a badger, defying elegance. "I'm sorry. I don't mean to cast doubt on your existence, but you look quite young for being the man you claim to be." Most unladylike, she smoked and drank beer.

"Ah, I'm sorry. I don't mean to be rude, but what honor do I have in meeting such a stranger?" Alfie said.

She smiled, "My name is Frances Benjamin Johnston. You may have heard of me. President Roosevelt commissioned me as White House photographer. I stuck my fingers in your niece's vagina and she liked it."

Angelique twittered out a nervous laugh. "Oh *Frannie*! You are *scandalous*!" Her husband cleared his throat, sputtering indignation.

"I duly apologize. I, ah, haven't been in contact with my niece in quite some time." Alfie said, heart racing.

"Ah. Well, as a very close friend of Angelique, I think we could benefit from a group photo of this meeting of such providence?" Miss Johnston asked. "Unless you disagree, Mister (ahem) Wilde?"

Angelique gasped, "Frances! I implore you! Our guest here—"

"No, no," Alfie said, "If I am to put myself in your trust, I must do it with both feet. Please, take a group photo. But dear Miss Johnston, please accredit my appearance as 'unknown'."

"You have my word," Miss Johnston said. As she set her camera equipment up at their table, Angelique chatted up Alfie.

"I'm quite interested in this 'Earnest' play you say you wrote. If it succeeds, perhaps we could put on this "Fortunate Accordionist" theatrical drama you speak so highly of at the local theater?"

"That would be delightful. But I require nothing but a small recompense and anonymity."

"I have the perfect idea," Angelique said, "There is a local fellow named A. Baldwin Wood. He has a magnificent idea to drain the swamps with this thing called a 'screw pump'. He claims to be able to drain the swamplands with his contraptions. Julien and I are buying up the unusable land quite cheaply. How would you feel if we set up a fund for the lad and use your famous play as a fundraiser? You could use the time to write your squeezebox play."

"Maybe we can form a trust for Mister Wood, and I'll help bring in donations. Well, I wouldn't want you in a compromising position. " Alfred said.

With stony faced bitchery, Frances replied, "Any position can be compromised." Alfred's stomach dropped into his tight shoes.

"You dirty girlie!" Alfred said, letting out a nervous laugh.

"What a splendid idea!" Angelique squealed in excitement.

"Say fromage," Miss Johnston said as the flash tray fired.

Nobody smiled.

Chapter 12:
Faster Cat-Hole, Kill! Kill!

> In the first bar, things would stop and stare
> In this bar things were lasses-faire
> and I was dancing in a lesbian bar...
> I was dancing in a lesbian bar...

> *I Was Dancin' at a Lesbian Bar*
> Jonathan Richmond

In London, 1904, George Cecil Ives spanked his personal bodyguard, Edward Shelley, lightly on the behind and said, "Come along, then. We are attending a poetry reading. What a smashing time! I do wish we had more culture in our little club. It's dreadful when they all move away." Edward knew it was true. With Bobbie in France, Hirshfeld and Brand in Germany, England grew lonely.

"Why are we going to a poetry reading?" Edward asked. "If we wanted poetry, we could simply visit Yeats's house. For a heterosexual, his beard hides more genitals than--"

Ives burst into laughter. "Well... regardless of what a beard hides, this is a bit more sensitive. I know you don't contemplate the intricacies of poetry, but your services may be helpful in this new... venture."

The carriage stopped at the mouth of a long, greasy alley. At the other end of the alley, a fishmonger's sign stood flapping in the draft: a man with a rain hood standing defiantly in a boat.

Edward and George stepped out, gazing at the moist clutter before them. Mangy stray cats hissed and ran off as the two men approached. On a small placard beside a door in the narrow path, a simple sign read 'poetry reading'. The dirty windows showed the pub busy, too busy for a tea-sipping poetry reading. The delicately hand-painted sign squeaking over the door announced the name of the place: THE CAT HOLE.

"Ah, I thought we'd never find it," George said at the hairy end of a dank alley. "Our kind never know where to look. I'm actually surprised to find this special spot under a canopy atop the entry way."

"Well, we never would have found it without some guidance from the women," Shelley responded. "Please stop me if I seem too aggressive. I understand these women are a bit more fair than the fairest sex. I'd rather not find my end with a neck snapped between the thighs of a woman in the throes of bloodlust."

"Ah, bloodlust only occurs one out of every four weeks." Ives said, checking his watch. "I think timing is on our side."

As Shelley and Ives prepared to enter the lady bar, A woman hurtled through the front window, landing face down in alley sewage. From the hole in the glass, a woman yelled, "I'll cut your sagging tits off and use 'em for stockings!" The shrieking wench wiped scraggly hair from her face, noticed the two men, and ducked back inside—where the sounds of shrieks and breaking glass hushed instantly. Shelley holstered his piece.

"This looks like my sort of locale," George said, smiling his icy smile. He turned to see Edward picking up the spurned woman from the puddle of alley droppings.

"Don't look at me!" She cried, running off through the streets.

"What are you getting us into, Ives?" Edward whispered.

The cold confidence Ives exuded sluiced into Shelley's dirty courage as Ives said, "Quite all right,

Mister Shelley. Dr. Hirshfeld, on one of his lecture tours, acquired the friendship of a marvelous songstress. Perhaps you have heard of her...Lady Maybel Batten? Miss Batten told Herr Doktor Hirshfeld that she knew about our Gentlemanly club. This is privy information, but the Sisters from the Isle of Lesbos have played this game much longer than we, and they seemed to discover us and require our active participation. I just love gossip. Come along..."

Edward followed close behind. On the other side of the creaking door, a room full of women glared, eyes full of man-hatred. A top-heavy gal behind a small music rack read some mangled, intolerable verse, and not a man in sight. It was the perfect cover for their operation, for no husband would ever venture to a poetry read, and hadn't for thousands of years.

As an eye is wont to do during a slow poetry reading, George Cecil Ives examined the patrons. In the smokiest, whiskey-reeking corner, he saw a familiar face he never met before. She was seventeen, at the very most. The girl spoke with a familiar Irish brogue, reminding Ives of Oscar Wilde. *No, It can't be...*

When the performer saw her only male guests, she incoherently hurried through the final stanzas and sat down. The females gave a deadpan clap, never taking their eyes off the men.

"We have to get out of here." Shelley whispered. Ives ignored him, exuberantly applauding the sad performance. His clapping tapered to an uncomfortable silence. Edward noticed every woman in the Cat Hole held a blade, glinting in gaslight. Ives and Shelley watched the audience turn into a shark maw, ready to swallow them whole.

Ives smiled toothily, throwing his voice through his teeth to Shelley, "Don't do anything rash, dear boy." The two would be ribbons before Shelley fired the first shot.

An elegant courtesan barked, "Get outta here or we'll cutcha cocken balls off and shove 'em down your throat until you shite out your own cock and bugger yourself to death!"

Ives looked to the seventeen year old girl, smoking a cigarette in a holder, who neither antagonized nor defended. Instead, she said two words to the lady beside her, who burst into laughter. *It's her. It has to be her.*

"I'll abort you in this back alley!" A beautiful woman in a red satin dress seconded.

Edward opened his vest and leaned back, revealing his gun and sighed "You can kill me, but six of you are coming wit' me." They looked so small to him, like fire ants ready to skeletonize a tiger.

Ives raised his hands. "Ladies, Gentleman. Calm yourself. Allow us to discuss this as civilized human beings. I'm looking for Jack."

A whip cracked like a gunshot.

The women parted, forming a path for Jack: A tall, thin woman in a man's tight tuxedo. The bill of her top hat shadowed her face, Curly-q sideburns kissed her creamy cheeks. She exchanged her eight-foot bullwhip for a rider's crop. She raised her face to her guests, letting her monocle drop. She tossed aside the tiny table in front of Ives and slapped the crop between Ives' legs, nipping the lip of his chair. Ives remained unflinching. Her riding boot slid under his groin. She lifted Ives' chin with the crop. "Look what the pussy dragged in."

"Hello, Jack." Ives said dryly, "How's Maybel?"

She pulled her toe out of Ives' crotch with a shrug and a smirk. "They're all right, girls. They don't want any of *this*." She said, grabbing her crotch. Edward watched as the tense crowd dissolved, as did the switch blades; the women hid their knives in every garter and frill of lace imaginable. 'Jack' pulled a cigarette from the silver case and struck a match off her teeth. "You didn't come here for the poetry. (puff, puff) Maybel said I could expect guests who could aid our, ahem, dilemma, though you don't look much like a German Jew doctor." With her toe, she spun a chair around, sitting on it backwards in one smooth movement. She sized Ives up. Ives smiled. Shelley tensed.

"Well my dear I just *love* your security!" Ives said. 'Jack' smirked, exhaling a thick cloud of cigarette smoke on him. Ives continued, nonplussed, "I come here on behalf of Dr. Hirshfeld. He is indisposed, as I am sure Miss Batten is as well. His people and her people should come together. You and I, if I may be boastful, are those people. My name is George Cecil Ives, and this is my business associate, Edward Shelley."

"Charmed. My name is Marguerite Radclyffe Hall. This is my personal army, The Bulldaggers. We look out for our own." She turned to a barmaid and snapped her fingers.

Edward Shelley crossed his arms in contempt at Miss Manpants and her rag-taggers. There's nothing worse for a bodyguard to know his own ineffectiveness. "Double D Dee, bring it over here." R. Hall said. The Rubinesque Double D Dee woman sneered, stomping off to the back room. R. Hall quipped, "It appears you boys may have a situation on your hands you might not be prepared for."

"Forgive me, Miss Hall, but I seem to be ill informed of your little organization." Ives said.

Ms. Hall threw her head back and laughed. "*Little* organization? Ha! You see, the girls here and myself are part of a larger organization, The Sisters of the Isle. We've been around since the dawn of western civilization. But since our subjugation by our male oppressors, we've become even more secretive than your, ahem, pervert parade. The Sisters fall into arranged marriages, into prostitution, lack basic civil rights. Even slaves have--"

"All right, all right. I understand." Ives said, his icy smile never fading, "How may we assist you ladies?"

A long exhale puffed out R. Hall's words. "I'm offering a peace treaty between The Sisters and The Gentlemen. You see, being under the heel of many a man, we specialize in information. Behind every great man is a great woman, and under each great woman, you'll find a Sister. We cover yours, you cover ours."

A the curious seventeen-year-old girl handed Hall a not-so-dainty pour of whiskey. The young girl met Ives's intrigued stare and intentionally broke it.

"An excellent idea. I will even encourage the more witty of my compatriots to befriend friendly women-- Sisters or not—to share information." Ives said. "If we find two Gentlemen sharing the same sister...Oh, I forget..." Ives said, "Edward, what was Gaelic term Oscar tossed about?" At the mention of Oscar Wilde, the seventeen year old launched interest.

"Fa ghag," Edward said, "It's Gaelic for drainage ditch. He also used to say it's the sound one makes when choking on a guy's--"

"--Exactly. We'll look after so-called faghags." Ives said, proudly.

144

From her tuxedo, Ms. Hall pulled out a small purple book. "Does this look familiar?"

"My word!" exclaimed Ives, "Where did you find such a relic? That is one of the address books of the Gentlemen of the Shade."

"Yes, Mister Ives… You are here on page 2, though your age is inaccurately telling. An agent in Paris, the smart writer of Claudine books, found this in her husband's sock drawer. He's on page 62. Countess Margot Asquith, the wife of England's Prime Minister has a far more detailed little lavender book, which includes high profile members of The Sisters. That is something we cannot allow. Unfortunately, that Industrialist dolt, Noel Pemberton Billing, acquired one of these very address books. He calls it the 'Mbret of Albania' or somesuch nonsense. My word, he thinks Lesbia is a *place*…" R. Hall threw her hand to her chest and released a peel of laughter Ives himself partook in.
"I don't think Catullus would mind," Ives said. Ives and Hall laughed. Edward felt left out.

"Do you think you can get one of your merry men to retrieve this document from Billing?" Ms. Hall said, putting her own address book back in her inner pocket.

"I know just the man." Ives said as Double D Dee returned with a photo and placed it in R. Hall's hand. "Now, what is this problem of ours you speak of?"

Ms. Hall said, "Apparently Oscar Wilde faked his own death and is living in New Orleans." The photo Frances Johnston took of Alfie Wood and the LaFittes landed in Ives's hand.

"That's not Oscar. Trust me, he's dead. I was there." Ives said, handing the photo over to Shelley. As Ives handed over the photo, the eyes of the seventeen-year-old girl never left him.

Shelley said, "Yeah, that's Alfie Wood. I remember him. He used to be in Brand's stable at Cleveland Street. Sodding wanker, he is. Spilled about saving up and starting over. I guess this is what he talked of."

Ives sighed, "Can nothing good come of that boy? Mister Shelley, do be a dear and see to this?"

"Oh, I've wanted to kill that pisser since he had hair." Shelley said with a smile.

Ives stood, smiled and replied, "Thank you, Miss Hall. This has been a most fortunate encounter. I will take care of the Lavender Dossier. I thank you for your assistance. Is there anything I could do, as a token of my gratitude?"

Ms. Hall smiled. "One of our agents in America, Jane Adams, opened up a battered women's shelter. I have a lot of books, so many in fact I usually keep two copies of my first editions. Miss Adams has an excellent library. Pay her a visit on my behalf. And...If you have an equally large library, I recommend you place your most valuable first editions there. A generous donation will ensure your copies will maintain... integrity."

While Ives and Hall shook hand, Ives leaned in to her ear. "I am not a man to ask a woman of her business, for surely I have little need or reason. However, I must ask about the curious seventeen-year-old girl in your midst. She seems... familiar to me."

R. Hall pulled back, confused. "I know everyone here, and yet you speak of one I am unfamiliar with."

"Her..." Ives nodded, only to find his gaze land on an empty bar stool. "Never mind, then. I must be catching the red tide."

R. Hall furrowed a devilish brow, "Careful, Georgie..." R. Hall burst into laughter and pushed George out the door, into the alley. George Ives stared at his mud-soaked hands as he pulled them from the puddle. On his knees, he found himself kneeling before the seventeen-year- old-girl with shock-red hair. Shelley was still inside.

She looked at him.

Ives looked up to her, speechless.

"Did you kill my uncle?" The seventeen-year-old girl said.

"Who is your uncle, my dear?" Ives said with his charming smile. The smile failed to charm. Still smiling, Ives panicked for the first time.

"You killed my uncle. You never helped. He went to jail for your cause and you fashioned him to the laundry line. Mark my words, George Cecil Ives, when I control The Sisters, I shall set your intestines as my garters. Under me, every Sister shall damn every Gentleman, and your traitorous nature shall be dragged from the shadows into the light, where your damned soul will burn in the light of god. Remember me, for I am Dorothy Wilde, and I will not rest until you, personally, pay for the betrayal and abandonment of one of our own."

"Wait! Dorothy! It's not that simple!" George pleaded as he wiped the sludge from his eyes. A door slammed behind him.

"Everything on the up-an-up?" Shelley asked.

George cleared his eyes, and with it, Dorothy Wilde. Blessed with his bodyguard's presence, the tide of security and confidence returned.

"Shelley, I've never been so bloody terrified in my life." Ives took a deep breath, as if nothing happened, and continued, "Edward? I shall wire the Captain and Tennille." He clapped his bodyguard's shoulder, "You're going to the states."

As the two walked from the narrow alley, George Cecil Ives looked over his shoulder for the first time.

Chapter 13:
The Mouth at Big Muddy

In High School I was a punching bag
When I got out, I was a punching fag
You fuck with me, I'll fuck with you back
Ain't gonna fall between the cracks.

Asskickatron
Fagatron

New Orleans, 1906. Alfie saw the same August moon as last year from the balcony of La Rue de la Splendour. Rene LaFitte slept in bed, but Alfie's newfound insomnia kept him from enjoying his companion. Whoever he was as Oscar Wilde dare not admit or enjoy success.

He faked his way through directing his first play as most do. *The Importance of Being Earnest* was as good as it would get and the writing of *The Fortunate Accordion* neared completion. Lying to actors was good practice for the outside world. To actors, he was nobody, a poser named Alfie Wood. To the producers, he was Oscar Wilde with a wink and a nudge. He thought it would be hard to direct, but at least the actors had scripts where Alfie lived improvisationally. Since his inception as a social fixture, the distant friends of the LaFittes already dropped $100,000 into the Baldwin Wood Levee Fund, an unimaginable amount to Alfie. Angelique kept her darling Alfie in her pocket, much to the impostor's dismay.

Julien tolerated Alfie's existence. Once after too many brandys, Julien said to Alfie, "My boy, I know you and my brother a *ka-weeah* for each othah, and I much rathah have him tied to you than stinkin' up his clothes with all them nigrahs."

149

When he wanted to start over with Oscar Wilde's identity, he achieved what he wanted, but not how he wanted. He was growing up. Alfie flicked his cigarette into the cobbled streets below from the balcony and stepped back into his room.

"Where were you?" Rene said groggily. Bourbon, jambalaya, and humidity seeped from Rene's skin into the ambrosia of pungent seduction.

"Out for a smoke."

"Are you okay?" Rene mumbled from bed, "You seem distant."

"It's the play. Your relatives aren't doing very well at keeping my identity a secret. I worry someone will recognize me."

"What, that little pissant Douglas?" Rene said.

Alfie laughed, remembering Lord Douglas and his small penis and wispy blonde pubic hair, "No, Rene. A man of my stature created enemies far more terrifying than a spoiled little rich boy."

"What do you mean?" Rene said, "I don't want my baby boy to be in danger."

"Worry yourself not." The secret burned Alfie's tongue. Love and truth are horrible companions. Those who love truth are always suicidal widows. With all relationships, Alfie compromised. "This is between us. You cannot tell anyone. Do I make myself clear?"

"You're scaring me," Rene said.

"I cannot put you in danger." Alfie said. "Before I say anything, I must know if you love me to the end."

"Well, you shouldn't get worked up the night before your big day. We'll talk about it later." Rene said. Alfie curled up away from Rene, who failed him.

The next day, Alfie bounded from bed. *Opening night,* he thought. Last night's spat would have to wait.

"Let's get a big breakfast." Alfie said. "It's a most exciting day."

"Of course, Oscar." Rene said with a smile.

As they passed through the lobby, Anne Dewey, forever on duty, read the paper as the morning sunlight scorched floating dust, incensing the room with the smell of old books. L'il Orville Wright slept on the sofa, little pillbox hat askew on his forehead.

Rene and Alfie sing-songed, "Hi, Miss Dewey!"

"Hush up, now, don't wake the boy," Miss Dewey said. "Good luck on your show tonight. I'd go, but I have... engagements. But I got you something." She dug out something from a cigar box. "Here. It's for good luck." Miss Dewey handed over a fresh boutonnière, a green carnation. "They were real hard to find round here, but you been such a good guest and a good man ta everyone, I did me some book reading and found yous wore these all the time."

Alfie looked to the green carnation, as if it were a blessed omen. "Why, thank you. Thank you very much, Miss Dewey. This means a lot to me."

"Now you boys go on and git! Mighty big day for ya!" Miss Dewey said.

Rene and Alfie sat upstairs at the Old Absinthe House, away from the teeming crowds below. The sun at just the right angle made Alfie appreciate the beauty of Rene's loyalty. For the first time in Alfie Wood's new life, he let his guard down—just for one breakfast. It was an amazing spread of sausages, eggs, bacon and pancakes. For those 45 minutes, life was perfect. Hard silence, built with tearful courage brick by brick, was now a monument to satisfaction. Staring at the empty plate, Alfie put back on his game face.

On route to the theater, Alfie read the local paper in the carriage. A reviewer saw the preview claimed the production was so true to form that "It seemed as though Oscar Wilde himself was on hand for the production." The irony of being a fake playwright directing *Importance* was not beyond him. He could almost hear dead Oscar's deep chuckles echo through the flyspace, goading the imposter to take it even further.

As the audience milled about before curtain, Angelique approached Alfie in a blushed frenzy, "Mister Wood! You would not believe who is coming to opening night!"

"Who?" Alfie said, his stomach turning.

"Did you read the review? It's your old friend Loudon Clear, the theater critic--"

"Are you mad, woman?" Alfie hissed, "Have I told you nothing about the importance of my new identity?" Alfie looked at Angelique, her face mortally wounded. She fanned herself rapidly.

"Well, Mister Wilde, for all I have done for you, one must not make a scene, especially at a theater... Good day." Angelique huffed. Alfie regretted his outburst. This would be one more thing to smooth out as a lapdog of the wealthy.

From across the room, Loudon saw Alfie's outburst. Angelique walked over to Loudon Clear. "I'm sorry, Mister Loudon. He seems to have a touch of the pre-show jitters."

"Who?" Loudon replied.

"Why, Mister Wilde, of course." Angelique said.

Loudon Clear answered, "Is that so?"

The house was packed. Julien assured Alfie would go unnoticed, but this was of no consolation. Rene walked up to Alfie, "Hello, my dear boy, Oscar. How do you feel?"

"Terrified," Alfie said out of character, honestly, "for all the wrong reasons."

"Imagine how the actors feel," Rene said, sapphire eyes twinkling. "Fret not, darling. You've worked quite hard at this."

Alfie chuckled and shook his head, "You have no idea."

"Sit back and enjoy the show. Think of it this way, you won't have to entertain anyone for two hours. Quite a break, if I must say." Rene said. He was right. Alfie wore himself out, keeping track of truths.

The audience took their seats. Rene leaned a knee to his lover's, relaxing the playwright into the moment. It was a good performance, after all. Alfie gave himself some credit for once, even if he still didn't get all the jokes he apparently wrote. Rene smiled out of the corner of his mouth and whispered in Alfed's ear, "I'm so proud of you." The house of cards grew taller and more fragile.

Alfie and Rene snuck out before curtain call. Alfie noticed a burned out streetlight. The sudden dark spot blighted the breezy spring night. No matter how much Alfie wanted Rene, Alfie couldn't take his eyes off that darkly wounded street.

"Let's get out of here. I have a bad feeling about all this." Alfie said.

Rene looked quizzically, "Why? This is your night!"

"Rene, "Alfie said, "Look, I left England in a bit of a rush. There's an ex-boyfriend…"

"The one you went to prison for?" Rene said, doe-eyed.

"Yes, that one. If he discovered I'm alive, he would hunt me down. He had many friends of power and influence. This whole situation is grossly out of hand."

Rene said tersely, "You must let this go! You are with one of the most powerful houses in New Orleans. No one will touch you, Oscar. I tire of your melodramas." Alfie feared the LaFittes almost as much as The Gentlemen. He's seen swamp justice first-hand often.

"Let's go back to Julien and Angelique's for the after party." Alfie said, "I've got a bad feeling about staying here. I'd feel safer with Julien's guards about."

Alfie stared into the shadows, feeling as though the shadows stared back. They did.

***

On the moonlit banks of the Mississippi, a small raft from the Mary Roger rocked through kicking waves. Tennille ferried Edward Shelley quietly to a creaky dock.

"What the deuce is this place?" Shelley said.

"This is Port LaFitte," First mate Tennille said, "It's a smuggling hub that's been around for a hundred years or so. Everybody knows about it."

"Then why isn't it shut down?" Shelley asked.

"Everyone knows about it." Tennille said. "When you get to the French Quarter, you'll understand."

"There's a French Quarter?" Shelley said. "*Great.*"

"Don't worry. You'll be provided with an escort. We know a fellow, tough I'd use that term loosely." Tennille said.

The port was slightly more than a gnarled dock and a hole punched in a tree line. A glint of a harness in the main road's black portal caught his quick eye. Shelley pulled his gun.

"Don't shoot!" a baritone called out. Blue moonlight showed ten rings and open palms of an ebony drag queen.

"You nearly shot your guide, Edward. Don't tell her anymore than you have to. She won't ask."

"Thank you for bringing me this far." Edward said.

Tennille pawed the air. "Stop flirting, you cad. I must return to the mother ship. Oh, and watch out for gators."

"A gator?"

"It's a mighty big lizard that'll cut you in two," A strong black woman said, holding the reins of two horses, built like a wrathful Nubian goddess in her telling wig.

"Are you my contact? My name is Edward Shell--"

"You can call me Anne Dewey. I don't want to know more than I need. Go on now, Mister Edward." Miss Dewey said, "Let's get you set up." They rode back mute.

Miss Dewey stopped at her boarding house, La Rue de la Splendour. "So what's the word on the street these days?" Edward said. L'il Orville waited behind the desk, sensing unease.

Miss Dewey said to L'il Orville, "Now baby, I need you to tell my suitor that I will not be able to make dinner arrangements." She handed him a slip of paper.

The urgency in the boy's face tipped his hand. L'il Orville bolted from the Inn and Miss Dewey returned her attention to her new guest. "There's a big play put on tonight. A lotta rich white folk are going. Sold out for weeks."

"I can't imagine why." Edward said with a smirk. "Tell me, where's a good night spot? I've been on a boat for three weeks. I need to unwind."

"The Old Absinthe House. It's only a few blocks from here. Miss Dewey said. "You want me to take your bags up to your room?"

"That won't be necessary," Edward said. "Let me sign in first."

Carefully, Auntie opened the ledger, turning it to Shelley. He flipped back a dozen months, seeing Oscar Wilde's name in various handwritings. Without signing it, Shelley closed the book. "I'll sign when I return."

Walking towards the door, Shelley felt two vices clamp round his neck, lifting him off the ground, helplessly smashing his face through the lobby window. His nose snapped. He felt his feet leave the ground.

He pushed against the wall, but she slammed him to the floor with bestial brutality as she sat on his chest, choking him. Gravity seeped into his body with immobilizing velocity. Her linebacker thighs blocked his pistol. His good eye spotted one of her size sixteen heels discarded in the charge. His eyes bulged.

Shouldn't have gotten those heels, baby, Edward thought, hammering the shoe into her eye. Auntie shrieked back as air rushed into Edward's lungs. Feeling reached his fingertips, now on the trigger. He spun to the wall. Miss Dewey bellowed at a terrifying volume.

"You stupid bitch! Why did you have to do that?" Edward said, vision still grainy and unreal. "You could have just kept your mouth shut and let me do my job!"

"I had to! I had to protect Oscar!" Anne Dewey sobbed, holding her eye.

"Oscar's been dead for years. Alfie Wood is a con artist."

"What?" Miss Dewey said. It all made sense to her now. Edward shot her between the falsies, freezing the betrayal on her face. In the new quiet, Shelley sat on the couch exhausted, staring at disaster. A drop of blood from his face dripped onto his pants, knocking him from his trance. A wave of regret loomed like a hurricane on the horizon. In the mirror behind the desk, Edward Shelley knew he would never look the same; the cheap glass sliced away the pretty. The broken window, the gunshots, and the dead trannie on the floor all cleaved away precious minutes; a hacked up face like this in a strange town with no connections tallied up a death trap. *Shut up and think*, Edward thought, hearing his pocket watch tick tick tick tick tick.

Focused, Shelley knocked the little pane of bloodied glass in. Shelley pulled the drapes, flipped the closed sign, and locked the front door. Now with more time to panic, Edward ran upstairs to the rooms. No one staying in a boarding house would be in on a Friday night. Then he saw Alfie's door.

"What an imbecile." Shelley muttered at the ratty peacock feather tucked under the room number, C33, which was Wilde's prison number. Shelley picked the cheap lock and let himself in. It was a ridiculous, pseudo-dressing room filled with dead sunflowers, tattered peacock feathers, and random bargain-bin books.

A typewriter revealed the last page of a manuscript called *The Fortunate Accordionist: The Lost Play of Oscar Wilde*. Edward Shelley stuck the manuscript under his shirt as a trophy for killing someone so asinine.

Relieved, he found bourbon, but the sour mash burned his choked throat, depositing gravel forever.

He gulped through the pain, drinking to the sobering conclusion of murder.

A mule kick later, he prepared his escape. Alfie playing Oscar required cosmetics. Rifling through the dresser, Shelley found concealer to mute his horrific beating, though his hands shook applying the make-up. No one could put it on for him. No one could kill Alfie Wood. They sent the wrong man for the wrong job, but that can't be stopped now. Edward pulled himself up, alone.

Shelley dragged the innkeepers massive body behind the desk and emptied the register to look like a robbery. The back office doubled as Miss Dewey's room, full of decapitated wig heads and feather boas. Alfie's room was above Miss Dewey's. Shelley bored a hole in the ceiling and ran the fuse through. Upstairs, Edward ripped off his clothes, slipping into Alfie's ridiculous southern fashions. After throwing the treacherous clothes away, Edward was ready; an altogether new man with a new face and a new name, just like the man he would kill.

In Oscar Wilde's room, Edward Shelley leaned back in the rocking chair, terrified. With gun drawn and a fuse at his feet, he waited.

Chapter 14:
Incident at La Rue de la Splendour

> *One cannot serve this Eros without becoming*
> *a stranger in society as it is today; one cannot*
> *commit oneself to this form of love without*
> *incurring a mortal wound.*
> --Klaus Mann

Guests had yet to arrive at LaFitte Manor.

"Opening night is over, Oscar," Rene said at his brother's lavish plantation home, "Calm your pretty little head. You are amongst friends."

"I don't know. I feel like I'm living a lie, faking my death. After all that I've been through, you're the most important thing to me. To lose you would be devastating to me."

Rene said, "You know how dreadfully dull I find your suspicions? Why do you insist on these matters? My brother owns a personal militia. Should any harm befall you, the measure of his wrath would strike down your adversaries--"

"This is not some dinner club--" Alfie growled, taking out the A. Baldwin Wood Levee fund bankbook, "Here," His hands shook. "If anything... If anything occurs too dreadful to mention, I want you to have this."

Rene whined, "Why must you be so bothersome with your antics? I cannot stand this on-and-on about these shadowy Gentlemen! You simply cannot follow along with the rest of us, can you? You always have to allude to our lives being in danger! Waltz through life with me, and I will hear no more of your imaginary problems! When guests arrive, I do expect you to put on your best smile and sincerely enjoy your evening."

Rene collected himself, "How can we prove the legitimacy of our love if you consistently make things difficult? We must always be the ideal couple. Strike envy in the hearts of those who find us sinful. We cannot maintain if you keep carrying on! Now drink your bourbon and put on a happy face. Our guests will be here any moment." Rene said, straightening Alfie's bowtie. "I do believe I hear the carriages."

Alfie shoved the bankbook to Rene's chest. "Take it." Rene reluctantly took it to his inner pocket of his baby blue suit jacket. At the foyer bar, Alfie slammed the sweet whiskey blaze. Listening to the guests file in, Alfie-as-Oscar-as-Alfie put on a fake smile and obeyed the love of his life, once again. When there was no one to depend on, he obeyed what he knew.

LaFitte's bodyguards arrived first; two dozen ugly, toothless, hell-bent, nigger-killin, tobacco-spittin', hard-hittin' rustlin'-up-a-mean-bunch-of-trouble bastards. Tied to upper management, the bodyguards never gave Alfie trouble, but no respect either. Seeing these good ol' boys lined up to protect this house calmed the imposter Oscar. Any European Gentlemen would meet quite an opposition with these savages protecting the plantation. It suddenly dawned on Alfie that the only one who took his paranoia seriously was Julien LaFitte. After all, Julien's ancestors were pirates.

Angelique entered as Julien stayed on the front porch. Alfie and Rene moved through the house, sampling the appetizers the negro maids placed about. Angelique and her entourage found Alfie and Rene with fan a-flapping. "Oh my! It was such a marvelous outcome, Oscar! Surely, you should have stayed to receive such precious accolades. Loudon Clear wanted to shake your hand, personally."

"Oh, but my newfound sense of modesty would have permitted me so," Alfie said as he scooped sour cream with broccoli with his rough peasant hands. Angelique twittered on as her personal retinue filed in, each one more banal as the last. Rene was all "dah-ling' this and 'dah-ling' that and Alfie questioned his entire existence: Why fake your way into a place you don't belong, or feel comfortable in? He just wanted the dull party, thrown in someone else's name, to be finished.

The loud pop of a pistol echoed through the humid night, sending guests scurrying to the front porch. Alfie's stomach dropped, fighting the urge to run—after all, there was no reason for Oscar to be under attack. A curiosity calmed the audience as Julien LaFitte walked back from the drive with what looked like a sack of potatoes. He dumped the body of a small black boy on the porch. Shot through the head, the gore was unavoidable. The gasping ladies retreated to chaise lounges, leaving the mess to the men.

"What happened?" Alfie said.

"The nigra came a-running up to the house, prolly gonna rape onna the women," the security head, Leroy, said. Alfie opened his mouth to object, but Rene tossed a stern glance. Leaves whispered in mourning. Leroy continued, "Happens all the time. Reginald, Bocephus—dump him in the swamp. Jerry, you get them colored maids to clean this blood off the porch." Alfie shuddered, nauseous: it was L'il Orville Wright with a slip of paper in his waistband.

"Here, let me help." Alfie said, awkwardly picking the mangled body up. Wet, warm, light and tiny.

"Now Mistah Wilde, you don't go messin' your hands with this," Leroy said, pulling Alfie away. Being a good pickpocket in London, Alfie pilfered the paper. Rene noticed.

"If you prefer, I'll console the ladies." Alfie said.

"This kinda thing happens all the time. They nigras just don't raise their kids right," Julien said.

Alfie turned and walked into the foyer, where he pulled the bloody note from his pocket.

Oscar—old friends are coming for dinner.

The emergency code dropped Alfie's stomach into his toes. Alfie's hands violently shook, covered in L'il Orville's blood.

"Oscar, what's wrong?" Rene said, taking Alfie's shoulder. Alfie spun around, sticking the letter in his pocket. "Nothing, Rene. Just a little shaken is all."

"Oh, you shouldn't think of them as people, Oscar," Rene replied. "Nigras are no more than scuffed furniture."

"Of course," Alfie said, "I don't feel well. Perhaps too many spirits. I should leave."

"Please don't," Rene said, "They'll think you--" Angelique said, gliding up to assess the situation, "Yes, it has been quite an exciting evening for us all," She batted her fan contemptuously.

"Rene, please see me to my carriage," Alfie said, "to protect me from other nigras who might be out there." This won Rene over, who walked him to his carriage. Sickened, Alfie was ready to quit.

Rene stopped Alfie. "Why are you acting so strange? It was just a little nigra boy."

Alfie broke. "I've never been Oscar Wilde. I've always been Alfred Wood, a London street tough looking for a way out. I found that way out and when I did, I found you. They will try to kill me. Do not follow. I will explain everything when I see you tomorrow." The whip cracked and the carriage rode onward.

"Wait! I don't understand!" Rene wailed to the carriage fading into darkness. Rene LaFitte felt his breaking heart and the bankbook covering it.

Angelique strutted up behind Rene, "Come along, Mister Rene. It's best we associate with our kind, back at the house, where there is a wonderful party. Many people are asking about you. Do come back inside. We no longer need to associate with the improper."

"I suppose you are correct, Miss Angelique," Rene said and, without hesitation, joined the gala event. At the end of the night, Rene Lafitte was plagued with a new emotion—genuine concern—which forced him to saddle a horse and ride into town.

***

Alfie Wood stepped from his carriage at the Rue de la Splendour. He swallowed hard. At the closed sign in the window (Anne Dewey never closed), Alfie wrapped his hand in his coat and punched out the door's windowpane. He reached in, unlocked the door, and entered.

A smear of blood ran from the foot of the chaise lounge to behind the desk. Alfie followed it. "Oh, Miss Dewey..." Alfie said, seeing the confused expression on the dead. She knew. He walked carefully upstairs, seeing his door opened. He heard his rocking chair creak. He pushed the door open. Shelley sat in the dark, cherry of a cigarette dancing in the black.

"Alfie Wood. They didn't think it would be you." Edward Shelley said, "Your testimony sent Oscar Wilde to prison. And (heh) here you are! Pretending to be the man you damned. Are you paying homage?"

Once, they met as mere children. Now they met as full-grown adversaries.

"Shelley, is it? Yes, I think I recall you being at my trial," Alfie said.

"You can't fool me, Wood." Edward said, smoking a cigarette. "You know why I'm here."

"I can't do anyone any harm, here. Leave me be." Alfie said, feeling his cockney accent completing a welcoming return. "Just go home, Shelley."

"You know I can't do that." Shelley said. "You've bitten off more than you can chew. Make sure you swallow." Shelley said, letting his cigarette fall to the fuse. "Oh, and you never shoulda teased me on Cleveland Street."

The fuse burned through the hole in the floor as Alfie lunged at Edward, slamming both through the French doors to the balcony. Alfie beat Edward against the railing, trying to throw the assassin over the edge. Fire belched from the ground floor lobby as Edward struggled to hold Alfie close. Flames buckled the second story floorboards and vomited flame over them both. Edward ducked behind Alfie as the blast raked over Alfred Wood. With unknown grace, Edward fell to the side as the blast threw the half-dead Alfie over the rail to the cobblestones below with an unsettling thunk. The barbecued cinder twitched for a moment and fell limp.

Alfie remembered that morning's breakfast, dying happy.

Edward stumbled over to the neighbor's balcony with a simple explanation about the next door boarding house catching on fire. They took him to a white hospital for his wounds. In his delirium, Edward told them his real name. The police came by, but to them it was nothing more than arson, most likely of a 'Cuckoo Klan" nature no one wanted to pursue very deeply.

While in the hospital, he received a telegram.

Thank you STOP the Hull of Houses
requests your presence STOP.

Edward Shelley bought a one-way ticket to Chicago. Passing the time, he read Alfred Wood's fake play.

***

As Rene approached the French Quarter, the unsettling scent of smoke hung thick as mist through the street. He turned the corner to see firemen pumping water into the gutted building once called La Rue de la Splendour. Rene dismounted and stumbled to the blackened, exposed body of his lover and shrieked a torturous refrain of loss, releasing a rage few know. The police tried to console him with phrases like "tried to jump from the blaze" and "nothing could be done." In the orange flame reflecting Rene's tears of mourning, the scorned lover took a blood oath to strike down the Gentlemen of the Shade and anyone in his path.

Chapter 15:
In the Shade of Gentlemen

Just when I thought I was out, they pull me back in.
--Michael Corleone, *Godfather Part III*

A man of Rene Lafitte's status considered the repercussions of overextending his reach. At the advice of his sister-in-law, Angelique said, "Well, it doesn't matter who he was or what caused that fire. That chapter in our lives is over, and it's best to just continue on." The warning remained perfectly clear. He belonged, of course, to respectable society.

For the next year, Rene dated around the bayou, with a nagging boredom. Some nagging sensation forced the men in his life away, unaware of the cause: Rene never got over Oscar. Sensing a certain withdrawn melancholy, Angelique suggested they go on vacation to Washington D.C., where Frannie Johnston, the White House photographer, invited them to a fundraiser hosted by President Theodore Roosevelt. Rene accepted with indifference.

In Washington, D.C., Angelique, Julien, and Rene walked into the lavish dining hall with their invitations, placing them at table 80, which sat eight people.

"Frannie! My word, what a marvelous display here." Far up at an enormous table sat none other than President Theodore Roosevelt, Vice President Charles Fairbanks, and Presidential hopeful Howard Taft. Rene felt nothing.

"So good of you to come all this way to support Taft," Frannie Johnston said. "I'd like to introduce you to our fellow guests. This is my good friend from England, Olive Custance Douglas and her husband, Lord Alfred Douglas." Olive was an attractive woman with wavy brunette hair barely contained in a bun. Her husband merely looked around the room with contempt, smiling spitefully at the LaFittes. "I deeply apologize, sir, but I have not previously met your acquaintance." Johnston opened.

A young, funny-looking man with a poor haircut entertained a woman twice his age. With a nasally twang, he replied, "Pleased to meet you, Miss Johnston. Please call me John Hoover. This is my mother, Annie." John beamed with pride. Mrs. Hoover nodded, out of place at her son's little soiree.

Angelique nodded to the matron, hiding insult among an old hag and a nobody. Julien kissed Mrs. Hoover's hand, tickling the older woman with flattery. An intrigued Rene sat between Lord Alfred Douglas and Frannie Johnston. Julien continued on about weather and politics to a disinterested John Hoover. The main course of Cornish game hen arrived. Frannie turned in hushed tones to Rene, and asked, "I know this is not polite dinner conversation, but I was just curious to know if there was a suitable outcome to such an unspeakable tragedy as yours."

"Thank you for your concern, Miss Frannie. Unfortunately, Oscar's killer was never found." Rene said. Lord Douglas's silverware clattered. "But I try to move on."

"What exactly do you mean, 'Oscar's killer'?" Alfred said.

Angelique cut the smallest bite possible and responded, "I hardly think murder is an appropriate dinner conversation. *Dreadful.*"

"No, no Miss Angelique. It's quite all right. Best to clear the air, now that the situation is finally over." Rene said. "Oscar Wilde faked his death and moved to

America. Then his hotel blew up. He perished in the fire."

"That's a most unusual situation. He died eight years prior." Alfred Douglas said.

"Perhaps that is what you heard in Europe," Rene said. "Sorry, Mister Alfred. But, where are you from exactly?"

"You will address me as Lord Douglas," Lord Douglas said with thinly veiled rage.

Olive breezed over it, "Me and my husband eloped and have not returned to Europe since. Isn't that romantic?"

"Quite." Julien said, shoveling in another bite.

"Are you suggesting that some kind of malicious organization killed the exiled playwright?" Lord Douglas asked innocently. Frannie choked a bit.

Rene shrugged and said, "He kept mentioning an ex-boyfriend named Bossy." Lord Douglas threw his head back in a howl of laughter. President Roosevelt looked up disconcerted from his dinner. "What is so funny?" Rene asked quietly.

"I know this Bossy, and Oscar dragged that poor child through the mud. Oscar was a most terrible person, a corrupter of youth and a slanderer of good names."

"Alfred, please…" Olive said, patting her lips with her napkin as if to silence her husband instead.

"I did not have the opportunity for such an impression at all." Rene said, thinking of all Oscar did for him.

Lord Douglas collected himself, demanding an upper hand. "A man as insidious as Mister Wilde would surely involve himself with something as unwholesome as faking his own death. Such actions are not without their consequences, especially if some horrible conspiracy of Homosexual deviants becomes involved. Something should be done about them. Why, I just spoke with my good friend, Noel Pemberton-Billing, who claims there is such an organization affecting English Parliament as we speak."

"Oh? Do you have any information on such a perverse organization?" Rene said.

Lord Douglas smirked and said, "Mister Pemberton-Billing claims the organization is called The Gentlemen of the Shade, headed is by a man known as George Cecil Ives."

Olive spoke up, "Oh really? I hear he donated a significant sum of money to the Hull House, up in Chicago not long ago."

"Olive," Frannie Johnston said quickly, "That is mere conjecture."

Olive smiled, "I am sure it is. Yet who knows, Miss Johnston? Every faction works an angle."

"Whatever do you mean, Miss Olive?" Rene said.

"Oh, it's just girl talk, Mister LaFitte," Olive said. J. Edgar Hoover ate silently, filling up on conversation. President Roosevelt stood at the far end of the hall. The LaFitte's table missed every word through poor acoustics and cigar smoke. John Hoover strained his attention.

"What is he saying?" Angelique asked.

"Roosevelt's endorsing Howard Taft," Hoover said. After a roar of applause, another man stood, Attorney General Charles Joseph Bonaparte. Bonaparte looked to Hoover and motioned for Hoover to stand. Hoover complied, waving to the crowd. His mother blushed with pride.

"Terribly sorry, but what just happened?" Julien said, placing his napkin over his finished meal.

Hoover beamed and said, "President Roosevelt employed many special agents over the years and he just announced the creation of the Bureau of Intelligence, or the B.O.I. under the Justice department. I've been placed as head of human resources and staffing." The homosexuals at the table chuckled to themselves at the man from B.O.I.

Offended, Hoover defended, "I care little for your crazy talk. Degenerates lack the human capacity to organize. Less than beasts, those perverts are. As the he who receives the head of B.O.I., I will pound every degenerate into the ground with my last gasp. They shall fear my greasy fist! I only wish you hadn't mentioned such repulsive creatures in front of my dear old mum."

"Oh, I don't mind, my little fuzzy lumpkins," Mrs. Hoover said, "I just go along with the times."

As dessert came and went, silence stayed. When time came to depart, Lord Douglas hurried off. Sure enough, Rene followed. "Mister Alfred! Mister Alfred!" Rene cried through the crowd. Alfred Douglas smiled to himself.

"Oh? What is it, Mister LaFitte?" Douglas said.

"We must do something about them, the Gentlemen, by any means necessary." Rene said. "What can I do to assist?"

"From what I understand, the men we're up against are very, very wealthy. You shall need as much financing as possible. I know you come from good standing, so that shall not be worrisome. Tell me, do you have sufficient funds?"

"...Yes." Rene said, thinking of the A. Baldwin Wood Levee Fund, which remained on hiatus since the incident.

"Perfect. Clean it out and meet me in New York." Lord Douglas said.

"When?"

Lord Douglas looked at him with deep condescension. "When the time is right, young man. When the time is right."

Olive rushed up, "There you are, my love! I swear, I turn my back for one second and..."

"Oh, believe me, my darling, I'm never far from your side. Not very far at all." Lord Douglas said, squeezing her arm in the vice of his grip, "We have *much* to discuss."

From the dinner table, John Hoover watched as the Douglases walked off arm in terse arm. Hoover caught Rene's prolonged glance. Angelique chattered on about the stuffiness of the leaving crowd, preferring the open air of her stately home. Rene smiled and turned away from Hoover's yearning glance.

Unaware of what Rene's glance meant, John Edgar helped his mother out of her seat. "Mummy, would you wait for me outside? This heat is too much for a woman of your condition and I have to say a word to Attorney General Bonaparte."

"Why of course, *special agent,*" His mother replied before peeling out a fit of giggles.

John Edgar pulled the white handkerchief out from his breast pocket and dabbed his forehead. He moved against the crowd's current through the maze of chairs and tables to the President and the Attorney General. President Roosevelt was all teeth, smiling away with his cadre of men's men. John Edgar gathered his strength and said, "President Roosevelt, it is an honor to have dined with you this evening. I trust you are in good health?"

"Good as ever!" President Roosevelt said, sticking his barrel chest out, smiling wide. "Congratulations on your new appointment, Special Agent Hoover."

"Might I borrow Attorney General Bonaparte for but a moment?" Hoover said. The gaff fell like a bag of rocks, which Hoover immediately regretted.

"Of course, my good man!" President Roosevelt said, slapping John Edgar on the back so hard the small man used every ounce of strength to stay on his feet. They all laughed at Hoover's feigned strength, a slight that would not go unchecked.

The Attorney General walked with John Hoover a dozen paces, "What's this all about, Special Agent?"

John Edgar's palms dampened. "Sir, I received a lead that could be of some use to us somewhere down the line. There's a Settlement House up in Chicago, The Hull House. It might be misappropriating funds from overseas that could very well be used by Illegal Immigrants... by seemingly systemized criminals and you know charity is communism."

The Attorney General looked at John Edgar with disbelief, "You want to *audit* a settlement house because you think criminals have a sense of organization? Don't make me doubt your appointment, Hoover."

"Since the Communists took over Russia, we have to be vigilant to see we have no Bolsheviks in our country, and the Hull House may very well be a funding hotspot for Communists."

"Good eye, Special Agent. However, that is not your primary concern. You just make sure we get some agents in the BOI. I want so many boys packed in there so tight, you'll have to come in through the back door to get to your desk. After you fill those tight leather seats with men, you can do whatever the hell you want. Now if you'll excuse me, I must tend to my photographic opportunity," The Attorney General said.

"I have no problem with that, sir." Hoover said.

"Good man. Way to take one for the team," The Attorney General said, quickly returning to the President's side with Taft as Frannie Johnston fired the flash.

***

In those first years, John Hoover waited patiently for the time to strike. The simple human resources man hired, fired, and promoted handsome friends he could count on for a favor. After a few months of keeping his head down, an agent knocked on his oak door. "Say, J. Edgar, you know that lead about the Hull House? Well I'll be damned. That little old lady sure enough has been keeping two sets of books! Imagine! You want me to go and bust the old maid?"

A smile curled across J. Edgar Hoover's lips, "No, Agent. Leave it to me. Just sit on it for awhile. I'd like to see how deep this one can go." Hoover's next step was to contact Lord Douglas's friend, Noel Pemberton-Billing, a military contractor. Pemberton once bragged about the Lavender Dossier, now stolen by a mysterious Arab. Hoover never understood why someone would boast about owning a homosexual address book. Most entries were of dead men, but George Cecil Ives' name still stood proudly on the second page.

On Sunday, June 28 1914, Gavrilo Princip shot Archduke Franz Ferdinand. In a single week, every country in Europe chose sides for the Great War. John Edgar Hoover called to his male secretary, "Roderick, get me a boat to London. Send a telegram to a Mister George Cecil Ives. Tell him I come in peace."

Part IV:
Rough Trades

Tod Crouch

Chapter 16:
Frienemy of the State

Dancing on the speakers, are you peaking with tweakers?
Bigger, tanner breeders on the scene.
The night don't last forever, so get your shit together.
Open arms are never what they seem.

--*Any Which Way*
Scissor Sisters

London, 1914. Ives was a pleasant man who compromised on his own terms. Those failing to see such privilege met his wrath.

The outbreak of the Great War required concessions few adhered to, let alone comfortably. In every shadow, Dorothy "Dolly" Wilde planned the demise of George Cecil Ives. But she was the least of Ives's difficulties. Some Yank from The States, J. Edgar something-something, demanded to meet with Ives with all that American pomp they are known for. Most uncouth, even for an inelegant American. Yet J. Edgar something-something knew all too much about Gentlemanly operations and must be dealt with accordingly. Looking for an excuse to reinforce his relationship with The Sisters, Ives decided on a neutral-ish meeting place, the Cat Hole, in hopes to find Dolly Wilde again.

George Cecil Ives and Edward Shelley waited for J. Edgar Hoover in the unsuspecting ladybar. In walked the slight man with a weak jaw and a horrible impression. The Bulldaggers cocked an eyebrow high enough to support the roof as the mama's boy noticed the only other men in the venue. Ives faked a smile and waved Hoover over. George Ives held his contempt close, "Mister Hoover, I presume?" while thinking of the most humorous way to disembowel him.

"George Cecil Ives, is it?" Hoover replied extending a hand, "Hi." The mass of scar tissue and raw power known as Edward Shelley chuckled. Hoover flinched.

Ives responded with indifference. "Please, seat yourself and have a drink on me. You travelled far to meet me. I am honored you find my presence so valuable. But I must humbly ask, what makes *you* worthy of my time, Mister Hoover?" Hoover failed to notice R. Hall's Bulldaggers secure the room. Dolly wasn't there, thank God.

"I bring you information for consideration, in exchange for a favor."

"Oh? Is that so?"Ives said, grinning toothily.

"I know all about your faggot organization. To be honest, I could care less." Hoover said with a garish southern treble pitched too high for Ives's ears. "We are both men with an interest in power. I look to gain more and you, I assume, wish to keep yours."

"You are correct in your assumptions. Please, explain to me the nature of your visit in a manner-of-fact fashion. My time is valuable, as I am sure yours is as well."

Hoover crossed his arms, seeming even smaller. "America needs to be in The Great War. Could your reach could extend far enough to allow this international situation?"

"I have an army. I have a navy. I have secure finances. It, theoretically, could be done quite feasibly." Ives said through a malicious smile. "As we both know, my prices are not within the realm of money.

What, may I ask, would I benefit from our mutual arrangement?"

Hoover responded, "First, a token, as it were, of trust. Although they were unaware of my importance, Lord Alfred Douglas and a fellow named Rene Lafitte look to usurp your position."

"And why I am I to believe that there would be dissention in my ranks?" Ives said.

"Ah," Hoover sealed, "that, my friend, is the very definition of trust. Do with that as you see fit. However, I have a larger vision, for both you and myself."

"Please. Share your vision with me." Ives said.

"I currently have a negligible position in the Bureau of Investigation, which I find detestable. It is not something for which I am suited." Hoover said before taking a light sip from his warm beer. "Taft wants into The Great War, but lacks a reason to go against the Germans. If I can provide such an introduction, I will give you and your people amnesty in America when they promote me."

With a chuckle, Ives responded, "You climb the American Intelligence ladder, give us free reign over stateside fringe businesses, and we find a reason to get America into the war? Is that the deal you are bringing to the table?"

"That is what I am presenting to you and your Gentlemen of the Shade." Hoover said.

"Enticing as it is, I must ask for the alternative." Ives said.

"What?" Hoover said.

"Allow me to rephrase: What will you do if I choose not to participate?" Ives said, smiling.

Hoover threw a manila envelope on the table. "These are not originals, of course. But I have it in my authority to audit a small settlement house called the Hull House. Jane Adams, I believe, runs the commie pinko degenerate halfway house for criminals and so-called 'battered women'. They have a, uh, elaborate bookkeeping library. It is a library I would simply *hate* to find your name in."

Ives laughed. "For an American, you are quite the effective businessman."

"I hope we can do more business in the future."

"As do I, Mister Hoover. As do I." Ives said. Hoover rose and extended his hand. Ignoring it, Ives responded, "Thank you Mister Hoover. I accept your proposal. I'll have my people be in touch with you soon."

Delighted, Hoover's eager, ugly smile repulsed Ives. "I will do all I can. Because If I don't you'll... you'll have me killed! Am I right? Am I right?" Hoover chuckled alone.

Ives grinned. "Oh come now, Mister Hoover. We are Gentlemen. What we do is much, much worse."

***

It took very little time to find Lord Alfred Douglas. Adolf Brand put his boys on the manhunt and Ives received an inconspicuous letter, reading, "Sydney and Britten meet on a corner in Chelsea. There, they meet a lad walking an irritable donkey."

At the corner of Sydney and Britten streets in Chelsea, Ives found the irritable donkey, or rather a terribly painted awning of a donkey with a giant winking asshole. The name of the bar, *The Engorged Ass*, seemed entirely suitable environs for Lord Alfred

Douglas. Ives smirked, wondering if the bar were named after Douglas.

Ives held his breath as he opened the door as a cloud of flies poured out into the sunlight. Immediately, George decided that upon returning to his domicile, he would burn his clothes and scrub himself red. Homeless, unwashed derelicts rutted against the bar as the eye-patched bartender rubbed the grease further into the glassware and chuckled through black teeth. An old leper in the corner masturbated under the table in vain. In the long narrow rectum of a bar, Lord Alfred Douglas sat in the colon: a single candle lit his santorum-smeared table.

"My word, Lord Douglas, you look a fright," Ives said, "Even for this place."

Douglas lurched forward, knocking over empty pint glasses. "You know what they say, Georgie. Surround yourself with unattractive elements to appear righteously beautiful."

"I trust your newfound heterosexuality is becoming you?" Ives said, inhaling through his mouth with great distaste.

"What do *you* want?" Bosie said.

"I want you as my parabatai," Ives said. "I know your plans to wrestle control from me. As much disdain I have for you, I would rather you join us than join against us."

"I already lead what you never had the balls to continue." Lord Douglas replied, trying to pick up his greasy mug and failing sadly. "Tell me one thing: did Oscar fake his death?"

"No."

Lord Douglas continued, "That information is valuable enough to me to consider your proposition. But I have not said yes."

"Fair enough." Ives said. "Can I count on you for such a legacy?"

Douglas scoffed. "Ah, so keep your enemies closer? Hmph! Well, I second that philosophy. So tell me, what brings to you to ask me for assistance?"

"I would like you to keep an eye on our detractors when the war breaks out, like Mister Billing," Ives said, "and the Heterosexual Germans. Especially the Germans. I think your (ahem) reformation, marriage, and subsequent lifestyle decisions could provide usefulness to us still."

"Well, look who comes crawling back." Lord Douglas slurred.

Ives smiled, "This is not the first time I've been in control on my hands and knees."

Douglas grinned the same dangerous smile that made Oscar Wilde fall in love. "I'll lead the Gentlemen, one way or another. Your offer suits me, for now."

"Marvelous." Ives said, "Well, must be going. Fear of the plague, you understand."

"Good luck," Douglas said, "That would be the least likely demise for a man in your position. However, I guarantee that the reaper shall not come to you in my form."

"We shall be in contact soon," Ives said, turning and leaving. As Ives walked into the opposing sunlight, he scrubbed his hands with a kerchief, knowing there was one parasite that he could not sterilize.

***

1914. At the mouth of the Elbe River in the North Sea, a small ship, the *White Swallow,* bobbed in a beautiful day. First Mate Tennille stroked his swarthy goatee and peered through his telescope at the small yacht approaching. The cabin boy, Sweetcakes, dangled his feet over the deck, splashing his feet in the waves.

Sweetcakes looked at the landlubbers: George Ives, Adolf Brand, and Dr. Magnus Hirshfeld wore red-striped swimming suits. Brand flexed and preened before swan diving into the water, increasing his vigor with each powerful stroke. George Ives and Magnus Hirshfeld sat in deck chairs, sunning themselves. Only two gentlemen, Robbie Ross and his parabatai, Noel Coward, wore suits. Legs crossed and fingers templed, Noel Coward had a fondness for the sea breeze, while Robbie Ross clung to the guardrails nervously.

Below deck rested 900 Mauser M1871 11 mm rifles and 29,000 rounds of ammunition. Surrounded by such illustrious men of high value flattered Noel Coward. Robbie Ross, tired of his illegal dealings, felt a forced obligation to Oscar in his role as a Gentleman. Handing over the reins to an eager child was too easy.

"I still don't understand why we're donating guns to a bunch of Micks," Brand said. "Seems like a waste of arms. We'll never hear the end of it from Captain Silvermane."

Dr. Hirshfeld wiggled his toes, "Well, the life of an arms dealer is significantly safer than his previous profession as a poet. Ironic that a man with a bullet in his wrist would pick such a profession as gun running."

First Mate Tennille lowered his telescope, "My friends, your words—but like my captain's bullet—

strike too close to the bone. Please find a more suitable topic of conversation."

"Quite right. Companions, my donation is not without subterfuge. As I explained about this vacuous Hoover fellow, I find aid from the Irish an absolute necessity. America wants in the war. Having no African colonies, they have quite the difficulty," Ives said, face burned lobster red. "There is a man who I think might have a good idea—Sir Roger Casement."

Robbie Ross choked on his cigarette, "You mean 'Congo Casement'?"

"That's the one. We scratch his back with these guns, he scratches ours." Ives said.

"Why would we want to help a bunch of Yanks, let alone the Crown?" Dr. Hirshfeld said.

Noel piped in, "Well, I love a good Yank just as much as the next fellow." Adolf Brand climbed back into the boat, slicked the water out of his hair, and proceeded with calisthenics to prove his virility. Noel continued, "Marvelous specimen, Herr Brand."

Brand stopped and said, "No one asked you, *child*."

"Mister Ives, *The Asgard* approaches," Tennille said.

"Excellent. Thank you." George said.

At the helm of the oncoming yacht, a man threw towropes to the curly-haired blonde cabin boy to *The White Swallow*. A tall, slender man with a full goatee, Sir Roger Casement, looked the perfect image of the stoic warrior. Casement smoked a pipe, leaning with one leg propped upon the bough. Ives waved from the wrist. Adler Christenson was a mutual friend. Ives saw why Mr. Christenson supported the fey rugged Irish Nationalist.

Casement stepped across the planks. His curly brown hair fluttered in the strong salty wind. "Mister Ives, Thank you for coming to our aid Without your help, I doubt our uprising would be possible. I would like to introduce you to Bob and Molly Childers, co-captains of *The Asgard*." Casement said. The couple seemed unusually happy for revolutionaries, smiling with a squint against harsh sun.

Ives extended a smooth hand. "These are my associates. This is my German contact who supplied us with the goods, Adolf Brand. These are Robbie Ross and his second in command, Noel Coward." Ross seemed misplaced on the boat, his nervous disposition revealed his distaste for seagoing travel. To Casement, Noel appeared as an eager child feigning importance.
Several Irishmen climbed from lower decks of *The Asgard* and carted crate after crate from *The White Swallow* to *The Asgard*. "Say, Sir Casement, might I have a word with you? I do believe we are in need of your services." Ives said.

Casement tapped out his pipe with furrowed brow.

"Anything to help repay the incredible debt I owe you."

"We need reasonable excuse for America to enter the war, and perhaps killing a few Englishmen in the process." Ives said. Casement relit his pipe, much to the amazement of the other Gentlemen, who could barely stay on deck in strong winds.

Casement puffed and continued, "Well, without a territory being invaded, it's significantly more difficult to rally public support for entering The War. I assume you want the Germans to win?"

"Of course," Ives lied.

"It would need to be big, with heavy civilian casualties," Sir Casement said.

"What if we sunk an ocean liner and blamed it on Germany? Or England?" Noel Coward said, "Just a little friendly fire, sending those less fortunate by being wealthy to a watery grave?"

Casement laughed. "It would have to be a titanic vessel, probably the world's largest ocean liner."

"You mean, *The Lusitania*?" Coward said. Coward, Casement, and Ives cast knowing glances to one another. Ives and Noel watched Casement crunch numbers in his head. Casement knew the Irish never truly trusted him for his work under The Crown, and The Crown would never take him back ever since he miraculously faked his death. Maybe if Casement pulled this off, the Irish would finally believe him.

"It would be impossible to take the ship head on. We must sabotage it from the inside out, which is still impossible. Even if we pulled that off, how would we survive the wreckage?"

Ives looked to the deck beneath his feet. "I can provide such transportation."

"It would take a lot of financing and some of the most talented people in Europe." Casement warned.

"Excuse me, Bobby?" Ives called across the deck. Robbie Ross clutched the guardrail and inched his way over to Ives. "What was the name of that fellow…the one exiled for those Black Masses…you know the one, the gent who bought the real Mona Lisa from you? The Franco-Italian chap."

A quizzical expression soured Ross's face, "Adelsward-Fersen?"

"That's the one! Could you send him a telly when we get back? I think he would be delighted at our little escapade." Ives said.

"Very well," Ross warned, "but he's bloody loony, that one."

Ives smiled his strange, vacant smile, "Sir Casement, is there anything else you require?"

A devilish grin crossed Sir Roger Casement's weathered lips. "I shall require a team."

Chapter 17:
Casement's 11

Can you tell what's on my mind
She's with him it drives me wild
I'd like to hit him on the head until he's dead
The sight of blood is such a high
Oh, oh, oh, oh, He gives me head...

Jet Boy, Jet Girl
Elton Motello

Noel Coward looked to the shores of Capri with wonder. Mountains skirted with trees led down to ancient ruins haphazardly scattered with betraying modesty. The tight body of the delicate young man rowing Noel to the tiny isle heated the passenger's blood. The ferryman's muscles tensed and relaxed with great definition. Noel took his eyes off the sun-bleached arm hairs of the olive-skinned eighteen-year-old and focused on the mythic isle of Capri. Tiny clouds of sheep darted about timeless foothills. The sky even stood aside, allowing the pastures breathing room. Noel fantasized with ease that Homer himself was on that island, somewhere.

The boat pulled into a tiny, ancient dock. The cinnamon-skinned youth looked away from Noel's hungry eyes, too familiar with the guests and their advances. The youth responded, pointing to the top of the steps, "Lysis House." Noel found the young man's embarrassment quite darling as he dropped a pound in the youth's supple palm.

"Thank you, Nino," Ross said as Nino Cesarini tied up the small rowboat. From the dock, a weatherworn staircase trailed exhaustingly upwards. Nino bounded up the stairs and waited for Coward at the top. The lemon trees, pendulous with fruit, framed the entryway while cypresses hid most of the building from view. Over the front door rested a plaque dedicating the house to love and sadness. As Nino led Noel inside, the vaulted ceilings sprawled over impressive paintings and wide windows bathing the enormous sitting room in crisp light. At the far end, a semi-spiral staircase down led to a rear, smooth landing outside. Before Noel knew what occurred, multiple explosions popped and echoed through the compound. Noel dropped to the ground at what sounded like sixty trees snapping in less than a second. Nino was unaffected by the terrifying noise.

"My dear word!" Noel said, "Whatever could that be?" Nino gestured a pistol. "Well, I have never heard of such a firearm." Noel followed Nino down the stairs and out the back door. On the other side of the glass, Robbie Ross chatted over a cigarette at a marble table with George Ives and Roger Casement. Ives laughed hysterically at Robbie's Mona Lisa story as they both nipped from a large mountain of cocaine. Further out on the landing was a naked man with two unusual rifles in both hands. The naked man pulled the triggers and fired off a few rounds of the familiar, deafening clatter. Casement seemed pensive, smoking his pipe with a mix of suspicion and curiosity as he studied the naked, armed man.

Even into his early thirties, Jacques D'Adelsward-Fersen had the slight body of an eighteen year old. He stood completely nude on the wide, white patio. Fresh bruises lined his thin chest and wiry arms from where the two firearms kicked into his blue-blooded flesh. None of his virtues showed signs of deterioration. Everyone fell in love with Jacques, and Noel preferred

189

to be the exception, reminding himself Fersen was a nutter. Ross knew Fersen was an art collector and minor pornographer, but also an incredibly wealthy industrialist, subsequently kicked out of France for black masses with teenage boys.

Ross and Ives noticed the new arrivals and beckoned Nino and Coward to participate. Through the door, Noel heard Jacques D'Adelsward-Fersen blow another load with a full, throbbing erection, "God damn, that feels good! The guns just shudder through your whole body! God *damnit*! (Grunt!) That gets me hard enough to peel the skin off my rodger! It vibrates my like a goddamn lighting rod! The only thing that could make this better is to bugger someone up the ass while I fire off two rounds into the air and another round in some tight throbbing brown eye! Get me another magazine, Bobby! I love these automatons!"

"Automatics, Mister Fersen," Ives corrected. Ross nervously tossed another magazine to Jacques as Ives beckoned Coward to sit. Noel felt a peculiar glee doing drugs with a superior.

Ross coughed lightly with a powdered moustache. "Jacques Adelsward-Fersen, this is Noel Coward."
Glassy-eyed, Adelsward sauntered up to noel, "God! I just wanna grab those ears and rape your face!" Noel looked to his nonplussed companions.

"Mmm, yes..." Noel said with an air of displeasure, "Tell me, what sort of device have you been creating all that racket with?"

"Look at these! Such a radical design!" Adelsward said through grinding teeth. "These are Thompson Machine guns. I acquired a few prototypes and *god damn* they turn me on!" Noel couldn't help but look at the man's erection wagging in the light like a berserk dowser's wand.

"Perhaps our conversation would be best suited at dinner time. I am dreadfully parched and in need of refreshment." Noel said. Ross and Ives smirked among themselves at the embarrassment of the young protégé. Sir Roger Casement sat, drinking his tea as the adult of the group.

Adelsward laughed to himself and gave a few irreverent strokes to his half-erection. "Quite all right. You had a long day." Adelsward said, firing off a few rounds with his rifle with his left hand and a few rounds of his gun with the other. "I'm calling some boys over. Are you interested?"

"Always." Noel replied.

"Great. I'll send one to your room," Adelsward said, "We'll get to business tomorrow morning. For tonight, let's just enjoy ourselves."

To Noel's surprise, the beautiful ferryman arrived at Noel's room promptly at nine in the evening. The guest basket Noel received included a fine scotch, a tincture of cocaine, Chinese opium, and Tangerian kif.

The male prostitute held the indifference of a temporary employee, not that it mattered to Noel, now twisted seven ways to Sunday. After a truly athletic screwing, Noel passed out in a perfect stupor.

The following day, the previous night's poisons still in his veins, Noel felt oddly refreshed. Adelsward wore a kimono at the afternoon breakfast table. Ives and Ross looked as hellish as Noel felt. Sir Casement showed no such signs. Breakfast consisted of fresh eggs and thick slabs of spiced bacon with mimosas on crushed ice by the pitcher. Imported oranges and grapefruits tumbled down from the centerpiece in a sea of thick afternoon sun. George Ives balled a melon, for a change.

Adelsward dissected a grapefruit with restrained annoyance, "So, now that I have entertained you properly, I ask you to do the same. Please, entertain me."

Casement took a deep breath and continued, "We would like to sink the Lusitania."

Adelsward tittered out a laugh. "Sink the world's largest luxury freighter? Quite a boner you are pulling on me. Continue, as I am folly's largest fan."

Casement pushed forward, "The United States government wants to enter the war and requires a third party to do it. It requires a small group of top-dollar saboteurs. The Gentlemen here have employed me to spearhead the caper, as they have interest in branching out to The States. They, in turn, wish to include you at a modest percentage to wartime profiteering."

Adelsward interrupted, "And what do you get out of it, Sir Casement?"

Casement's steely eyes sliced Adelsward, "I get to kill a lot of rich Englishmen responsible for my exile." Even the mad millionaire squirmed in his seat.

Noel took the stand, "The RMS Lusitania is a 32,000 ton, four funnel vessel spanning 785 feet. She accommodates three thousand and fifty passengers. 540 first class, 460 second class, 1,200 third-class and 850 crew. The hull is made of a new type of high-tensile steel and outfitted with electricity, which can seal its watertight doors at a moment's notice should a hull breach occur. To give you an understanding of what we face, I would like to inform you that the kitchen makes ten thousand meals a day. At full steam, she runs sixty eight thousand horsepower with a top speed twenty-five knots."

Adelsward smirked, "I'm listening."

Casement added, "This would be impossible, save for Lusitania's penchant for smuggling arms to England under the guise of a passenger line. The explosives are already on board. According to the charter and everyone involved, the arms do not exist. The crates are located in the hull."

"How do you have access to such sensitive information?" Adelsward said.

Coward informed, "Quite an amusing fellow over at the Washington capitol supplied all we need. As for the ship itself, I have passed as an entertainer on the Lusitania for several months now and understand the floor plan intimately. In fact, I have done so many *dreadful* tours back and forth on that washtub, the captain calls me 'Mr. Bridger.'"

"What are we talking, finance wise?"

Noel Coward rushed in, "Fifty thousand."

Adelsward laughed. Ives pipped in, "Fifteen percent of the smuggling trade. During war years, quite a steal, if I may say. We are willing to lose a penny-farthing for the political benefits it will bring us, if you decide to invest in our business venture."

Adelsward snorted up a line of Congo Rouge and launched into a coughing fit. "So how are you going to do it?"

Noel quickly picked up, "Ah. Yes. Our team infiltrates the liner. Master Ross's forgers will provide passports, and we will purchase tickets for the fated voyage. All on the up-and-up, you understand."

Coward unrolled the blueprints of the Lusitania. "Now, these blueprints point out fourteen electrically-sealed watertight doors are only on upper levels. The magic trick is going to be detonating these three beams—one at the bow and at these two beams on both starboard and port—and get out in time without setting off the watertight doors. There will be enough explosives *already there* to do the job, thanks to the English and American contraband. When the detonation occurs, our party will have about 18 minutes to get to the deck. The ship has electricity; if we set charges to the emergency generators and puncture the starboard hull with explosives, she goes down like you gave her a quid. The flood doors stay open, allowing our party to make it to the main deck without hindrance."

"Once on deck, how are will you survive the sinking?" Adelsward said.

Noel lit a cigarette, which bobbed with his every word. "A young fellow, Louis Vuitton, fashioned for us some armoirs; buoyant, air-tight, pricey mind you, and large enough to hold an hour or two of air. We slip into the empty luggage and drift off, picked up by First Mate Tennille and the crew of the Mary Roger." Noel said, "We skip out scot-free. The States enter the war with the ambition of ending it, you get a cut in the contraband. The Gentlemen have acess to move the operation to the colonies, and we all dash away splendidly."

Casement stood from the enormous table, "If I may say, Mister Adelsward, I am responsible for every player accounted for. I will find a way to shave off that five minutes if it guarantees England's ultimate disgrace. You ask this soldier to do a duty during wartime, this soldier will not falter. If there is but one casualty on my watch, I will not collect my fee. Fund this venture and your influence overseas will be infinite."

Adelsward smiled. "I will talk it over with my accountants, but I want you to consider this project green lit and go." A wave of relief swept over the Gentlemen. "But tell me, do you have your group collected?"

Sir Casement smiled, "I would not come empty handed."

***

Within a few weeks of his original meeting with Ives on the boat, Roger Casement entered a tight little Parisian bar called Trou de Poisson. Liane de Pougy was rumored to sing there Wednesday nights. He pressed the wood door open into the smoky bar. Liane was a member of the Sisters of the Isle, under the Natalie Barney house known as The Women's Academy. The room reeked of stale beer and tobacco without a man in sight. There, on stage, was a woman who could turn any dandy: Liane de Pougy. As Liane sang, idle chatter transformed into the breathless, focused silence of a unifying moment. She sang a siren's song to the room, who held chests in baited breath at her every movement, every note that passed through her quivering lips. As she finished her song, a brief pause allowed her audience to catch their wind and launch into rapturous applause. She was the most beautiful woman in Paris, and therefore, the world.

Too much a soldier for her feminine charms, Casement liked Liane. She commanded every room she entered like a general. She changed in a small back room with the door ajar. She sat like a queen in her makeup chair, the gaslight lamps flickered against each cheek. The room, heavy with perfume, seemed like an opium den of seduction.

Without turning from her mirror, Liane replied, "Sir Roger Casement, I presume? Miss Barney said you would request my services," Liane said. She turned, the gaze of her beautiful green eyes cut through the Casement's soul. Electricity sparked between the two; where Casement denied, Liane de Pougy ignited. "She said you might have a job for me?"

"Yes," Casement said. "Your services would be most beneficial in allowing The United States to enter the war. We will pay handsomely, though there might be significant danger involved." Casement explained her place the plan.

She answered with deafening silence. Her lips separated; then, she spoke. "Where do I sign up?"

***

Roger Casement walked into the insane asylum of London's west side, at Virginia Woolf's recommendation. Virginia said the boy was a troubled poet, but made no mention of his institutionalization. Screams vibrated the walls as Casement delved deeper through dim and dirtied walls. For all horrors of the Congo, the insane frightened him. Kill a tiger with a gun, but man's own delusions turn the pistol back on the gunman.

Casement walked down the long white hall and stopped in front of Rupert Brooke's cell. Through the small opening in the door, Casement saw Brooke sitting despondent at a desk, staring at an empty sheet of paper. He still wrote beautiful poetry. The light brown eyes locked Casement in place with the beauty of lust.

"Are you here to see me?" Rupert Brooke said.

"Yes." Casement said, seeing in him a bright future under Casement's guidance. There was a young man who Casement could confide and guide, to teach and train to become the man Casement could never be and give this boy all the wisdom Casement's hard life could have never been. To caress, to cuddle up too vulnerable as he ages, Roger Casement smelled Brooke through the bars: the musk of ammonia, dead roses, lilac, and irrefutable lust. Only then did Casement realize Rupert Brooke had this effect on everyone, and felt cheapened for believing in charisma. Casement blinked, remembering where he was; Casement fell under the boy's tragic spell.

"Are you a patriot, are you not?" Casement said.

"I am." Brooke responded with a silence so pregnant, Casement expected twins.

"I need your help to bring this war to an end." Casement said.

Rupert Brooke said, "Please, give me something to do. I can't stand helplessness. That is my great tragedy. What can I do? These are just… walls, here. Bugs, crawling in the city have more respect among themselves. I wish to be a soldier, another bug. Not being so, these walls are my… battlefield. The corners, they tell me war is not eternal."

"Of course…" Casement said. "What would you think about being a real soldier, a soldier without walls?"

A beatific glance swiped the side of Casement's face, "I would like that very much."

***

As the list grew, Casement filled out his roster. Edward Shelley, Ives's right hand man, was onboard as muscle. Sir Casement spoke with the elegant courtesan, Liane de Pougy. Adelsward-Fersen approved the expenditures. For reconnaissance, Noel Coward spent months aboard *The Lusitania* and would be present for the curtain call. Captain Silvermane would do the pickup, while First Mate Tennille would help execute the escape. The disturbed yet handsome soldier, Rupert Brooke, was onboard. With the peculiar inside source, John Edgar Hoover, Sir Casement tallied nine.

Only two more and Casement would get his eleven. Roger Casement and Noel Coward weaved through the streets of Taormina, Italy. The squat Sicilian woman they asked for directions from suggested the Teatro Greco to find the photographers.

"I do not understand how you can find your way through this *dreadful* city," Noel said, feeling claustrophobic, "My closet is wider than this."

Casement smirked, "You'd feel more comfortable with tight spaces if you stepped out of the closet."

Noel rolled his eyes and waved Sir Casement away with a flick of the wrist. Upon finding the old open stage, Casement smiled and ushered Coward in. "Ah, here we are." Coward had been photographed a few times in tight studios, but this was quite an unusual set up, like watching a play from backstage. Between two columns, a bronze-skinned youth held his hands to the sky and wore only a wreath in his hair and a thick slathering of unusual body paint. From this sun-baked Adonis revolved odd satellites of photographic equipment. A young Italian man held up a fill card while another diffused the sunlight with a white sheet.

"Just hold the pose a few more minutes," The photographer said, hunched down under the camera's drop cloth. "Is that plate ready yet, Guglielmo?"

Guglielmo was unusually short with a black and greasy receding hairline.

"Yes, Wilhelm. It's right here." Guglielmo said to the gangly photographer.

"I think you should put more glycerin on Pancrazio."

"Of course, Wilhelm," The assistant said, noticing Casement and Coward. "Sir, I think we have some company."

"You can rest, Pancrazio. Vincenzo, will you please fluff the artist?" the photogrphaer said.

Vincenzo, a simple photography assistant, approached the model with the awkwardness expected from giving a dispassionate hand-job to a friend. The lanky Italian turned to his guests and spoke perfect English. "Hello, Gentlemen. What can I do for you?" Wilhelm said, as the second assistant jerked the bored model behind the photographer.

As Noel was easily distracted, Casement stayed on point. "Sir, our mutual friend Jacques Adelsward-Fersen had you photograph his lover, Nino Cesarini."

"Ah yes, what a *handsome* boy," Wilhelm said with a twinkle in his large brown eye. "I have a feeling you are not here for portraits. How are they doing in that little villa over in Capri?"

"They are quite well. We plan on visiting them indubitably soon," Noel said.

"Yes, yes. Quite, quite." Baron Gloeden said.

"Quite, quite. Yes, yes," Noel responded.

Sir Casement knew this would deteriorate into a catty loop of small talk he had no tolerance for. He intervened. "Sir, we are undertaking a certain event where a man of your understanding of chemistry and electricity would become quite useful," Casement said, "as well as your particular predilection for discretion. Tell me, Baron von Gloeden, are you familiar with certain explosive compounds?"

"My cousin here, Guglielmo Pluschow, is better at understanding chemistry. However, I have been working with what I am calling replicated light, using the magic of electrical lanterns and flash powders. I have not exposed my research, for it is still quite revolutionary in its processes." Wilhelm Von Gloeden said proudly.

"Do you believe you could disarm an electrical grid of a luxury liner?" Casement said.

"A ship? That would have to be one bloody large ship to have electricity." Von Gloeden said.

"The biggest." Noel said.

Pluschow, Von Gloeden's defeated cousin, walked up to Von Gloeden, "Sir, we're losing light and the second assistant's wrist is cramping."

Casement said, "I shall hasten my proposal. As an exile myself, I understand the deep need for vengeance."

Baron Von Gloeden arrogantly declared, "You know what? I care little about Germany. As you may notice from my dashing good looks, I am quite wealthy and that is better than youth, strength, or wisdom. I spend my idle time behind a camera aimed at teenage boys." "Though I find the images quite arousing, I feel I haven't really contributed to The Cause as I should have for my fellow Gentlemen. Certainly, I supplied European Gentlemen with my illustrious art, but here I am, hiding my beautiful face behind the camera. I shan't join your company for your paltry shillings, but for The Cause! Yes, I Baron Wilhelm Von Gloeden will assist you in this international act of homosexual patriotism, one nation under the pink flag!"

Pluschow sighed, "Sir, you aren't a Baron. We've been over this."

"Come, my noble assistant! Let us aid them in their plight!" Von Gloeden said.

"I better come along, too. He's liable to get himself killed." Pluschow added, knowing the delusions of his rich cousin all too well.

"Delightful," Noel said. "We will supply you with the details soon."

As the two walked away, Noel said to Casement, "So it looks like the easy part is over."

Casement responded, "The hard part has just begun."

Chapter 18:
The Sissy Seven

The enclosed notice will appear in forty local papers Saturday, May 1st. The Lusitania is going to sink on May 7 and the American populace should be warned. I want the allies to win with minimal civilian casualties.

Patriotically yours,
R.R.

"Notice! Travelers intending to embark on the Atlantic voyage are reminded that a state of war exists between Germany and her allies and Great Britain and her allies; that the zone of war includes the waters adjacent to the British Isles; that in accordance with formal notice given to Imperial German government, vessels flying the flag of Great Britain, or any of her allies, are liable to destruction in those waters and that travelers sailing in the war zone on ships of Great Britain or her allies do so at their own risk."

It was obviously a hoax. Two months later on May 1st, Ambassador Bernstorff's stomach felt a lead weight of panic resting against his irritable bowels. The ominous feeling grew with each newspaper clipping gathered. By afternoon, he was up to thirty-seven newspaper clippings. Bernstorff went to the Special Agent Hoover at BOI at an office no bigger than a water closet. The German Ambassador said, "Sir, I think the German army is going to break treaty and sink the RMS Lusitania," Hoover looked the postcard and gave the newspaper clippings a once over.

"Don't you worry about that, you heathen kraut," Hoover said, "You are just trying to set us up with your backwards sense of logic." *Drat!* J. Edgar cursed to himself, *Someone spilled the beans.*

Captain William Thomas Turner of the RMS Lusitania was a good-hearted man with a crew that respected him. He checked his pocket watch. His crew was nervous. Even though no one told him what might be aboard his ship, he knew. Captain Turner looked out to the gentle sea. "Are we going to be okay?" Turner's first mate said. The worry leaked through the Captain's face.

Captain Turner replied, "Yes. We'll be just fine." No one believed it. Captain Turner synchronized his pocket watch. He looked up to see his first mate eye the life preserver. Turner signaled his crew for departure. The dark horn blew.

Smoking a cigarette on the saloon promenade, Noel Coward watched the New York pier overflow with passengers. After months at sea, he wanted to sink the wretched liner and be done with it. Among the hundreds clamoring on board, he clearly spotted Liane de Pougy. He snuffed out his cigarette and turned from guilt as the ship boarded. The dark trumpet blew.

From under her frilly parasol, Liane de Pougy strolled down the center of the pier as men and women parted for her. The women looked to her with envy while the men looked at her with lust. Behind her, four seamen struggled with her enormous cargo of seven Louis Vuitton full-length Armoires. "I'm sorry, Miss de Pougy, but your luggage is oversized. I'm afraid we can't accommodate your entire luggage." The deckhand said.

"Oh, is that so?" She said, batting an eye. "Be a dear and strap it onto the top of the boat? I do so hate to inconvenience my... fellow passengers," Liane said, handing the deck hand two crisp hundred dollar bills.

The deckhand's eyes lit up. "Why of course, Miss de Pougy," The smitten deckhand responded. Was a beautiful day, and Liane's grace would not falter to the nervousness of her fellow conspirators. Whereas others dealt with explosives and espionage, all she had to do was spend large sums of money and coerce men to do her bidding. None did it better. She was the most beautiful woman in Paris. As one fine lad assisted her up the gangplank, the dark horn blew.

Roger Casement prepared himself for passing as a Special Agent for British Intelligence with his two Italian prisoners, Baron Wilhelm Van Gloeden and Guglielmo Pluschow. They were sorry looking prisoners, raised by nannies. Their hands were smooth as river stones. Their faces were impeccably clean with primped moustaches. Casement looked down at the two fidgeting with their handcuffs.

"Stop that! You're hardened criminals, remember?" Casement said.

Pluschow answered, "Sorry, sir. They're just so dreadfully uncomfortable."

Casement barked, "They're supposed to be!"

"Well, that doesn't seem right," Von Gloeden said, "What if we start to chafe?"

Casement pinched the bridge of his nose and let out a sigh, forcing every ounce of tension to relax, "Please do not speak when we get to the gates."

Baron Von Gloeden was a stilted, tall man with a bourgeois posture. "Really, Constable Gustafson," Von Gloeden said with a wink at Casement's cover name, "If we are to be prisoners, could we have a back story that were not so droll? I mean, murder? Hmph! The very idea! What if instead we were both on trial for breaking artistic convention?"

Pluschow huffed, "Oh you've been reusing that Greek chestnut in your work for years, sir."

Von Gloeden replied, "You make pornography of my art. And your female nudes are more wooden than the trees you hide them behind." Pluschow gasped.

"Will you two silence yourselves?" Casement said through clenched teeth to the Germans. Wounded in fake striped prisoner uniforms, Von Gloeden and Pluschow looked even more pathetic. Casement said, "And where did you think to get those pencil thin moustaches? You both look like French ruffian puppets."

"I thought it made me look *dangerous*." Baron von Gloeden replied. Pluschow nodded in agreement.

"But does it make us look like *mean* puppets? You know, the scary kind?" Pluschow said, baring his teeth as though checking for food in the gaps. Pluschow growled, weakly pawing the air. "Grr... Grr..."

Von Gloeden smacked the younger cousin's hand, "Are you mad? Criminals don't do that. They hold their hands out like this..." Von Gloeden placed his hands out as though catching a medicine ball, "...And then you have to laugh like you're catching someone off guard like this... ha-*ha*!" Pluschow tried mimicking it, but failed miserably. The two prisoners bellowed "ha-ha" in various intonations for ten minutes before boarding the ship of fools. Casement now accepted his eventual arrest. The dark horn blew.

In the belly of the Lusitania, Rupert Brooke brushed the gold hair from his face and jutted out his strong chin, aiming his cigarette closer to the flame. He looked sharp in his cute little bellboy uniform, waiting for the onslaught of wealthy demands. Being at sea for two months without contact from Casement or the others, he hoped to reach the promenade for a place to escape. Even though Noel was often on deck, Rupert never spoke with the singer. The floor hummed as the coal engines roared when dark horn blew.

Deep in the bowels of the ship's hold, Edward Shelley's sooty, sweaty body glistened in the furnace's red light. As he and the other unfortunates risked exhaustion, shoveling coal into the gaping furnace's maw through deafening humidity, it was as good a place as any to die, knowing whatever follows does not compare to the endless labor and the accompanying terror when the dark horn blew.

Roger Casement showed his papers to the customs agent. The fat agent blathered, "State your business."

Casement cleared his throat, hid his Irish brogue, and said, "I am part of the British Counterintelligence Division. Quite a hush-hush operation. I'm informed of your holding cell aboard and I'm to take these two criminals back aboard the safest ship in the seas. They are… quite mad."

Baron Von Gloeden threw his hands out in front of him, catching the invisible medicine ball, and said, "Ha-*ha*!" Pluschow bared his teeth and pawed at the air, mewling out a growl like a surly cat.

The customs agent wasn't biting. "Well, I didn't get the memo."

"Of course not. You've seen the papers. Do you think these paying customers want to know your ship is not even safe to carry imprisoned terrorists? If you think your ship is so doomed to not even carry hardened international war criminals, which I have under my absolute protection, it would be quite the travesty to report to your superiors, which is my next stop if I don't get these boys to holding. What was his name... Captain Turner? This is a top-secret mission of international importance. He knows this ship is not going to leave without these two, as a matter of national security. They are due to answer for war crimes in two weeks. You don't want to make the Captain turn back when you could easily allow us through, do you?"

Casement showed his British Secret Service badge. The tin badge had a chip in the scrolling at the top. Casement's eye noticed this shoddy handiwork, but still flipped the badge out, poker faced.

The customs agent said, "No, officer. I would not want them to turn the boat around."

Three members of the security team stood behind the customs agent. The first smiled a mouth full of busted teeth. The second had a lazy eye. The third had a six-pack, stretching his white uniform. "You," Casement said to the third one, "Show us to holding." Van Gloeden and Pluschow watched the ceiling and followed the black wiring. Casement dropped the prisoners off in holding on the shelter deck between the engine room and the infirmary.

Pluschow and Baron Van Gloeden sat in their cell, quizzing each other on the details, when an entirely different British officer (in an entirely different uniform) entered with the jack-toothed guard and two additional prisoners.

Pluschow asked in Italian, "Did they double book us?"

Van Gloeden responded in broken German, "I don't know what you are talking about," which translated between the cousins as *Shut up and let's see how this plays out.*

As the cell door closed, the two *real* German spies sat in silence for a moment before saying, "Gutentag."

The sudden lurch of the ship leaving the dock spiked terror into every last one of them; Roger Casement, Rupert Brooke, Baron Von Gloeden, Guglielmo Pluschow, Edward Shelley, Noel Coward and Liane de Pougy. Each and every one of them knew this was the last voyage of The Lusitania.

Having unfettered access, Sir Casement brandished his papers at every turn under the guise of inspecting for stowaways and spies. Casement's quarters were on deck E in third class in the middle of the floating city of seven stories of the massive ocean liner.

Casement headed to the boiler room. He flashed his badge to the coal master, "Just a routine Q&A, you understand. Just want to ask your boys if they noticed anything unusual." Casement walked through the baking heat, looking for Edward Shelley, but found it impossible as the dozens of sweaty, hard bodies all looked the same under coal dust. At the front of the ship sat Edward Shelley, pouring water over himself to cool off, the furnace light glistening on his rippling frame.

"Excuse me sir, might I have a word with you?" Casement said.

Shelley gave an ugly grimace. "Sure."

Casement said, "Have you noticed anything out of the ordinary, perhaps some unusual cargo?"

Shelley rubbed a blackened towel on his chest, smearing grit into his abs. "Why no, Officer. I have seen nothing on *this* floor."

Casement tugged the brim of his hat and went about his business to the next floor up to third class to the main cargo hold. He searched the room in its entirety, finding an unobtrusive cargo hatch. He lifted it and looked down; crates of ammunition, guns, and mortar shells waited. He didn't find the expected explosives, though several crates marked with chemicals seemed out of place among the guns and shells. Casement stormed into deck C, where the German prisoners waited. "Tell me what you know about Potassium Perchlorate!" Sir Casement said, backhanding Plushcow again and again.

"Stop hitting me!" Pluschow whined, eyes welling up with tears. "I don't know what you're talking about!"

Von Gloeden spoke up, "Combined with aluminum powder, it becomes a highly volatile compound. It is used as flash powder in photography. Even the slightest spark ignites it." Pluschow wept from blackening eyes.

"Thank you, sir. I will see that your death sentence will be quick." Casement said, slamming the bars behind him. The other spies looked on with respect at these heroes of the Empire.

Casement walked down to his tiny room in third class, a floor which he shared with the ship's staff, and proceeded to the hindquarters, where he pretended to inspect the room service employees. There, he ran into Rupert Brooke, whose delight in seeing one of his own nearly betrayed him.

"Tell me, young man, have you seen anything out of the ordinary?" Sir Casement said.

"No sir, nothing at all." Rupert said.

Casement slipped him a few coins and a small piece of paper. "Thank you, young man. This is for your trouble."

"No trouble at all, Constable," Rupert said with pleading eyes.

Moments after Casement left, The Bell Captain bellowed, "Hey Rivers!" Rupert perked up at the mention of his pseudonym, "You got a request from someone in The Regal Suite. Towels to Room B44."

Rupert Brooke headed up two flights of stairs to the deck B Promenade and knocked on Room B44.

"Come in." a woman's voice answered. Brooke entered, where Liane de Pougy sat, fanning herself as the porthole light shone on her magnificent lap. "I trust you brought me my towels?" Brooke smiled and delivered the towels. "Thank you, sir. Here is a little something for your trouble." She tipped Brooke before he left. She unfolded the towels and found a slip of paper.

11 p.m. 6th day.

Taking the long way, Brooke walked up to the main deck, where he could see the luggage strapped down on the roof of the hurricane deck above.

On the first night, Noel Coward sang his hits with a full orchestra. As he performed, he scoured the audience, nervously anticipating Liane, Casement, and Brooke. Liane arrived late with great bravado; men clamored over each other to buy her drinks. She popped her fan, waving it slowly 23 times, then with pause, fluttering six more times. Upon eye contact with the singer, Noel nodded slowly, and orchestrated the band with the phrase "a two and three and a six!" He turned back to Liane, who nodded politely.

All Liane had to do now was live through it.

Chapter 19:
Going Down on the Lusitania

And the crowds stagger sleeplessly through the boroughs
As if they had just escaped a shipwreck of blood.

From *Dawn*
Frederico Garcia Lorca

Upon the sixth day, Liane de Pougy sat at the Captain's table beside Alfred Vanderbuilt, whom she befriended in her rare moments of forgetting the ship's fate. The moral implications of sending thousands to a watery grave were lessened by the overabundance of lifeboats. From the massive dining hall on the main deck, Liane looked through the skylight to her luggage on the roof of the hurricane deck. Across the room, Noel Coward gave a smashing performance before the wealthiest of dancing passengers. As the large clock clicked ten, Liane De Pougy excused herself with such grace no one noticed... save three. Noel felt a wave of relief cross over him, watching her exit out the side door. Sir Roger Casement's eyes panned the room. Noel nodded to Casement, who departed to the lower levels.

Liane walked out to the promenade, searching for a way to get to the luggage elevated atop the hurricane deck. The embroidered Edwardian monstrosity she wore hid a network of zippers, allowing her to shed the petticoats with ease and reveal a binding black cat suit she wore only for this final act. A long silk rope snaked along the inside of her skirt, which she unhooked from the dress, fashioned it into a lasso, and threw it over the topmost mooring.

As a courtesan, Liane mastered many arts, like scaling walls, should her profession require avoiding wives (and sometimes husbands). She pulled the serrated knife from her garter and sawed through the thick rope restraining the Vuitton luggage. After cutting the final restraint, she began tethering the armoires together and emptying the cased of her extensive wardrobe.

"What are you doing up there?" She heard. Liane's heart stopped at her throat. It was Alfred Vanderbuilt, looking up at her curiously. "And what on earth are you wearing? Good lord, are those pants?! I can hardly see you."

"Well, after seeing what all the other women are wearing, I couldn't live with myself with last season's fashions." Liane said.

"Come down from there! A lady as delicate as you could seriously injure yourself, and I will have none of such nonsense." Vanderbuilt said. For as polite as he had been, her grip tightened around her garter-knife.

Liane said from above, "What about your wife? Should you be looking after her?"

"Oh she has withdrawn for the evening, rather earlier than usual. But then again, she started early." Alfred said. Alfred Vanderbilt's wife was the heir to the bromo-seltzer company, and her drinking embarrassed Vanderbuilt to no end, especially after she acquired the cruel nickname *Alchie-Seltzer*. Liane's heart sank. She threw her clothes on him. "Careful, my love! You are dropping your unmentionables upon me!"

"Oh I'm terribly sorry, Mister Vanderbilt! I can't see very well see where I'm throwing them." Liane pulled out a pair of frilly bloomers. As she released them, a gust of ocean wind carried the undergarments to the main hall's skylight, where several guests underneath the glass looked up in confusion. Liane looked to her unmentionables, spackled with rain, holding tight on the skylight. As the courtesan of high society, she indulged in the lower-class act of swearing by muttering under the rain, "*Merde...*"

Noel Coward looked up to see a pair of bloomers laying flat on the skylight, and a small crowd looking up in wonder at the scandalous night sky. In mid-song, he feigned a coughing attack and walked backstage as the band played an instrumental. He waved the stage manager over and said, "I do believe one of the bell boys has stolen my cold medicine. I believe his name is Rupert Rivers."

In the Bell captain's quarters, The Bell Captain said to Rupert Brooke, "Hey Rivers, did you take Mister Coward's cold medicine?"

"Oh," Rupert said nervously, "I thought it was empty. I just returned from his quarters. I'll fetch the bottle."

"You're fired!" the bell captain said.

Under his breath, Rupert replied, "Fire is no different than water when death brings his deck of elements."

"What was that?" The bell captain said.

"Nothing. On it, sir," Rupert responded, dashing to the main deck and saw the large crowd gathering under the skylight, staring up at Liane's bloomers. He hurried back stage where Noel wrung his hands nervously. Noel grabbed Brooke by the forearm and whispered to him. "Get to Casement as fast as you can. We're ahead of schedule."

Rupert bolted through the halls, down the stairs by the engine hatch and straight to the holding cell, where

Von Gloeden and Pluschow waited patiently. Outside the holding cell, Brooke picked up a fire axe and walked into the small office outside the holding cell, where a guard sat behind an out of date paper. Hearing the door open, the guard dropped the paper, seeing the young Rupert Brooke wielding an axe.

"What the holy hell?" the guard said. The axe came down, blade lodging in his split skull. The guard fell back twitching.

Brooke fished the keys off the guard. Von Gloeden and Pluschow stuck their hands through the bars and Rupert, half his face covered with blood, unlocked their shackles. Von Gloeden massaged his wrists and said, "There's going to be a lot more where that came from, son."

Rupert said to his Italian consirators, "Now is the time your mettle is forged."

"What about us?" The two real spies yammered in terror, shackled to their benches as Brooke unlocked the door.

Pluschow took the gun out of the dead guard's holster and said, "You're part of the 'lot more'." He fired two quick rounds into the prisoners. Rupert stared at what remained of their heads.

Von Gloeden smacked Brooke from his daze. "Chop chop. We have a boat to sink. See you at the extraction point."

"Go, you damned fool!" Pluschow said.

As Rupert left, Von Gloeden and Pluschow headed two floors down and entered the clockwork belly of the *Lusitania*. Pluschow held his pistol close as they dodged various oblivious workmen. Cutting through the engine room up to the electrical room, the Italians were responsible for sabotaging the watertight doors.

Brooke ran off to warn Shelley and Casement in the bulkhead.

Three floors down, Casement and Shelley struggled to open the crates of explosives. Shelley stripped the dormant wire above the watertight door, leading a fuse to a makeshift mixture on the floor. Casement pricked up his ears. "Did you hear something?"

In the Grand Hall, Captain Turner looked up at the white bloomers on the skylight and excused himself. His first mate came up beside him. "What of it, sir?"

"It could just be another drunk like that Alchie-Seltzer Vanderbuilt woman, but we should get back to the bridge, just to be safe. Get the boys to close the water tight doors, slow down to 18 knots." Captain Turner pulled the first mate close and whispered into his ear, "...and get as close as you can to the banks of Ireland." The first mate nodded and hurried off down the corridors.

Reaching the electrical room, Pluschow heard the first mate's order through the communication tube in the engine room. "We have to stall them, Wilhelm!"

Meanwhile, Rupert reached the door of the cargo hold. "Casement! Shelley! We're ahead of schedule!"

"What are you talking about?" Casement said.

"Everyone saw Liane's bloomers!" Brooke yelled.

"Now or never, brother. Now or never." Casement said.

"What?" Shelley said as a sudden lurch forward and starboard shifted the storage, pinning Casement between the ship and a crate of explosives. "Roger!" Shelley tried to move the crates off the trapped soldier. "Are you all right?"

"Get out of here! We're all going to hell if you don't." Casement said, a tired certitude crossed his face.

As Shelley dragged Rupert with ease away from the door, "We'll dig you out!"

"Get out of here! You haven't much time! Do not sacrifice yourself for the sake of the misson! That is an order, soldier! Get everyone out safely!" Casement yelled, feeling the shards of bone grind against each other.

With ease, Shelley grabbed Rupert Brooke by the scruff of his uniform and dragged him away.

"What are you doing? We have to get him out!" Brooke yelled.

"It's too late, Rupert! We have orders! Come on!" Shelley called back.

"I'm not leaving without Casement!" Rupert yelled, "God damn you for not saving him!"

Shelley backhanded Brooke, "Get a hold of yourself! This boat is going down and I am not going down on it! Neither are you." Rage glared in Brooke's eyes.

In the electrical room, Von Gloeden and Pluschow pulled fuses from the circuit boards. In the wheel room, Captain Turner pulled the heavy lever, closing the watertight doors, but to no avail. At the bottom of the ship, an alarm blared, but the doors failed to close. As the misdirected energy from the engine belched fire through the engine room, Shelley and Brooke raced up the stairs of the floating citadel. Noel Coward felt the dance floor rumble.

Sir Casement felt the cold sea through the steel hull. He chuckled to himself, feeling the stabbing pain of his broken leg pinned with explosive crates. Abandoned by the British Government, abandoned by his fellow Irishmen, this time around Casement would be doing the abandoning. The aluminum powder twinkled in the air as a red glow came from the furnaces far down the hall. He chuckled as the watertight door failed and the air blazed white-hot.

A crowd gathered around Liane as she threw her expensive clothes down to the onlookers. Vanderbilt still tried to convince her, "Honestly, Miss de Pougy, come down from there! You'll catch your death!"

Under her breath, she said, "Quite the opposite, my love." A great rumble groaned through the leviathan lurching starboard to a murderous shriek of panic. The hull blew, continuing to shovel ocean water into the lower decks.

Vents from the holding floor vomited boiling water on passengers. As the deck listed, passengers toppled over the railing, crushed by those who lost balance. Lifeboats swung out too wide for passengers. Liane was in awe of her own naïve wrath. As she watched the front of the Lusitania erupt in a gulf of flame and nosedive, passengers shrieked and pleaded for sanction.

As the murderous waves smacked the innocent to the sea, Liane unfettered the luggage in a terror few comprehend. Black wave after wave consumed the bough, when she heard her name. It was Noel Coward, his young face twisted in terror as he ran against the crowd. Behind him, people clamored into lifeboats. Liane looked to the lifeboats, which banged and smacked down the sides like tin cans, spraying people like droplets of flesh while the ship tilted.

The explosion roared through the ship, detonating the high-pressure engine rooms and the aluminum powder. Directly one floor up, Von Gloeden and

Pluschow watched as the soles of their shoes melted. The Baron looked to his cousin as the steel floor turned from pale grey to glowing red. Pipes and gears shuddered as the room imploded, taking Pluschow and Von Gloeden instantly.

The Lusitania rocked again as Brooke and Shelley climbed through third class, chased by the cold ocean. The ship continued forward, drinking water through the breach in the hull. "We're not going to make it!" Edward yelled over the shattering glass of flooding rooms.

"I have a plan!" Brooke yelled, cutting against the currents of people and water. "Get to the elevator!" Shelley never left the coal room and had a trust the man who hated him.,

"How long can you hold your breath?" Rupert Brooke, waist deep in freezing water. "I know this layout! We can get to the surface if you trust me! How long can you hold your breath?"

"I don't know!" Shelley remembered all those times his johns face raped him. "About four minutes, I guess!"

"Follow me!" Brooke yelled. A small ladder in the elevator shaft led all the way to the deck, though the water level quickly rose beneath them. Never fast enough for nature, they were quickly submerged. Shelley followed close behind, unable to see the man before him through the dark, cold water.

After riding the flooded shaft up, the two spilled out onto the polished wood of the promenade deck. Rupert Brooke saw Noel and Liane with all that damnable brown luggage on the hurricane deck: the final destination.

Shelley and Brooke pulled themselves up a flapping towrope, watching the megalithic structure's end rear up at full speed. Socialites slid down the polished deck to a death Brooke blamed on Shelley. Liane and Noel spotted them and waved as the Lusitania lurched once more, sucking countless innocents into the cold black sea. Hand over fist, Brooke and Shelley worked up the rope to the luggage. Shelley knew the propellers were now above water level, and the ship could break in two at any moment.

"Get in the cases! Get in the cases! We're the last! We're the last!" Shelley bellowed, knowing the worst was yet to come. Noel and Liane were both in tears as they climbed in and latched the armoires from the inside. Within moments, Edward Shelley and Rupert Brooke climbed into their coffins.

"See you on the other side, Rupert Brooke." Shelley said.

"Pray to god I don't."

Seven tethered armoires slid from the ship to the darkness, surrounded by the screams of the dying. Just as Shelley felt sleepy from asphyxiation, the decisive moment arrived. He opened his Vuitton casket to the light of dawn. He pulled himself over to the other armoires. Three were empty. Three were full.

From the floating armoires, they watched the innocent drown. They watched children freeze to death. They watched the unnatural speed at which a shark carries off a live prey. They watched. They watched as the brutish push the weak into shark-infested water. They watched a society void of money and full of survival. It was no less brutal.

They floated in a sea of junk and corpses. The pink water served as the dinner table for a grisly shark frenzy. Noel and Liane cried in silent horror around six a.m. Off in the distance, a small fleet of fishing boats picked up survivors. Before long, the *White Swallow* made its way towards the little floating island of Louis Vuitton armoires after all other survivors were collected.

A rakish man with a plumed hat leaned over the edge. First Mate Tennille stroked his goatee and said with a smile, "Did I miss anything?" The four survivors said nothing, floating beside three empty cases. Tennille somberly took off his hat, placed it to his chest and—

"God Damnit," Noel yelled, "Get us out of here!"

Lianne's hand never left her mortified mouth. From the deck of the Mary Roger, she watched as the cases for Pluschow, von Gloeden, and Casement turn up and sink into the watery grave. "I'm doubling my fee," Liane said through her fingers. On deck, Edward Shelley lumbered up to her and put a hand on her shoulder as she dotted tears from her eyes.

Edward Shelley played his 'dumb oaf' card, "Miss Liane, I ain't no good with words and I's even worse with numbers. But we lived through something a lotta folks didn't. I know I ain't much to look at and I don't expect nuthin' in return 'cause you already done enough. I think you did more than you expected, maybe more than you bargained."

Liane stared out to sea, unaware of the shawl Shelley placed over her shoulders, "Yes... Yes, I do believe my desire for adventure has ebbed as the tide, which shall never rise so far up this shoal again."

The other mates on board *The White Swallow* looked to the mast, where Edward Shelley, the ugliest man in the world, comforted the most beautiful woman in the world. Shelley pulled the shawl over her other shoulder. With that simple motion, Liane De Pougy crumbled in tears.

"For what it's worth," Shelley said to the sobbing ragdoll in his arms, "I will make it my personal responsibility that you never have to worry about a man to take care of you. That is a Gentleman's oath."

Liane sobbed, "Oh, but even you... You make me indebted to *a man*."

As Shelley held the quaking beauty in front of the sunrise, he consoled her as *The White Swallow* rocked in the waves. "Miss Lianne, after what I just went through, I'm not so sure I'm much of a man."

Chapter 20:
The Cast Party

> *Good times for a change*
> *See, the luck I've had can make a good man turn bad*
> *So please please please…*
> *Let me get what I want this time*
> *Haven't had a dream in a long time*
> *See, the life I've had Can make a good man bad*
> *So for once in my life, Let me get what I want*
> *Lord knows, it would be the first time*

> *Please Please Please Let Me Get What I Want*
> The Smiths

Robbie Ross gripped the sides of the small catamaran to the Island of Capri. Before him, the curly blonde-haired cabin boy, Sweetcakes, endlessly chattered on about the joys of being a pirate. Captain Silvermane promoted Sweetcakes from loblolly boy to 2nd mate. Though the cheery disposition charmed the most innocent, Ross feared the reality of the fair haired-child: When a young boy joins the ranks of pirates as a loblolly boy, he saws off wounded limbs and generally performs the most wretched of tasks.

The swiftness and endurance of youth placed Sweetcakes as one of Silvermane's top pirates. When not cauterizing wounds with boiling tar, Sweetcakes also functioned as an exceptional cook. "Do you want half of my sandwich, Mister Ross?" Sweetcakes said with all his blinding ivory teeth. "I made the sausage myself!"

"I'll pass, But thank you." Ross said, white knuckling the boat's sides.

"Oh Mister Ross, I'm gonna have my sword and it'll be splendid and then I'll--I'll swing from the mast and take over my own ship! And--and I'll be all 'arrr!' and they'll be all 'Oh no! It's the dreaded Sweetcakes!'" Sweetcakes said, giggling maniacally. His bronzed muscles glistened in the sweat of exuberance. "Contingency!"

"I am sure you shall, Sweetcakes." Robbie said, closing his eyes at his taint-clenching terror of small boats. At any moment, the small catamaran would fling Ross into the open sea or instantly dissolve underneath him. "So how fares Captain Silvermane and Tennille?"

"Contingency!" Sweetcakes squealed. Robbie Ross remembered why he refused the company of seventeen year olds anymore. Sweetcakes continued, "Captain Silvermane teaches me so much about the sea... and Gary Tennille is (giggle) handsome." Sweetcakes erupted in the same laughter he probably used sawing gangrenous legs off cannonball victims.

Ross corrected himself. "How big is the fleet these days?"

"Oh gosh, probably thirty or forty. We lose and gain a few ships every month. The Great War is hard, Mister Ross." Sweetcakes looked off to the horizon. "Mister Ross, a lot of the old salts don't know much about steam or petrol. The future is a different sea with steely tides."

"Uh... I suppose you are correct," Robbie said. Sweetcakes returned from whatever ruminations distracted him, vacuously as cheery as before. "Tell me, uh, how many guests are to be in attendance at the Villa Lysis?"

"Well ol' Captain Silvermane didn't want a lot of attention drawn to Capri, since Italy isn't involved with The War." With a straight face, Sweetcakes added,

"The Captain says docking in the back can wear out the port."

Robbie Ross smiled, "There is some truth to that."

"We've been using Capri as a midway point between Africa, Europe, and The States. A lotta people want guns these days. You'd think people who shoot each other would eventually die off, but no. More and more of 'em every day." Sweetcakes said, pulling the small catamaran into the shallow dock.

Robbie Ross walked up the terribly familiar steps to the manor as the barefoot child effortlessly bounded onward. Approaching the open and indifferent doors, Robbie hated such a detail; any animal could just walk in. Yet Fersen was the type of man to wander inside and announce, "Oh look Bobbie! A badger in my bathtub!" Adelsward would proceed to choke the life out of it in a cocaine fueled rage. Such an affectation of madness exposed Ross's own insanity by association.

Sweetcakes pushed open the door into the cavernous foyer. On a chaise lounge, a fit young lad with cinnamon skin roused from his naked sleep. His curly drapes matched the carpet, and those of the room as well.

"Hello Mister Ross," the uncircumcised young man said.

"Hello Nino," Ross said, showing his English prudery while hiding his semi. Sleepily, Nino stood, rubbing his glistening eyes. Nino led them through the arching ceilings to the back garden. Though the architecture stunned Ross, he couldn't take his eyes off Nino's perfect ass. The tension of each cheek traded off like a hypnotic metronome.

Nino sing-songed, "Ja-aque... Bobbie's here..." Nino Cesarini's bare feet slapped on the white tile floor.

Villa Lysis felt quiet, as much of the help left went to the continents for better jobs. Adelsward and Nino lived in a remote mansion on an island, undisturbed by the war as they explored the deepest realms of intimacy without any sense of responsibility or limitation of desire. Admittedly, Ross was jealous.

As Ross entered the patio, the guests cried, "Bobbie!" A spark of camaraderie ignited calm as Ross greeted his dear friends. The Victrola spun out a gay tune, where Liane de Pougy waltzed with Noel Coward, who sang over the song's weaker strains. With the indifference of a supermodel, Nino Cesarini walked to Adelsward, kissed him, and then took a small coke spoon to his nose before lounging outstretched in a lounge chair, as if inviting the lusting guests.

Adelsward tossed a card out. The Captain bellowed, "You fuckshtick of an ashpump! Thasht's the fifth hand in a row!" Liane laughed infectiously. It was a beautiful day.

"Come join us, Bobbie," George Ives absently as Tennille dealt him in.

"Where are Rupert Brooke and Edward Shelley?" Ross said. Adelsward cursed his hand.

Ives cleared his throat. "Rupert joined up with the English Military. Shelley is on another job right now. I wouldn't concern yourself with it."

Noel said, "Oh do stay for a spell, we simply must have you! That Hoover fellow has done us quite the favor."

"Yes," Adelsward added, "Looks like this little fellow opened up some highly profitable contracts for your pirates and myself."

Captain Silvermane threw his dead hand into the table, "He contracted me out to run contraband.

Twenty of my ships are shcurrying back and fourth acrosh the Atlantic as we shpeak. By the time thish war is over, we'll be millionaires."

"Make that multi-millionaires, all for 'The Cause'." Ives said.

"A lot of good it does Roger Casement," Robbie Ross muttered.

"Must you be so droll," Noel said, "He wasn't in it for the money. He wanted to die a warrior's death."

"Don't be so hard on yourself, Mister Ross," Liane said, breaking from her dance partner to puff off a hookah.

Adelsward joined in the conversation. "Ross, this melancholy must cease at some point. Our lot in life is one of strife--Nino? Go to the cellar and bring us more champagne... No, from the *champagne* cellar, not the wine cellar--and if we do not take advantage of predicaments, they will take advantage of us. We are at war with those who imprisoned Wilde. You seem to forget that." Adelsward said, snorting a railroad tie of cocaine, "But if you just want to sit back and let the Germans rape Belgium, let England throw you in prison for buggery, become blacklisted in the art world—be my guest. But we're not going to stand for it. Neither should you, of all people. Your take is in the Tiberius Room just beyond the China Room downstairs. You can't miss it. We'll telegraph you if we need another outing ruined with your whining."

"I should probably go then," Ross said. This was the first time he understood how ungrateful he must appear to those who believed in him. Ross knew this was Noel's welcoming party--and Ross's bon voyage. He wondered how long they humored his self-righteousness. George Ives looked up from his cards, as if to object, yet did nothing. Ross bade farewell to all but Adelsward and left.

Ross walked down through the China Room, littered opium pipes strewn about the oversized cushions and rugs. A wall hanging hid a sliding door. On the other side was a stone room with carvings of unmentionable acts of depravity, old as the Roman Empire itself. Adelsward built this place over a love nest belonging to one of the exiled Roman emperors, Tiberius, whose hunger for depravity was legendary.

The musty cell always spooked Ross, even when the real Mona Lisa, not the one in the Louvre, stood proudly on a far wall over a carved stone shrine caked with centuries-old black blood. The warm, dry room also housed crate after crate of Captain Silvermane's contraband weapons. Among the ancient and modern, the art and the filth, rested a small carpet bag. Ross wasted no time retrieving his money.

"Oh hello, Mister Ross. Are you going so soon?" Nino said, surprising Ross from behind. Nino wore pants now, made of nearly transparent billowing gauze. "You know how Jacques can get when he gets in one of his moods." The words came out slow and sweet like molasses.

"Yes, Nino. I fear I have worn out my welcome, or what was left of it." Ross said.

"Would you like me to ferry you to the mainland?" Nino said. It sounded like a proposition. Ross's heart fluttered.

"Yes, Nino. I would like that very much."

Ross and Nino walked down to the catamaran. Along the channel, Robert Ross felt he could safely leave these dirty dealings behind him. The waves bucking the tiny rowboat along the bleak horizon made him feel more alive than mere art could, for mere art never portrayed the scent of brine and fish permeating his bare travels. With Noel entering the business, Ross could focus on his legitimate art dealing, putting this murderous game behind him. He finally felt at peace.

Ross looked over to a metal rod sticking out of the water. Perhaps it was a trick of the waves, but the pipe seemed to be move closer, before dipping below the waves. "How queer..."

He carefully stood, noticing a strange v-shaped wake heading straight for them. As soon as Ross figured out what it was, the German U-boat rose out of the water, stranding the catamaran on the steep tip of the steel submersible. The small boat tipped over, spilling a soaked Ross and Nino onto the cold metal. Ross pulled Fey Dunaway from his holster and prepared for the worst.

The hatch opened, revealing a skinny blond man popped out, "Hi Bobbie! Miss me?" the man said, "Feeling a little stupid for not letting me in your club now? You'd never believe what an outrageous turn of events has taken place."

"Lord Douglas," Ross said, "What the Devil are you doing in a submarine?"

"The Germans are paying top mark for the Lusitania saboteurs. Looks like I found them." Douglas said. "Adelsward is an embarrassment to the Italians. I'm doing them a favor." Douglas stepped out, wiping wet hands with a handkerchief. Ross fired Fey at his nemesis, who laughed when the wet bullets clicked against the hammer.

"Come on, Bobbie. You should know better than to fire a wet pistol... unlike this one," Douglas said, pulling his own handgun. His bullet punched a moist hole in Nino's head.

Five German soldiers marched out and disarmed Ross. "It was easy to hunt you and those inverts down. For a secret society, you sure make yourself easy to find."

"But you're one of us!" Ross cried.

"If it were me, *I* would have been me leading the Dieppe House! *I* would be me up at the Villa Lysis! It would be *me* in charge of Wilde's estate! It would be *me* who had his money! It would be *me*... who had his heart." Ross rolled his eyes. "Don't you dare mock me!" Douglas screamed. Handsome German soldiers swarmed in around Ross. Douglas laughed, "Where are your Gentlemen of the Shade now?"

"They'll kill you for this, Bosie."

Lord Douglas smirked, "Not if I kill them first, which is happening right now. You see, Mister Ives made me his Parabatai, but shuns me! Everyone should know by now, I am not a man to be shunned!" The German soldiers descended, beating Ross within an inch of his life.

On the island, Silvermane and Adelsward first heard the gunfire, which took Nino's life. "What the hell devil that?" Adelsward said. Noel shrugged at Liane and took her hand in dance.

"Contingency!" Sweetcakes said, tearing off into the woods.

Noel said, "Well, aren't you going after the little scamp?"

Silvermane chuckled, "I gave up long ago keeping up with the little bashtard."

Ives, Tennille, and Adelsward ran to the overlooking cliff to see the massive black metal submarine not far from the shore. "What's a German U-boat doing in Italian waters?" Tennille said. "Italy isn't getting involved with this war. They have enough problems."

"Whatever the case, I doubt they're here to give us a gift basket." Adelsward said.

The trio ran back as the guests stopped what they were doing as the three men ran over to the others. Concern spread through the crowd. "What's going on?" Liane said.

"Get inside. We're under attack. Drop everything and get inside. There's a German u-boat out there."

"Why?" Liane asked, "What's happening? Who's attacking us?"

Silvermane tossed his cards and drew his pistols. "Tennille, get Ives and the Liane to the Mary Roger."

Tennille drew both pistol and rapier. "Come, my fine ladies. We have a boat to catch."

"But…but what about me?" Noel Coward replied. Adelsward and Captain Silvermane shot him a look.

"Don't be such a Nancy, Noel," Adelsward said, "If you don't feel like growing a pair, grab the Thompsons from the Tiberius room. We're going to defend our spot, Italian-style."

***

The black bag came off Robert Ross's head. Strapped to a chair, a bare bulb's light fell harshly on the wheezing Ross. Lord Douglas stood proudly over the prisoner. Douglas aged smugly since their Wildean trysts, but maintained better shape than the captured underworld diplomat. Ross looked at Wilde's gun in Douglas's hand with subdued rage. Ross's left hand was crushed like a wet napkin.

"This... should have been mine. I'm surprised you would still carry this old relic," Douglas said, playfully spinning Fey Dunaway on his index finger. "Looks like the one thing we have in common..." Douglas said, taking the gun by the barrel bashing Ross's face repeatedly, "Is that we just... can't... let... Go!"

Ross spat teeth and blood on Douglas's white suit. Douglas laughed. "Oh, Bobbie. After all this time, I bet you thought you were quite clever, always taking the high road. Hiding behind your friends isn't going to help you now. You see, the Kaiser and I have grown close. Very, very close. And when I told him a gaggle of fairies were going to sink the Lusitania and blame it on him—and then you actually pulled it off—he started listening to what I had to say. The more I told him, the more he listened. And finding the culprits responsible for bringing those ghastly colonies into something that was not even their concern made your selfishness *his* concern!" Douglas hissed, spraying spittle onto Ross's face. "All your friends on that island, they're already dead!"

A pounding on the steel door interrupted them. Douglas threw a small tantrum and answered the door, where a German soldier stood. "What do you want? Can't you see I'm busy!" Douglas screamed. Ross's hand throbbed. Another few seconds and the hand would swell too large to slide free. Ross coughed up a spattering of blood as he slipped his hand out of the shackle behind him. For a second, he lost consciousness in agony.

"No no NO!" Douglas screamed, jumping up and down, "That's not how this is supposed to happen! Do something about it!" Douglas sneered as he looked to his captive, "I'll be back, Bobbie. Don't go anywhere."

The twittery laugh echoed through the metal walls as Douglas returned to the bridge with his men.

When the right distance stood between Ross and Douglas, Ross leaned forward, free. In his childish rage, the traitor left the steel door unlocked. Ross leaned over and vomited a bright red pool. He limped towards the door unarmed, badly beaten, and up against more than a dozen German soldiers. There was only one thing left to do.

***

"Where the blasted hell is it?" Noel Coward said, looking for the sliding panel in the China Room leading to the Tiberius Room. Finally, he pushed the fake wall open to that creepy chamber. In the corner under an unsettling tapestry of children and donkeys, Noel found the crates and threw the gun straps over his weak shoulders.

Topside on the island, Adelsward watched through the telescope as the U-Boat bobbed against the current to the island. "What's the shtatus, Jacques?" Captain Silvermane said.

"It can't submerge so close to the shore." Adelsward pulled the telescope down, "I believe they are unaware of the other dock. Obviously, whoever's captaining that contraption doesn't have the nautical foresight to circle the island first. Where is that blasted Coward?"

"They won't make it to the dock," Silvermane said, pulling a funny looking gun out of his inner vest.
"What the hell is that?" Adelsward said.

"Get down." Captain Silvermane said, pointing the gun overhead, and pulled the trigger. A shrieking noise exploded in brilliant sparks overhead. A single white star floated down over the salmon pink setting sun.

On the other side of the island, Liane, George Ives, and Tennille ran down steep stone steps to the seaside dock. "What's that?" Liane said, pointing to the flare in the sky.

Tennille replied, "It's the dire wolf signal, letting the *Mary Roger* crew know we are retreating. But you're not." Tennille shot George Cecil Ives, point blank. Liane screamed and backed away from Tennille.

"Tennille? Why? Why?" Liane cried, throwing herself back against the stairs.

"Do you think I'm going to be replaced by a sodding cabin boy? Oh, you pretty wench, quite a shame you had to die beside these wankers, so confused among these savage socialites. I would dare not see the Mary Roger simply become ferrymen for upper class dilettantes. The kind Lord Alfred Douglas promised I would attain captainhood at the death of everyone on this island. He enlisted the help of the German Emperor for this mutiny. Once the Germans land, they shall murder everyone in the Villa Lysis. With Lord Douglas commanding the German Gentlemen, Brand and Hirshfeld will fall under heel and I'll be Captain Tennille!" Tennille said. "Since I can't bear to strike down a lady, you are coming with me, Liane."

From high atop the trees, the living heard someone howl, "Contingency!" as Sweetcakes swung from a vine and knocked Tennille down the long stone staircase. The first mate's fight with gravity failed until he slackened like a bag of potatos to the dead bottom.

Liane de Pougy squeezed the blushing young man, "My hero!"

Sweetcakes giggled out, "Contingency!"

Ives winced in pain, "Argh! My word, that smarts." The wound in Ives's shoulder stung less than the unexpected mutiny.

Liane ran to the fallen Ives, "Dear sir, are you all right?"

"Darling, I have been *shot.*" Ives said.

"Don't worry, Mister Ives!" Sweetcakes said cheerily, "I've been shot three times! I can patch you up real good! I can plug any hole!" Sweetcakes eased Ives down the steps. At the small dock, a Finnish Pirate named Tom waited to pull up the gangplank.

"What happened to Tennille?" Tom asked.

"He fell." Sweetcakes said, "All Aboard! Set sail for the mainland and boil up the pitch!"

"But what of the Captain?" Tom Finn asked. "The dire wolf flare—"

"Orders are orders! Captain fired the Dire Wolf and we must depart! Those are Captain's orders and I am commanding officer!"

"But what about Tennille? Should we honor him with a burial at sea?"

"Let the scallywag rot for the vultures," Sweetcakes said, ripping Ives's tailored shirt with amazing efficiency. "Mister Ives, nothing will ever hurt this much again." After sopping up the wound's blood with a greasy rag, Sweetcakes slathered on the tar. Ives shrieked as Liane hid her face in Tom's chest. The color drained from Ives's face as he lost consciousness.

"He'll be fine. Set sail for the shore. We must protect these passengers at any cost."

Tom responded, "But... what about the captain?"

A devilish smile crossed the New Captain's face. "Contingency..."

***

Captain Silvermane stared at the black leviathan through a telescope. Adelsward barked, "Where is he? That Coward should be here by now!"

Noel Coward ambled down the steps, weighed down with six machine guns. "What, did you stop to polish the wood on your way?" Adelsward backhanded Noel. "You stupid incompetent! If we die here, it would expose the Gentlemen to the world! What were you thinking, you insolent child! If we didn't need you to fire on that vessel, I'd kill you right now!" Adelsward said, his eyes glossy with cocaine.

"Jacques," Captain Silvermane interjected, "That u-boat is 200 yards away. These guns can't take down a shteel beasht like that."

"Damn, damn, damn, damn it all to the abyss!" Adelsward screamed. "Well, what are we to do?"

Silvermane stroked his long white beard. "The boysh are shircling around. There can't be too many Germanshs on board. Twenty, maybe thirty topsh. We might be able to shnipe them off as they dock. My boysh will make sure they don't leave thish island alive."

Adelsward huffed, "So it's up to us, then?"

***

Aboard the U-Boat, Robbie Ross found a shovel for a crutch and worked his way out of his holding cell just above the engine room. He stumbled down the stairs, the roaring furnace muting his tumble. A young man lathered in sweat and coal dust diligently shoveled fuel into the belly of the beast. Ross wasn't made for this, which was exactly why he had to rise to such an occasion. At just the right moment, Ross threw his crutch-shovel into the coal porter's neck, sending the poor lad into the furnace. Ross rested a moment, coughed up more blood, and looked at the knobs and turning wheels surrounding him.

Understanding brought him to tears. Everyone dies saying, "Not like this. Any way but this." Robert Ross took the wheel in his good arm and spun. No matter how painful, it would never be this painful again. Scorching steam poured into the small room and Ross felt his flesh blister off in air too thick to breathe.

The hull cracked and the submarine lurched to the left. "Sir," the captain replied, "Our controls are useless! We're going ram the island!"

Douglas sneered. "Ross…"

Adelsward, Coward, and Silvermane watched the dark grey tube advance to the dock, showing no signs of slowing down. With the shriek of crumpling steel, the submarine plowed thirty feet into the shore's tree line.

"My begonias!" Adelsward squealed.

"Begonias? What about the Cypresses?" Noel said.

"Letsh take a look then," Captain Silvermane said and they worked their way down to the splintered dock.

"Don't worry," Silvermane said, "We'll shtrip it for parts and drag it out a few hundred feet." The hatch to the submersible swung open limply.

"I hope Bobby and Nino got to the mainland. Allow me to examine the contents of this wreckage," Adelsward said, climbing over the twisted hull to the hatch. Five badly injured soldiers climbed out. With a quick wave of his machine gun, Adelsward dropped them effortlessly before entering the U-boat. Not long after, Adelsward climbed back out with a sour expression. "I probably shouldn't have killed those men."

"Why?" Noel asked.

"I should have asked them how they survived. It looks like an elephant exploded in there." Adelsward said.

"What about Robbie Ross?"

"He's dead," Adelsward said when three bullets fired from the u-boat. Adelsward's face twisted in disgust as he looked down to the red stains on chest spread, sullying his suit. "Most inconvenient..." Jacques said before falling to the ground. Noel shrieked.

"Jacques!" Silvermane said, clumsily hobbling towards the wreckage. In a white suit flecked with blood, Bosie climbed out and shot down at Captain Silvermane.

"Ah, I suppose you must be Noel Coward, the Paraibatai of the late Bobbie Ross. Allow me to introduce myself. I am Lord Alfred Douglas. I would shoot you dead right here with Oscar Wilde's own pistol, but being that you are the last English Gentleman, I might have some use for you. And you certainly have use for me. We shall be in touch." Bosie Douglas turned and disappeared off the other side of submarine into the splintered foliage. Noel stared at where Bosie stood, dumbstruck. Captain Silvermane coughed.

"Captain! Are you all right?" Noel said.

"Please," Captain Silvermane said, "Call me one last time by my real name."

"What is it?"

The captain whispered it before his eyes slackened into the void.

As the Mary Roger sailed into view against the blood red sunset, Noel Coward sat beside the burning u-boat at the beach at the end of the world. With the villa behind him obscured by black smoke and the cleaved, lonely island, Noel Coward held the captain's body. "Fare thee well, Monsieur Rimbaud."

The Mary Roger would return, and with it, The Great War.

Part V:
The Great and Fabulous War

Tod Crouch

Chapter 21:
Poets with Pistols

"Everything is so dangerous that nothing is really very frightening."

--Gertrude Stein

His eyes snapped open in dim rain as a fighter plane roared low over him. The first instinct is always to scream, but Siegfried Sassoon learned to stifle this impulse. Waking up with night terrors on the front lines came costly to soldiers gone mad with sleep deprivation. After blinking rain from his eyes, he slowly looked around. Grey sky met grey mud consuming grey-skinned corpses. It rained. His head hurt. Shells thundered in the distance.

Observation balloons loomed on the horizon. Sassoon watched one ripple, deflate, and flutter down smoking. The war was far from over and far from here, wherever this was. Siegfried came back into his body, giving himself a moment's rest. He felt his soul sink for a second, causing him to lurch and keep moving. He shat himself, but did not notice under layer after layer of cold mud. His ice blue eyes glimmered, the only brightness on the blackened plain. He threw up yolkish stomach lining, steadying himself with shuddering hands. Down his left shoulder ran a streak of rust-red crust. He removed his pith helmet, feeling flesh rip. Blood splashed from his left ear, roaring in pain.

"Damn." He said, startled at the sound of his own voice.

Siegfried found another helmet cradling a small puddle of rainwater. He washed his wound as best he could, and the bleeding slowed to a trickle. His helmet took the bullet's brunt, grazing his skull. He understood why they left him for dead. He was hungry and could sleep forever. If he didn't start moving, he would.

Sassoon picked up his rifle and felt in his feet familiar blisters goad. He searched the ground frantically for something, unable to remember what. Something seized up in his mind, watching his bloody fingers dig through mud. Whatever he searched for was under all that mud. Siegfried's fingers tore into shrapnel, his arms shuddered in cold raw exhaustion— *It's not there!*

"Where is it? God damn you, where is it!" Sassoon screamed, his wet hair lashing across his forehead. His body was not his own. He distantly watched his hands move by themselves. A German soldier's arm flopped away from the reclining body. The singular movement spooked Sassoon, who threw himself back and fired on the corpse. The shots chipped chunks from the soft slab until wind's silence returned to the gun's empty chamber. All he found were faces of the fallen. By the time any cleanup crew would come through, they would be sun-ripened carrion. He stepped over Privateer Bobby O'Toole, gutted by some blast into meat. Sassoon remembered he hated O'Toole in life as he prodded a slow walk to civilization.

To what he assumed was East over the landscape of bodies and rubble, the war raged on. "Get it together, Siegfried," He said to himself, snapping back into the freezing vessel of his body. Sassoon walked away from the front lines' pillars of black smoke. Rain and uneven footing across the crooked graveyard were his only companions. The black skeletons of trees along the horizon were his best option. Unaware if he was still in France or crossed over to Germany, Sassoon assumed France lay safety behind scorched trees.

A strangely familiar foxhole came upon him. A river of blood and grey clay eddied along the flotsam of pink meat. He slid down the embankment to see Henri Lafleur's wide dull eyes with lips just as blue. Siegfried rifled through Henri's pockets, finding a tin of sardines. He ate them voraciously and drank the salty oil. The tiny feast made all the difference, diminishing the debilitating tremors to violent shakes. Planes roared overhead to the front lines like cheap death traps.

Siegfried hoped to follow the exhaust trails back to a launch base, scores of miles away.

The lost soldier climbed out of the foxhole, cautious of the partially submerged razor wire. To avoid stepping on the bodies became impossible. Occasionally, the not-quite-dead reached up to grab Siegfried's ankle. Siegfried shot them in the face and walked on. His terror had no remainder. Sassoon imagined himself in hell, but without Heaven's optimism.

After nearly two miles, the blackened trees came into close distance. Only a few corpses rested on the other side of the road. He vaguely recalled marching in from this road, but which direction his origin lay failed memory. A sparrow lit off a corpse with indifference and Sassoon almost laughed.

He slumped against a blasted tree trunk, exhausted. It was a risk to sleep, but Siegfried walked from the killing fields and felt he earned his life and the right to sleep within it. Should he sleep the sleep of the dead, he welcomed it. Constantly aware of the sinking sensation bringing death, Sassoon fell into the lucky arms of Morpheus and not Thanatos. As Siegfried

Sassoon snuggled into his reeking clothes and prepared for death or rest, the birds sang beautifully.

Sassoon stopped himself from screaming as he woke up in total darkness, listening. His mind raced his heart. A head wound could lead to blindness, and he suffocated in the fact. No breath and no sight—

Sassoon moved his arms and touched his face, happily not buried alive. Recounting his steps, he felt the tree behind him.

A small pop of light to his left showed the war, far off in the distance. Sassoon let out a chuckle—It was merely night! The soldier laughed and laughed until tears streamed down his eyes. What hilarious madness to confuse death with a moonless night! To prove his return from lunacy, he searched his pockets for his cigarettes and found a few survivors. Lighting one, the flare of his match caused him to laugh hysterically again, dropping the burning stick. Celebrating mercy's passing hand, Sassoon fell back against the tree, sighing with exhaustion. Getting the cigarette lit, It tasted like a five course meal.

Sassoon stripped off his cumbersome pack and crusty coat and felt the night wind kiss his wretched arms. He was fast asleep again in minutes. The dull roar of faraway war lulled him like a crib's soothing sways.

A motorcar sputtered and popped from the recesses of his slumber. Siegfried Sassoon saw the headlights advance and pondered strategy. He tried moving his arms, too tired even to risk death. As the motorcar grunted and bobbed along the dirt road, Sassoon slumped, hoping his head wound would prove a convincing feigned death.

The motorcar stopped, headlights fixed directly on him. Two stepped from of the automobile. A woman's voice twittered in French. A brash man answered her. It was easy for Sassoon to play dead, but when his curiosity flared, he flicked his eyes open and said,

"Gertrude? Alice? What the bloody hell are you doing here?"

"Saving your ass, apparently," Gertrude Stein let out a raspy laugh and said, "I'll be damned. Siegfried Sassoon. Shot in the head and still kicking. You old bastard, get your ass in our ambulance so we can fix you up." Gertrude said, wearing a bright red cross on her white tunic. She looked like a Medieval Crusader.

Beside her was a small bird of a woman, nervous and fidgety. Her place was the kitchen, not the war zone, but she would go anywhere with Gertrude. Alice B. Toklas's lantern shook nervously. "Oh, Mister Sassoon! We were so worried about you! Are you okay? That's a nasty gash on your head! Let me help you up!" Alice said. She obviously didn't have the strength to lift Siegfried, but Siegfried lifted himself up to comply with her sweet efforts. Gertrude stood by, propped up on a cane with an amber tip.

"Where am I?" Siegfried said, "I don't think I'm right in the head."

"No shit." Gertrude said. "Ever since you signed up for this. You're between Germany and Toul, France. That head is for thinking, thinking is for the head, says I think with my thinking head thinking and not getting blown off—which you so very nearly accomplished." Sassoon winced, unsure if he incurred brain damage or if Gertrude Stein tormented him with her blasted Modernism. "I would tan your hide, nurse you back to health, and tan your hide again for jumping out there to get shot at. Your mother is worried sick!"

"Sorry, Gertrude," Siegfried said, sheepish as a schoolboy.

"Well, no use wasting words on it. Get in Auntie with the rest of them."

"Auntie?" Sassoon said.

Gertrude held up her kerosene lantern at the clunky looking buggy of a Model-T, refitted with a chuck wagon bonnet on back to house the wounded.

"Siegfried, I'd like you to meet Auntie." Gertrude pointed just above the bright red cross, where a painstaking signature read AUNTIE. "You like that?" Gertrude said, looking to the battered soldier.

A bewildered Sassoon responded, "It's a nice touch. The lettering is... okay."

Gertrude belly-laughed, "It's a Picasso! Pablo did it as a sending off present! Honestly boy, you are a great many a thing, but stick to the words, kid. You don't know art from *merde*." Gertrude wrapped her arm affectionately around Siegfried's shoulder. She patted his blood-spattered hand, "It's going to be okay, my boy. We will take good care of you. Alice and I picked up two other stragglers, but they're all konked up on Morpha. Do you want some, perhaps cocaine? I would love to catch up for a few days one night."

Alice piped in, "Oh, but Gertrude! He's been through so much! Maybe he just wants to rest up a bit?"

"Sleeping in that contraption like being thrown down a cliff!" Gertrude barked, "I can barely read in that thing!" A loud boom roared in the distance, taking the trio off guard. They stopped like frightened deer.

Crackling gunfire closed in.

Alice looked to Sassoon and Gertrude as a brilliant flash of light in the distance dimmed and said, "Miss Stein, what was that?"

The ladies could not discern distance, but Siegfried's battle-sharpened senses calculated quickly as Sassoon muttered, "Nearly four hundred meters. The frontline is falling back this way. We've got to get out of here as fast as we can."

"Crank us up, woman!" Gertrude barked as Alice skirted shadows, grinding Gertrude's grill. Hand over fist, Gertrude's pistons fired up with a sputtering pop.

Alice skittered into the passenger's seat, "I really wish you didn't have to start up an automobile by standing in front of it. It's the worst place to be in an automobile."

Gertrude yelled, "Hang on, my lovely. We're going to outrun them!" as she whipped the enormous wheel around. The electric headlights spun over the dead field of limp limbs. Clouds of grey dust kicked up as Gertrude downshifted, barreling violently down the dirt road. In the enormous rearview, Gertrude saw shadowy lights glow clear. They were spotted. She threw it into fourth and gunned the gas. She prayed the forty miles per hour didn't shudder the car apart.

Auntie fought the jarring meekly as Alice stumbled into the bonnet with a lantern. "Just take a seat with the others, Mister Sassoon." Alice said. She hung the lantern up carefully, though it swung wildly with the teetering shadows. She joined Gertrude up front as Auntie bucked through the black.

Among the cupboards and crates of medical supplies, Sassoon joined four cramped and wounded soldiers. Siegfried's eye locked on a large man with a full face and a small moustache. The giant Frenchman held a worried look in his sharp eyes. He smiled amiably, "I see you have a head wound as well," he said,

"Allow me to introduce myself as Monsieur Guillaume Apollinaire." A huge blackened stitch over his left eyebrow sprawled into his gauze skullcap. "I judge you are with the English?"

"Yes. My name is Siegfried Sassoon. My platoon was killed and I was left for dead."

"Weren't we all?" Another soldier said. He was beautiful with the face of an angry child. His uniform fit tightly against his lean frame. "Privateer Rupert Brooke. Pleasure to meet you." Rupert said, seeming to fight back bitterness. His dark blonde hair was thick with mud, his lips caked from a once-bloodied nose. Grime rouged his cheeks. His eyes were glistening auburn pools, hinting at fallen tears. His greased skin shone in the lamplight. Sassoon feared two things: falling in love or watching him die.

Apollinaire continued, "Miss Stein and Miss Toklas were sent to find me and succeeded with rapid ease, but the route we used was left truncated. We drove about the front, waiting it out and found more of our boys. Alice stitched me up quite well, but we are having a *beast* of a time trying to outrun the Germans. Nothing personal, you understand. The enemy is just trying to clear out anyone still left behind, like us."

"Are you feeling well? We have some dried meats if you are hungry," another soldier said. He had all the charm and looks of a moving picture actor. His clean uniform strained against his powerfully large shoulders and biceps. "Try not to strain yourself." The soldier hid his shattered nerves with a debonair smile.

"Thank you. What is your name?" Siegfried asked.

"I'm Private Wilfred Owen," the soldier said. Sassoon's heart leapt into his throat. It was mutual love at first sight. "Tell me, are you feeling all right?" Wilfred Owen said, placing his hand on Sassoon's heart.

Touched, Sassoon replied, "I've never been better." Sassoon smiled, opening a wounded cheek, now oozing blood. Owen popped open a first aid kit and cleaned Sassoon's cheek. As Wilfred Owen gently swabbed the mud and blood from Sassoon's cheek, their eyes met.

"Jesus, what is this? The poofter patrol?" the last soldier said, sulking at the far end, arms and legs crossed with a railroad map of scar tissue for a face. He had a boxer's nose. His short, cropped hair and sharp jaw looked contemptuous to his fellow soldiers, though his uniform appeared to be a tailored imitation. Edward Shelley was battle-ugly and fight-handsome.

"Gentlemen!" Apollinaire barked. Being twice the size of both, both shirked away from the brute. "You'll have to forgive Edward Shelley." Apollinaire pulled Sassoon close, "He's been through a lot, even before the war. The Gentlemen's top man, you understand." Sassoon's paranoia exploded, realizing this was no ordinary group of soldiers. They were all Gentlemen of the Shade, and Sassoon was no exception.

Sassoon pulled away and moved to the front.

"Gertrude, where are we going?" The dawn broke slow over sparse trees.

"We can't get to the base camp with these bastards on our tail," Gertrude said. "There's an abandoned farmhouse only a few miles up the road. We passed it on the way here."

"Do you think the front will pass over us?" Sassoon yelled over the sputtering engine.

Gertrude looked Siegfried in the eye and called out, "Not a chance in hell."

Chapter 22:
Anthem for Doomed Youth

> *Oh, the wind, the wind is blowing,*
> *through the graves the wind is blowing,*
> *freedom soon will come;*
> *then we'll come from the shadows.*

The Partisan
Leonard Cohen

"...When they took me in to questioning, I told them I had nothing to gain from stealing the Mona Lisa, but Pablo Picasso loved it. Well, you know the French police--they never take a joke—and arrested Picasso for art theft! Long overdue, if I may say." Apollinaire said as the other soldiers burst into laughter. "After they released Picasso, he cursed and raged at me until he was blue in the face and I said, 'Pablo, ragging on me as you are, you must be on your blue period! Oh look, we're here."

Auntie sputtered, backfiring along the crumbling gravel path to a weatherworn estate. Swelling rainwater infected the building's bullet holes. The gouged eyes of empty windows were proof of the house's death. The ghost of home left through the axed front door. In the pre-dawn cast, the faint outline of an unused barn hid behind the disgraced architecture. With Gertrude at the wheel and Alice in the passenger's seat, Edward Shelley steadied himself, keeping an eye for ambush.

"Somebody's here." Shelley said as the dim candle-glint in the second story window snuffed out black. Halfway down the long drive, Auntie gasped her last breath. *"Merde,"* Gertrude said, climbing out.

"What is it, Miss Stein?" Alice asked.

"Damned if I know. Any of you boys know what to look for under the hood? That's a stupid question. You wouldn't even know to pull back the flaps." Gertrude said, popping the hood and exposing engine's meat.

The boys filed out of the back. Apollinaire spoke first, "What recommendations do you have for the present situation, Miss Stein?" Gertrude closed the engine up and wiped greasy fingers on her shawl.

"It looks like it overheated. I think we're going to be here awhile. Push Auntie into the barn. Edward, it's time to get out the toys." Gertrude ordered.

Apollinaire, Sassoon, and Wilfred Owen pushed the light vehicle quickly around back as Gertrude steered. Rupert Brooke and Shelley held their rifles out the back, searching for oncoming Germans. The boys rolled the car silently around to the large gravel patch behind the house. Gertrude hopped down and pushed open the rusty sliding barn door.

Gertrude commanded with her amber tipped cane, "Owen. Sassoon. Hide the old gal behind some bales of hay. Apollinaire, get on that wireless contraption and signal us some backup. Shelley, how are you coming along with the toys?"

Edward Shelley spun around holding Thompson machine guns in each hand, "Got 'em right here, Gertrude. The rest of us are going in." Apollinaire pulled out a large metal box and dragged it to the back of the barn. Alice grabbed the lantern. She didn't like guns.

"Incredible, Miss Stein! How did you ever learn so much about battle tactics?" Sassoon asked.

"Ever been to one of Natalie Barney's salons? The Germans have a lot to learn from a room full of crazy lesbians, especially if Rene Vivien is there." Gertrude said, ramming the round clip into the Tommy gun. "Okay boys, lock and load." In the distance, they heard the German automobiles. "I do believe we are expecting guests."

Alice opened the creaky backdoor gently and shone the lantern on the dusty floor. Gertrude waved the boys in. It broke Alice's heart to see a sitting room in such disarray: expensive furniture needlessly destroyed, bare hooks showed the bright square of paint once protected by well-hung art, a thin layer of dust covered the floor, and another thin layer over scuffled looter footsteps. Something dark and grey scuttled along the ground. Alice shrieked and Shelley tapped the trigger, deafening them all in a room of splintered wood and gun smoke.

"What was that?" Alice said and Shelley pondered her as a liability he was forced by duty to protect.

"Well... I believe it to be hamburger now, but I thought it to be a raccoon," Brooke said with a smirk, his beauty disarming the sudden tension. Rupert's heart pounded as something toppled upstairs. "Maybe it's another raccoon," Rupert said.

Through the dusty pantry, they entered the kitchen, which gave way to the hollows of the unlit dining room, where the table settings remained untouched. The dining room led to a book-walled sitting room. From there, Alice saw the foyer with the grand marble staircase, bathed in the baby blue of early morning radiating slowly from the busted front door.

A single transport truck was close enough to hear. Gertrude nodded in the silence, while Alice bravely-- and ever so quietly--walked up to the grand staircase leading with the lantern as they entered the master bedroom. The boys followed close behind.

Two windows framed an enormous canopied, unmade bed. Empty mason jars covered the floor, burnt out candle nubs scarred windowsills. Beside the door was a recently used bedpan. Gertrude turned a concerning glance and saw a mason jar roll by the closet. With a nod, Shelley stepped into the quiet.

Gertrude and Shelley flanked Brooke, who prepared for the other side, grasping the two doorknobs. They flung the doors open and saw a tiny little head, holding up two baby-fat hands in defense. Alice gleefully said, "It's a little boy! Hello little boy!"

"Don't shoot! Don't shoot!" the boy's voice cracked. The boy's sanity teetered from being hunted, living off cold canned food. He raised his pleading face to the lamplight.

Rupert said, "Hello, son. We're here to help you." The boy fastened himself to Rupert's leg. "What are you doing here?" Rupert said to the child.

"I'm waiting for them to come back," The boy said, his mad eyes reflecting the acceptance and resourcefulness of a child who grew feral too fast. It spooked Rupert.

"What's your name, boy?" Shelley snarled.

Gertrude stepped in, "Now, Edward. We are in the company of our host. We, as guests, should allow the young man of the house to introduce himself as a proper gentleman." Gertrude said, "You may call me Miss Stein. I must say that I have not had the pleasure." The little boy beamed with the flip of a switch, finally feeling something even as familiar as etiquette.

The young aristocrat responded, "It is a pleasure to meet your acquaintance. You may call me by what my friends call me, which is Richie, but my proper name is Richard Halliburton." The boy in the dirty knickers and soiled white shirt, he held up his grimy hand. Gertrude shook his hand as though he were a prince. "May I extend my invitation to your friends?"

"You may." Gertrude said, "This is Rupert Brooke, Edward Shelley, and Miss Toklas. Three of our friends are parking the car."

Shelley hated such posturing. "Ritchie, how have you survived? I noticed your candle light from the window. The Germans could have easily found you. Why didn't you stay blacked out?"

"Damnit, Eddie," Gertrude said, smacking Shelley like a misbehaving child. "Sir Halliburton, I understand certain inconveniences affect us all."

"Yes. Yes they do." Ritchie said, holding down his shock.

"Surely one must not lose composure before guests." Gertrude said.

"Certainly not." The boy said, reeking of urine.

Gertrude took the leap. "While your parents are away, they wanted us to take care of you. May I condescend to your aid?"

"Yes please ma'am..." Ritchie said, his eyes tearing up with relief, until he remembered the necessity of a host's composure. Stein clutched her heart, smitten. "I could not extinguish the light because... because I'm afraid of the dark." Ritchie said. Fearless in the face of self-preservation during a German attack was one thing, but monsters in the closet were an entirely different adversary. Everyone understood and treated him as an equal.

Shelley said, "Don't worry, kid brother. We'll take care of you."

Gertrude noticed this was the only time Edward ever acted human, but she was also the only one present who knew of his upbringing. Shelley whispered to Alice, "He's going to be one messed up little popinjay." Outside, some unknown distance away, a German engine turned off.

"What's the plan, Gertrude?" Shelley said.

"Mister Halliburton, do you have a wine cellar?" Gertrude said.

"Yes, it is located in the hindquarters of the estate. I am not allowed down there." Ritchie said. "I can show you where. Will your friends be joining us, Miss Stein?"

"I hope so, Mister Halliburton, I hope so." Gertrude said, "and I do believe your recent trials allow you special priviledges. Your mother said she would have no other show us the wine cellar."

Ritchie Halliburton beamed, "She said I could go down there when I was a big boy."

Gertrude smiled, "Mister Halliburton, you are a big boy if ever I have met one."

Ritchie giggled and took Gertrude's hand.

***

As the search party found a child, the thin blue lines of daylight leaked through the barn's walls. Apollinaire watched Sassoon and Owen quickly stack bales of hay in front of Auntie. The large Frenchman unpacked the complicated field radio the size of a footlocker. "Certainly, I am no Luddite, but this damnable contraption eludes me." Apollinaire said, tinkering with the vacuum tubes and following the directions written on the inner casing.

Owen's heart leapt, hearing shots fired inside the house. He peeked through a knothole to see the other team intact, entering the manor. Sassoon threw down the last bale from the loft and joined them, raspily whispering, "What was that?"

Wilfred answered, "Nothing, yet. Apollinaire, have you found anything on that contraption?"

Apollinaire cringed as shrieking feedback screamed through the earpiece. He dialed through the static and looked for a French channel in the crumpled maps at his feet. Apollinaire barked code into the metal tube and read their position off the map when the growl of a German automobile stopped at the gate at the end of the drive. Apollinaire slid off the earpiece and stood up. "Americans are on their way, yet I cannot say with certitude their arrival will be in a timely manner. I do not understand why Americans find it fashionable to be late."

Sassoon peeked through the barn door and watched tall grass bend and ebb as German soldiers fumbled forward through the underbrush. "They plan on taking the house, privates."

Appollinaire said, "Going through the underbrush is no way to take the house, privates. Dreadfully musty, I must say as one who attempted such a tactic."

As German soldiers sprinted across the front lawn, the barn-dwellers heard Gertrude's battle cry ring, "Muerent Le Basieur!" and six forms slumped into the unkept grass, empty pockets in the emerald sea where the bodies fell.

Sassoon smiled, "I never liked her poetry, but she's a helluva shot."

"We've got to let them know we only have to hold our ground until the cavalry arrives," Apollinaire said. "How many do you think there are left?"

Owen spoke up, "I only heard one transport, but it's still on the move. That doesn't make sense. Where did those Germans come from?"

"They're doing a pincher attack." Sassoon said, "Come on, let us get down there and hold steady ground." Owen, Sassoon, and Apollinaire braced for the bolt across the lawn, seeing Stein's party leave the house--with a little boy-- heading towards the cellar.

The trio of soldiers opened the back door to the barn. Edward Shelley lead the group out, covering the front from the house's corner. Rupert stood at the cellar doors, getting Gertrude, the boy, and Alice in first. Shelley followed, covered by Brooke.

Seeing the civilian child, "This just gets better and better." Sassoon said.

"Any word?" Brooke rasped to the barn-stranded patrol.

"On their way," Apollinaire said. "We wait it out."

Sassoon whispered, "Pincher attack!"

"What?" Rupert Brooke said, when a red mist sprayed from his head, tumbling down into the cellar.

Shelley grabbed the corpse as bullets zipped overhead, boxing them in. Staring at the grey morning sky through the cellar doors, Ritchie shrieked.

"Shut that goddamned kid up!" Shelley yelled, "Everyone to the back of the cellar! Go! Go! Go!"

Outside, Apollinaire hosed the tree line with bullets. Owen and Sassoon climbed into the hayloft. Apollinaire laid down cover fire, but metal beats wood every time. Metal beats wood every time, and the Germans shot through his cover, dropping him among the splinters. The gun dropped out from his hand, looking to his new wounds with confusion as he fell, heavy and empty.

"Private Owen," Siegfried Sassoon said, "We're pinned in." Inside the barn, Owen and Sassoon watched as half-dozen soldiers stepped from their cover into plain sight to the open cellar doors. Two German soldiers met their end peeking into the basement.

"No…" Sassoon said, seeing a grenade in a third soldier's hand. As he pulled the pin out, Sassoon opened fire on the remaining four and dropped them, but not before the grenade slipped onto the grass and detonated outside the wine cellar.

Heavy fire punched holes in the side of the barn, forcing Sassoon and Owen away from their perch. Even from inside the barn, they could still hear that little boy screaming.

"We have to save them, Wilfred! It's up to us!" Sassoon said.

Wilfred Owen looked Siegfried straight in the eye, grabbed the soldier by his jacket and kissed him deeply. Sassoon warmed immediately, knowing this could be the last of everything.

"Let's do this, then." Owen said. They bounded down into a pile of hay and grabbed the round clips. With the remaining ammunition, they rained molten lead into the tree line. The automatics turned tree trunks into wood chips with unrepentant wrath. Metal beats wood every time.

Their hands blistered from the heat, shaking muscle from bone in a deafening cacophony when Wilfred flew back as a bullet zipped through him.

"Wilfred!" Sassoon screamed as Wilfred Owen fell back. With new resolve, Sassoon took his last stand, noticing a few fallen bodies from his apocalypse. From the shooting patterns, he realized too late: the German forces were in perfect positions to fire ceaselessly, piercing the barn and Sassoon's thigh.

Sassoon's hands were gun-numb. His wound leaked through the straw, dripping down from the hayloft to a growing red puddle underneath. No matter how he tried to work his hands, he failed to slide the last cartridge in. At the very least, he kept the Germans away from Gertrude and the others. As a final resting place for a soldier, this wasn't so bad. He held Wilfred's cooling hand, closed his eyes, and waited to be pulled out of his body. Fireworks exploded in his closed eyelids. He felt himself lifted up with the sound of angels in the distance. One of them sounded like Gertrude.

The matron said, "The Great War is over." She was smiling now, nearly crying. "You're going to live."

***

Gertrude Stein watched as they loaded Siegfried Sassoon into the transport. "How did you know we were coming?" the Sergeant said to the kindly nurse with the Tommy gun strapped over her shoulder.

"We didn't. It just so happened that those nice boys in the barn covered us. When the Germans tried a pincer attack, your men were waiting." Gertrude said smiling, patting the Sergeant on the hand. In the driver's seat of another medical wagon, Alice looked after Little Ritchie Halliburton, now wrapped in a wool blanket, drinking hot chocolate. With marshmallows.

"…Yeah," the Sergeant said apprehensively, "I couldn't help notice some of your firepower. I've never seen a gun like that before." The Sergeant looked at the gnarled tree line, freakishly chipped away to nothingness.

"Well, we are just a modest little mobile nurse wagon." Gertrude said with a wink.

"Mighty big guns for a motorized pharmacy," The Sergeant questioned.

Gertrude laughed and patted the sergeant on the helmet, "Such a nice boy."

"Don't patronize me, woman! What is your outfit?"

"Do you like this?" Gertrude said, holding out her Thompson machine gun. "You see, our mission is rather… esoteric. We brought these firearms in for trade, in case we needed a trump card. I'm sure they could come in handy with your research and development--"

Edward Shelley interrupted, "What my traveling companion is saying is that we are forever indebted to your aid and we want to give you these state-of-the-art arms as thanks for your assistance. Do we have an understanding?"

"I think an arrangement can be made," the Sergeant said, taking a step back from the Shelley, his boiled meat of a face scowl. "What is your outfit, sir?"

"Don't ask. I don't tell." Edward Shelley said, walking off into the morning. "See you around, Gertrude."

Gertude called out, "Is there anything I can do for you, young man?"

Shelley smiled, "Are you good with your word?"

"I'm a poet," Gertrude said, "I'm only as good as my word."

Shelley said without looking back, "Tell the boys I quit." With those words, Edward Shelley walked away from everything.

Alice Toklas was the only one paying attention outside the conversation between the Sergeant, Shelley, and Stein. They were unloading German prisoners from one truck to another. "Miss Stein? Look."

Gertrude looked to the crowd of German prisoners of war and saw *him* shuffle out. His tousled gray hair mocked both the young and the dead. Gertrude cursed under her breath. She turned back to Shelley, but he already gone. She did not pursue. Gertrude pulled Alice away from the Sergeant.

Gertrude responded, "With Sassoon in the hospital, and the others dead, it looks like it's just you and me, Alice. They'll kill him if we don't do something."

"Oh," Alice said, "How can we possibly break Adolf Brand out of a military prison?"

Chapter 23:
Brand's War

Too late, Too late
The Iron Horse hurrying to war
Too late to lament
Too late for warning
I'm a stranger, alone
In my country
Again.

From *Iron Horse*
--Allen Ginsburg

Adolf Brand stood atop the world and watched it burn. He pulled the binoculars down and looked at what remained of his unit. They were little more than hungry children with guns, weighed down with supplies. Forced onto a hill, they watched the English advance, and with it, death.

"Herr Brand, the reinforcements... They aren't coming. The war's over. We lost." Radio Officer Axel said. A bombing raid leveled the base camp, taking out the Major. As tents ruptured into flame and the grey dust coated trucks and men alike, the only color on the bleak slaughter was the red hues of fire and flesh.

The raid still haunted him. Adolf Brand's ears rang as he screamed *"Get up that damned hill now... Grab what you can and go! Go! Go!"* After the third day without sleep, that bloody moment seemed so long ago. The next thing Brand and four other NCOs knew, the ground shook underneath, jarring against their footsteps. The slaughter somehow left him unfazed, but the shuddering ground unnerved him, reminding him of hell absolute.

The medic tried to save what was left of his own leg and went into shock. Brand took it upon himself to lead the rest of the noncommissioned officers not towards victory, but survival. Trees burned to the south, the English advanced from the west, and that damned river pinned them in from the north. The trees behind only prolonged the inevitable.

"Are we going to die? We're going to die, aren't we?" Hartwich cried, "I don't wanna die! I don't want to die!"

Brand backhanded him, "Get a hold of yourself, man! We're not going to die."

"But we deserted! We'll be court marshaled, or worse," Jordan replied, his white eyes peering out from a mask of grit.

"Those soldiers out there..." Brand said, "That's not a front, it's a search party. I'm almost glad to meet them."

"What are we going to do? We can't take them out!" Jordan wailed.

"Don't you understand? The war is over! We can go back home!" Derk said. A faint whizzing turned Derk's head into helmet mush.

"Get down!" Brand screamed as they dropped into the pine needles. "Don't shoot! We surrender!"

"But they shot Derk!" Jordan screamed.

"They'll kill us all! They'll kill us all!" Hartwich said, convulsing in terror.

"Axel! Tell the General Lieutenant we're surrendering." Brand said, kicking Hartwich's legs out from underneath him out of the line of fire.

"But they shot Derk!" Jordan said.

"Don't you think I don't know that?" Brand barked.

"But they shot Derk!" Jordan said. The radio operator looked to Brand. One by one, they cracked.

Jordan lost it, too. The radio operator, positioned against a snowy tree trunk, knew the most mentally stable men were himself and Adolf Brand. The shellshocked quickly became liabilities. From the ground, Brand watched pockmarks chip tree trunks. Jordan stood unable to digest his perceptions. The radio operator nodded permission to Brand. With a confused expression, Jordan faced the English army, stumbling forward in a daze. Brand knew his small troupe was insane—his only comfort was to know the difference between the mad and those beyond sanity. Jordan walked towards to opposition.

Brand cried, "Don't do it son! You'll kill us all! You'll kill us all! Jordan! Don't make me do this!" Jordan walked on, eyes blank. "Jordan, No!" Jordan raised his rifle to the dozens of soldiers lined up at the foot of the hill. Brand knew if Jordan's madness left the barrel of that gun, the three remaining survivors on that hill were finished. Brand suppressed regret and drew his sidearm at Jordan and pulled. The pistol in Brand's hand cooled once more.

Brand turned to radioman Hartwich, who shook so violently in terror, his rifle jumped like a dowser's wand. Brand said, "It had to be done, Hartwich."

"And now you're going to kill me?" Hartwich said, "You're going to kill us all?"

"Don't do this, Hart," Adolf said, "We're going to get out of this alive."

"I'm not going to let you kill me, Adolf, not like how you killed Jordan!" Hartwich said, his arm tensing to pull the trigger. A gun went off. Hartwich slackened, eyes to God.   Radio Operator Axel slipped his pistol back in the holster.

"His suffering would never end, even after the war." Axel said, throwing his guns to the dirt at Adolf's feet. Adolf did the same at Axel's feet.

"Let's never speak of this again." Adolf said.

"Agreed." Axel said, stripping off his gear.

Brand and Axel walked down the steep hill, hands on heads.   The English army shouted unintelligibly.

Axel said, "Herr Brand, I have a bad feeling about this." The little men at the foot of the hill moved up. Brand envied the healthy-looking soldiers: well-fed, comparatively clean, well-rested, and far less insane.

"Too late now," Adolf said.   The base camp still burned in the distance. Four personnel carriers and a clunky looking jeep transported two dozen Germans from other battles. As Brand surveyed the decimation, six soldiers now came within close range, rifles drawn.

"We surrender."   Brand and Axel extended their wrists, accepting cold iron shackles.   The enemy marched them into a truck. Brand smirked and said, "I'd like to upgrade my room to the Emperor's Suite." The soldier laughed as the rifle butt cracked down on Brand's face.

When Brand came to, he convulsed in chills. His shuddering body forced the blood moving. His hands were behind the back of freezing metal chair. His neck hurt as he raised his head to look at the empty concrete walls. Brand realized the chill of his ass in the chair and pissed himself. A draft came from behind, raking his back with punishment. He begged for the will to die and failed. This struck him profoundly; he couldn't die. He would, somehow, get out of this alive. He accepted all these horrible facts. In hell, it comforted him to know temporary immortality. "Bitches! Where's the God damn room service?" yelled Brand.

"Shut up, you damnable fool!" a voice said from behind. "Are you trying to get yourself captured? Oh, right. You already are."

Under pain's veil, Brand turned his head,

"Gertrude? Is that you? You salty dog! What the hell are you doing here?"

"Trying to get your ass out of that sling you put yourself in." Gertrude said, "Now shut up, simmer down, and listen to me. I'm keeping you from getting killed when I could be at home with Alice sipping absinthe and eating her brownies right now."

"I hope you are referring to her baked goods," Brand said, feeling light headed, "Don't talk about food, Gertie."

"Call me that again and I'll shoot you in the face myself. I sent Alice to find the Captain and Tennille. We haven't been able to get a line out to the rendezvous point. What the hell have you boys been doing?"

"I'm so tired, Miss Stein. So very, very tired," Brand said.

"Hold it together you big Nancy," Stein said before storming off back to the medical tent. The English medics smiled at Gertrude, who casually pocketed a small bottle of ether. She calmly walked into the makeshift recovery room, where Alice Toklas tended to Sassoon's wounds.

"Alice," Gertrude whispered, "Get Auntie ready. We can't wait for a signal. We're going to have to go to the dropoff point and hope the Captain's there."

"But what about—"

"Siegfried's a commissioned officer. He'll be fine. And the cleaner their hands are in all of this, the better off they'll be."

Gertrude slipped Alice the ignition key and whispered, "Keep the Auntie running." She took a deep breath and prepared for treason, pushing an empty gurney down the corridor, past the soldiers who loved the dotty old woman. She passed the young guard, who smiled politely at the stout lady. Upon returning to Brand's cell, she feigned shock, "Officer! I do believe this prisoner has passed!" The young soldier walked over to the bars when the ether-soaked rag dropped him. She was surprised at her own audacity—not a shudder of nervousness.

The nurse dug through his pockets and pulled out the keys. It took too long to find the right one. Ah! Perfect fit, finally. Stein closed the cell door behind her, where she stripped the soldier and uncuffed the barely conscious Adolf Brand. Now came the hard part.

The soldier's uniform failed to fit Brand's robust build, but Gertrude managed to replace the incapacitated soldier into Brand's chair and filthy uniform. She placed the shackles on the poor boy and slipped the keys back in her pocket. Gertrude slapped Brand onto the gurney and threw a blanket over his ill-fitting pants. Moving unconscious men proved tiring, yet another reason she dismissed them as a whole, but the hard part was over.

She opened the door and wheeled Brand out. He asked, "Gertrude... What's happening?"

Through gritted teeth, Gertrude said, "Shut up, you damnable fool. You'll get us killed. Play dead for once."

"I don't want to sleep, Miss Stein. I'm afraid to fall asleep."

"Hang in there, Herr Brand." Gertrude said, wheeling him away. The two glided to the loading dock, where Alice waited nervously.

"Everything go accordingly, Miss Stein?" Alice said.

Gertrude placed her tinted spectacles over her eyes and replied, "Just drive." The ambulette bounced down the road with Adolf Brand in back while the Nurse Stein administered an amphetamine, keeping Brand's blood brackish, yet alive. Alice disliked driving, especially down these darned back roads of the demilitarized zone. They came to a small checkpoint tent. To Gertrude's horror, five soldiers, shot at point blank range, laid side by side on the ground, awaiting their shallow graves. "What the holy hell..." Gertrude gasped.

Panic came over Alice as she pulled in. "Do we go in, Miss Stein?"

"I don't think we have much choice. Stay here with Brand."

She took out her tiny pistol and searched through the campground. "Hello? Is anyone here?" Pulling back a tent flap, a lone man sat at a table, eating a can of cold beans.

"Hello, Miss Stein," Edward Shelley said. Gertrude holstered her pistol back under her red smock.

"What are you doing here?" Gertrude said, hiding her mortification poorly.

"Waiting to die, I suppose. I can't get to the rendezvous point, where the Captain was going to pick us up after extracting Apollinaire, Brooke, Sassoon and

Owen. I came walking through here, and they refused my passage. Things got messy."

"Oh, Edward," Gertrude sighed, "Must you always be so difficult?"

Edward Shelley smirked and said, "Difficult times require difficult men. But more importantly, what are you doing here?" Edward threw the empty tin on the floor. Gertrude jumped.

Gertrude asked, "Are you going to kill me, Mister Shelley?"

Edward laughed, curdling Gertrude's blood. "Oh Miss Stein, I would never kill you. I'm sick to death of death. But you didn't answer my question. What are you doing here?"

"I was trying to make my way to the extraction point. It seems we've hit an unexpected snag."

"Oh?"

"The English captured Mister Brand. The Geneva Conventions don't cover POWs. He's half dead, sitting in the back of Auntie. We failed to contact Captain Silvermane. We don't even know if the Mary Rodger will deliver us from the mouth of this hellscape. With the war over, our work here is done. We just have a few more miles to go and we can put an end to this sad travesty. Please, Mister Shelley, deliver us from the maw of war."

"Brand's with you?" Edward chuckled, "That old codger just won't die, will he?"

"He is a tough old coot," Gertrude said. "Come with us, Mister Shelley. They'll kill you if you don't."

"There really isn't an end to this, is there?" Edward sighed.

"You won't get out of the demilitarized zone alone, not after what you did to these poor men." Gertrude said.

"I don't really plan to." Edward Shelley said with a distant gaze. She saw an empty bottle of whiskey at his feet.

"You really don't get it, do you?" Gertrude said, "You're a free man, but you've never known freedom. I offer a ride out of this freezing hell and you sit there with baked beans on your chin, preferring defeat and death over the unknown. One way or another, you are leaving your old life behind you, right here and now. If you stay here, well, maybe you don't deserve freedom. Good day, Edward Shelley. You are a good man who never got a fair shake, and it deepens my sympathy to pitiable levels to know you would rather die than give up a carnage you look at with such disdain.

"A man of your caliber deserves a wealthy retirement, and you give that up, right now, right here!" Gertrude said, "I want you to walk away from this! I want you to live the normal life you never knew! I want you to live a life without fear! I want you to start over, far away from us! But the path from this war zone, a war zone you have spent your entire life in to a mysterious, idle existence—Alice, Adolf and myself *must* see you off at the pickup point. I know you Eddie, and you did not come all this way to fail at the doorstep of what you always wanted. If I'm wrong, then stay here and die before the firing squad and I will not waste a sympathetic tear on you. But you are better than all this!" Gertrude said, kicking a tin can. She grabbed a full gas can and walked out.

"Let me give you a hand with that," Edward said, taking the can.

"Such a nice young man," Gertrude said, patting his hand.

"Gertrude?"

"Hm?"

"Thanks."

Gertrude laughed and patted him on the shoulder. "You've always been a good boy, Eddie. Don't forget that." Gertrude said smiling admirably to her former bodyguard.

Climbing in back, Edward sat by Brand's cot.

Adolf Brand blinked into conscious along the crumbling road. "Edward Shelley? By God, it's been ages since I last saw you."

"It's been a long time." Edward said, "We've been through a lot since the Cleveland Street days." He opened tin of rations for Brand. Brand sat up, shakily shoveling cold meat byproduct under his moustache.

"Miss Stein told me you look to get out of the life," Brand said, his baggy eyes tiring. The food brought him slowly back to life.

"I mean no disrespect, Herr Brand. I'm just getting too old for this."

Brand's laughter ended in chokes. He cleared his throat, "What could you possibly do instead? Stamp collecting? You're a natural born killer. What would you do? Where would you go?"

"I've always liked The States. Maybe go and live out my life in New York City. Hide in plain sight."

"Are you sure you don't want to set up a Manhattan branch of Gentlemen?" Brand said.

Shelley responded with cold silence. Brand continued, "You knew I had to ask. When you get to America, there are two Sisters of the Isle who have a summer home in Bar Harbor, Maine. Jane Adams and Mary Rozet Smith. Good people."

Shelley smiled, "I know Jane. She's nice."

"Jesus, kid, we sure have been through a lot together." Brand said, "You did a long run. If you want out, I'll make sure Ives sets you up nice. I don't say this often enough, but you turned into something I'm proud of. I know you didn't choose any of this. I just... I just wanted to tell you that I'm sorry."

"Sorry? For what?"

"For all the wretched demands. Cleveland Street. Hanover. Sex parties. The Lusitania. New Orleans. Hauling my sorry ass out of military prison. I used to think that if someone violated you, they would incur Satan's wrath. How... pompous of me to think I could liken myself to the devil, and I could protect my soldiers from sin, when my demands were beyond sin or redemption. How arrogant to think I was more elite than Satan." Brand said, delirious.

Shelley laughed, "It matters little. We both live. That is all that matters."

"Bullsheissen," Brand said, "There's more to life than staying alive. I regret never showing you more to life than survival. You are a good, loyal man who didn't deserve this life. I regret we were never able found love for you, the only real work. I am thankful that you stuck with us as long as you did. You, over anyone, know my regrets. As heavy as a hand can land, I spread myself too thin. For all the homosexuals I tried to grant happiness to, your happiness should have been at the top of my list, and I failed you." Brand closed his eyes as his thick hand patted Edward's thigh. "I'm sorry."

"You're rambling," Shelley said.

"It's the amphetamines."

"Get some rest, you old dog," Shelley said, "It's hard to sleep at sea."

Auntie rolled along the back roads until Gertrude pulled up to a small dock, where a small sailboat waited. The Mary Roger waited further out at sea. Shelley, Brand, Tolkias, and Stein filed out of Auntie, doused Auntie with petrol, and set her ablaze. Stein crossed herself and said, "She was a grand old dame." The four walked to the dock, Auntie blazing behind them in the night.

"Silvermane! We're here!" Stein yelled at the ship. A young blonde man stepped from below deck. "I'm sorry. Silvermane could not make it. He is dead. My name is Captain Sweetcakes and I command the Mary Roger and her entire fleet."

Edward's jaw dropped to see such a young, platinum blonde, bronze muscled stud commanding the Gentleman's naval fleet. With a wiggling saunter, Captain Sweetcakes took his wayfaring soldiers aboard and said, "So sorry we were a touch late. We always end up a bit tight in the end."

Chapter 24:
The Lizas and Gagas

As long as society is anti-gay, then it will seem like being gay is anti-social.
--Joseph Francis

As 1919 rolled in, The Great War slowly lurched to a halt. Two Germans crossed Belgium to England. Magnus Hirshfeld hung his head and said a prayer for he decimation of Brussels. Scorn met them every step of the way. Adolf Brand shrugged it off, indifferent.

"Just think, Maggie," Brand said, "if they knew what our true intentions were, they'd kill us outright, rather than merely sneer."

"I wish George Ives had come to Berlin instead. This place sets me on edge." Dr. Hirshfeld said.

Brand chuckled, tossing heavy shoulders, "You know the English. Having us visit keeps them from verbally rubbing our noses in our country's loss."

"But you are German as well, Herr Brand." Hirshfeld smirked.

"Only by circumstance, Maggie. Only by circumstance."

"When are you going to stop calling me that?"

"When you start acting like a man," Brand said, "Anyway, do you know that kid that Bobbie Ross saddled us with? He's some kind of actor and playwright, so I gather. Who isn't? He pulls off one international scandal and starts thinking he's cock of the walk."

With sympathetic eyes, Dr Hirshfeld said, "I miss Bobby, too. But he named this Coward fellow as his successor. We must respect that."

"That doesn't mean I like it." Brand said.

The two cleared customs and stepped into the cold chill of English weather. Hirshfeld huffed. "Damn Ives. He said he was going to send a car."

Brand replied, "For all your research of sexual inverts, you still can't pick one out of a crowd? I'm embarrassed for you." Adolf nodded to no one in particular.

A fuchsia Rolls Royce roared up onto the sidewalk, carrying a garish lad with a wrist so limp a weak breeze could tear it asunder like tissue paper. "Yoo-hoo! Over here, darlings!" the young man said, swishing his hips and hands as though controlled by a frustrated puppeteer. Like a magic spell, the other tourists stopped in shock, as if the effete male magically appeared. Not only were the mannerisms flamingly gauche, but it was none other than superstar of the stage, Fred Barnes.

In his usual demeanor, Dr. Hirshfeld smiled wide, "I've heard so much about you, Mister Barnes. The pleasure is all mine."

"Oh, Papa! Call me Freddy," Barnes said.

Magnus said, "Did you hear that, Adolf? He called me Papa."

Brand grunted dismissively.

With a hand fanning them in rhythm with his speech, Fred said, "Now don't you two worry about a thing, darlings. I'll take your luggage and drop it off at the hotel after I take you to the Black Cat in Soho. You simply must! It is to die for!"

Brand expected to hate this.

Magnus took the passenger seat, while Brand stuffed himself in the back. Magnus politely provided an audience to Barnes' endless recitation of cabaret numbers. Brand fumed in the back seat, counting the seconds. With little regard to motorist etiquette, Fred Barnes roared up onto the sidewalk in front of the Black Cat as pedestrians scattered in terror. Magnus and Brand stepped from the loud car as Fred Barnes shrieked, "You boys have fun now! Toodles!" With a squeal of rubber loud as a queer's gasp, Fred Barnes swerved back into traffic to an orchestra of urgent honks.

"So much for subtlety," Brand said.

"It should not be our strong suit." Magnus said. Brand looked around the exterior of the Soho café called the Black Cat. The neighborhood seemed friendly to sexual inverts, though it appeared to be more pose than action. Brand already missed the aggression of the toughs of Berlin. Here, it was all advertisement and no product. The little tin bell chimed as they entered the faux French bistro of the Black Cat.

***

In a small booth enclosed in frosted glass, George Cecil Ives tapped his spoon against the supple mug, shaking milk from his tiny utensil. He checked his pocket watch. Brand and Hirshfeld were running late, as was Noel, though Ives secretly hoped Noel would never show.

The amount of trust needed to secure the legacy of The Gentlemen met increasing suspicion. With so many high-ranking members dead, old age sparing none, handing the reins over to the young became a harsh reality. Ives himself celebrated his fifty-first birthday, and the bullet wound never grew back clean. Noel was barely twenty, and Ives suspected he played a part in the Lysis Mutiny, though had no proof.

According to Coward, soldiers trying to escape the beached U-Boat shot Adelsward and Silvermane. Noel only survived because, he was in fact, a Coward.

Lord Alfred Douglas seemed unusually mournful at hearing at the death of Robbie Ross, and denied ever knowing a "has-been named Tennille."

Rounding out the newbies was J. Edgar Hoover, who at best could be considered a better ally than an enemy. Ives shuddered.

"Waitress! Might I have a spot of brandy?" Ives said. The waitress turned round, looking a terrible fright. Her face was a horrible shade of orange, her hair was a curly henna red. Blue eyeshadow circled her bright eyes. Her lips glistened cherry red above a chin raised at an obtuse angle. It was no secret this was a man. Afraid of offending the fellow charged with his table, Ives averted embarrassed eyes as the waiter approached.

"Terribly sorry, sir." Ives said, unsure if this creature was man or woman. The waiter's pride deflected both.

"Brandy is hardly worth apologies." The waiter said proudly.

"Damn it, Denis!" the brutish host bellowed. The host turned to Ives, "Please excuse our new waiter. He is a bit rough about the... edges. Favor from the family, you understand." The waiter gave the faintest of coy smiles, turning to the bar.

Enter Noel Coward in a white tuxedo. "Terribly sorry I'm late," Noel mumbled, "I just came from the most wonderful party last night and wished to sleep off most of the celebratory afterglow. Garcon? A martini, if you please."

The orange-faced waiter smiled. The malicious contempt did not escape Ives, but Noel failed to notice.

"But of course, *Master*." The orange-faced waiter said.

"That *is* a fitting title. Master..." Noel said. "Is it too much to ask that I be considered such in conversation?"

George weighed his advantages, "If you feel you are worthy of such a title."

"I did single handedly sink the Lusitania." Noel said, "Might I bring something to your attention before the remainder of the voting party arrives?" Noel asked, trampling convention. Every time Noel spoke, Ives missed Robbie Ross even more.

"You may always speak freely, Noel. However, if it is a matter concerning the Gentlemen, we must all voice our opinions and come to conclusions as a group."

Noel huffed, "How *dreadful*." The waiter delivered Coward's martini and Ives' brandy. Ives waited for Coward to continue his self-absorbed monologue. "Ever since the conference at Capri, I feel marginalized; my true abilities have not been placed at the forefront of our endeavors."

Ives asked, "And what are those endeavors?"

"Why, to make our kind elite. The Gentlemen should be the most powerful people on the planet. It is our right and our heritage. Perhaps I am phrasing it wrong. I am best suited for mere representation. I tire of running quaint errands. It's beneath me, I say. I need something larger."

"And why are you telling me this without other members?" Ives said.

Noel continued, "Because you are English as well. Brand and Hirshfeld are Germans. Lord knows what they think, especially after the war. They could come in, kill us both and claim power for all of Europe. But you and only you know how much money is involved with this. Are you going to trust the damnable Germans?"

Ives leaned in, "Listen, you *child*. Don't you *ever* disrespect a fellow Gentleman. I know you are new to this game, so I'm going to pretend that your attempted mutiny is merely a sign of your childishness. I cannot understand how you have still failed to see The Cause. If you cannot see it by now, I will take you out into the street and put a bullet in your bloody head myself, because such a disrespectful..." the small tin bell chimed. "--Oh look, our guests have arrived." Ives said. Magnus and Adolf took close seats.

"Well isn't this the most depressing armistice of Nancies," Adolf Brand said, looking at Ives's arm in a sling and the pomposity that is Noel Coward. Noel sat like a scolded child. George Ives smiled. Noel Coward smiled to Magnus and Adolf, who did not reciprocate.

Noel assumed Germanic dispositions prevented Hirshfeld and Brand from cordiality, though both vigorously shook Ives' hand with a warm greeting.

"All pleasantries aside, let us arrive at our conversational destination." Ives asked.

Magnus started in, "Now that the war is over and the new Weimar government is in place, we must strike forward." Ives caught Noel rolling his eyes. Dr. Hirshfeld continued, "We know there are others like us, and even more sexually unusual humans who are shunned and abused. I have been touring the globe and my research in the matter of sexuality has reached a saturation point. We must come forward for those who cannot. I request the Gentlemen fund an institute for sexual studies—a building which houses all our desires and great ideas."

Noel said, "And just where would you set up such a brothel?"

"Not a brothel, Herr Coward," Magnus said, avoiding disdain, "A scientific academy where we could intellectually reason with heterosexuals that homosexuality is natural, contemporary, and universal."

"Where were you thinking of starting this?" Ives asked.

"Berlin. The newly formed Weimar Republic is very open to the idea. I already have several museums and private collectors willing to donate historical curiosities to a museum. We'll have a lecture hall, a museum, a library, and clinics to help those with unique sexual identities. Did you know some individuals are born with both a penis *and* a vagina? Quite fascinating."

Brand chuckled, "Again with the trannies?"

Dr. Hirshfeld huffed, "I speak of hermaphrodites, Adolf, not transvestites. Be reasonable for once. Regardless, I already started in-talks with a real estate developer to purchase an entire city block. I anticipate a full staff of doctors, psychologists, and scholars from around the world to research and promote The Cause. That is still being worked on. I've been touring all across Europe and Asia, delivering speeches about inverted sexuality. The response is surprisingly positive—so long as the institute is not in their country."

That thing with the orange face and blue painted eyelids arrived at their table, "Good afternoon,

Gentlemen." The four diners panicked at the title. "Would you prefer a café au lait or perhaps a strong scotch?" The fairy quipped.

"Denis! Tell them the specials!" The gruff host barked from the seating podium,

Denis the waiter placed his slender fingers against his breast, threw his head back, and laughed so loudly that several patrons stared. Flustered, the host grew red with fury. The waiter said to the host, "If you are going to ride my ass, be a dear and pull my hair." Ives saw Noel's shocked eyes.

Denis, the waiter, snapped his queeny head to Noel, "Oh don't give me that look. You must have chosen that pomade for the ease it gives you when sticking your head up your own arse."

Brand, Hirshfeld, and Ives burst into laughter at Noel's embarrassment.

"You're done, Denis! You're fired!" The host screamed.

"I beg to differ. As a restaurateur, you should know the difference between rare and well done. I see how it could confuse you so. To clarify the matter, your customers are rare and I am, as it were, *flaming*." Denis said. As he walked off head held high, he casually stopped carrying his drink tray, which fell to the floor with a deafening clatter.

"Did you see the scrotum on that fellow?" Adolf Brand said, "Pendulous!"

The manager came over like a whimpering lackey, "Please forgive the disturbance. He has been trouble since day one. Please, let me get you anything. On the house."

Noel subdued his rage, upstaged by such a low-caste fairy.

"No," George Ives said. "Go apologize and rehire him. He was marvelous entertainment."

"But he was a fairy! A degenerate! And a rude one who didn't know his place!" The host said.

Brand leaned back, exposing the butt of his gun resting in the chest holster, "I'd be careful about the words you use at this table."

The manager turned a whiter shade of English and said, "I will go retrieve him at once, sir." The host scurried out the front door, feverishly looking for Denis. When the manager left, Brand cackled and pounded the table. Magnus cocked a huge bushy eyebrow.

Brand smiled. "I merely spoke for the unspeakable. You get my vote on the institute. Ives, you in?"

"Naturally." George said.

"And what about you, Noel? Are you in?" Brand goaded.

Noel looked at his companions and said, "Not that my vote matters at this point, but I think it ridiculous to spend money on something that will never make money. Absolutely absurd, I vote no. You men are quite behind the times! Practically dinosaurs, I say! Lizards--Lizas, even! Each of you! There's no power in community, only power in fame and money. Naturally, I have been keeping abreast of the new technologies and objects of interest, and an institute for sexual studies certainly is not one of them." Brand was ready to thrash the boy if he spoke another impertinent word.

"Do you have a more suitable idea?" Magnus said diplomatically, "Perhaps from the mouths of babes drool more than 'Gaga'."

Coward arched his manicured eyebrows. "I've heard of this place in California, over in the States. It appears there are these things called moving pictures. They are like pictures, but they move. They're calling them movies--"

"We know what movies are, Noel. We've been to California." Ives said, "Go on."

"I think we should get involved there and I would like to place myself as a representative over there. I'm most suitable to the arts, which is why Bobbie put me in charge." Noel said.

George Ives smiled wide, "Well, that seems like a marvelous idea. It's about time we jumped the lake. Wouldn't you agree?" Magnus and Brand nodded encouragingly.

"Really? You're letting me go to America?" Noel said, eyes wide with excitement.

"You should have said something sooner. We would have sent you months ago." Brand said. Magnus kicked Brand under the table.

"Well, then it's settled. Noel goes to Hollywoodland! Magnus gets his Institute. Brand, do you have any business opportunities to present?"

Adolf Brand pounded his meaty hook into the table. "I say we buy this place, fire the goddamned host and put that saucy fairy in charge. That kid's got exactly what our outfit needs—all pride and no dignity."

George smiled, "Agreed?"

"Agreed." Brand, Magnus, and Noel said in unison.

"Now if you don't mind, I'm off to prepare my more presentable arrival." Noel said, standing with great airs. The Master rose expectantly, avoiding eye contact. The diners and admirers of the Master stopped eating to watch the genius leave with such pride into the Great Wide West! This would not be a mission of fame and glory, but a mission of destiny! Leave the old men behind, Noel! Strike out for the unforgiving wastelands of Hollywoodland! Your tan shall keep you young! "Fare thee well, Gentlemen. May our bonds be strong," Noel said, turning a dramatic chin from his collaborators in the struggle of all lovers of the damned.

"Yeah yeah, Noel. We get it. Have fun. Good-bye," Brand said, thankful to be rid of him.

"How about that waiter, eh?" Ives said absently.

"He's young, poor, and doesn't give a damn what anyone thinks of him." Adolf said.

"Noel did have a point," Magnus said, "We are getting out of touch with the youth culture. The War made quite a generation gap and took many men between our age and those of the youth. Captain Sweetcakes is barely a man. We're Lady Lizas in a world of Lady Gagas. We're must adapt."

The owner ran up, puckered to kiss some ass. "Terribly sorry, sirs. Is there anything else I can give you?"

"This restaurant." Brand said, "We're buying it from you. That waiter is now your boss. I'm sure you will find our offer generous." Brand leaned back, reminding the owner of the firearm.

In terror, the host replied, "But of course, gentlemen."

The effeminate waiter sauntered up to the table like an underfed mule with his hand keeping the violently swishing hip from dislocation. The host whispered something in Denis's ear, transforming the waiter's contemptuous face into delight incarnate. Ives smiled, extending his hand. "It's a pleasure to meet you. I'm George Cecil Ives. These are my business associates, Adolf Brand and Magnus Hirshfeld. You said your name was Denis, was it?"

"Not anymore," the waiter said with a gleam in his eye. "You can call me Quentin. Quentin Crisp."

With his trademarked dead-eyed smile, George Cecil Ives proclaimed, "May I be the first to welcome you as owner of this fine establishment? This is your base of operations. Welcome, Quentin Crisp, to the Gentlemen of the Shade."

Epilogue

Dr. Magnus Hirshfeld and Adolf Brand shared a seventh pint inside the Black Cat as Ives rounded the alley to the backlit figure among the dustbins. The London drizzle passed, leaving the slick brick glistening in the gaslight. Under the streetlight stood a tall, slender man in a fedora and a smart tan raincoat.

"Well, how did it go?" The shadowy stranger sneered.

"They are unaware," Ives said. "Let's take a walk, Bosie."

Lord Alfred Douglas said, "You know how some power-hungry, backbiting bitches can be."

Ives inhaled, feeling the absence of muscle tissue serrate against his chipped shoulder blade. "If he succeeded, it would be a bigger problem for you than my corpse. Have you made contact with New York?"

"Mmm, yes," Bosie said absently. "My contact over there is, well, rather disappointing. He has a small gang operating out of a Negro neighborhood, which sits uncomfortably with his southern accent. New York is going to be more difficult to acquire than once perceived. Everyone has a gang there. The Jews, the Irish, the Italians. It is a highly competitive market, being the nexus of the world, but I think I have a man capable of stitching a place among what already exists, without too much difficulty. Let it be known, Mister Ives, that I have my sights set much higher than squabbling pedestrian turf wars in a cesspool."

"Promise me, Bosie. Promise me you won't touch Edward Shelley. What he's done for us..."

"He will not be pushed, filed, stamped, indexed, briefed, debriefed or numbered. His life is his own.

That being stated, I cannot assure his protection from third parties." Bosie said. "Fear not, Mister Ives. We might not get all of New York, but we will acquire what matters. This I guarantee. Sleep tight, Mister Ives. The Gentlemen are in good hands."

"Even your third parties will not *touch* Edward Shelley. Mince words as you may, but my word is the blade. If you wish for the full support, Edward Shelley is to be left completely alone."

"Oh George, why would I bother with yesterday's Gentlemen? With all your smuggling and flitting about, just because you stay busy doesn't mean you have any power."

"Promise me his safety."

Lord Douglas laughed, "You gave me the lancebearer status, something you cannot so easily retract. You *must* trust me now. Go home. Young as I may not be, I am still more effective at driving the Gentlemen to their ultimate goal, just as you suggested. Friends close and enemies closer? Ask me to keep Dolly Wilde from killing you—then we shall see who controls The Gentlemen of the Shade. What was that? Nothing, you say? This is my turn at the chessboard, old man Ives. Pray I let you live out your twilight days, for I am the Golden Dawn."

Ives replied, "Be warned, Lord Douglas, it is doubly hard to bite a forked tongue."

***

Over the clink of glasses and loud chatter, Brand spun his ale in hand to the wobbly bar table. "Maggie, I have a question I've been waiting to ask you."

"Well, by all means, it never stopped you before." Dr. Hirshfeld said, feeling the effect of alcohol massage his tongue.

"Have we made any progress? We spent the better part of our lives fighting for The Cause. And we still piddle for progress."

"Progress? Ha!" Dr. Hirshfeld said. "Between you and I, the only progress we acquired is in our bank accounts and business associates. Money makes excellent armor. How flippant we can be, believing in our open-minded superiority while the uneducated, confused, tortured, and beaten continue to live day-to-day without privilege. I hope my institute can break down the class barriers and untangle the exploitation of our own kind. We have survived by any means necessary, and men of our means will always survive."

"Nietzsche would agree," Adolf Brand added.

"I could care less about your passing fad philosophers," Dr. Hirshfeld slurred. "Eugenics, now *there* is a scientific principle I can stand behind."

"Heh, you'd stand behind anything, so long as he pushed back!" Brand said.

Dr. Hirshfeld laughed, "Oh, you dirty cad!" He raised his glass, "A toast, Herr Brand. "To surviving another day."

Brand smiled, "To a brighter day in the shadows…"

***

While Quentin Crisp delighted in running his own restaurant, Noel Coward packed his trunk for the next leg of his theatrical tour.

Across the Atlantic Ocean, J. Edgar Hoover slept soundly in Washington D.C., preparing for his promotion with his mother asleep in the next room.

Rene LaFitte, nestled in a Harlem firetrap, plotted his vengeance to the Negro music from a club he lived over. A half a dozen miles away on the same island, Edward Shelley threw a log into his potbellied stove and watched the people from the second story of his Greenwich Village townhouse. He felt something new for the first time in ages: tranquility.

Across the Western world, The Gentlemen of the Shade prepared, in their separate ways, to enter the Age of Assassins.

ABOUT THE AUTHOR

Tod Crouch (b.1978--) grew up in a small, isolated town and started writing at the age of 13 when he was afraid he was "gay-positive". He finished his first novel, *Cutting Teeth*, at 18 before entering Columbia of Chicago. From there he moved to New York, where he completed *The Immaculates*, *The Night Watchman*, *Gentlemen of the Shade*, and *The Accidental Protégé*. He resides in Brooklyn, living a quiet life as a bartender.

www.ingramcontent.com/pod-product-compliance
Lightning Source LLC
Chambersburg PA
CBHW060408260626
47160CB00006B/2470